The Runaway

The Runaway

Eleanor Rowe

The Runaway

This book is a work of fiction. Named locations are used fictitiously, and characters and incidents are the product of the author's imagination. Any resemblance to actual events or places or persons, living or dead, is entirely coincidental.

Published by
Lighthouse Christian Publishing
SAN 257-4330
5531 Dufferin Drive
Savage, Minnesota, 55378
United States of America

www.lighthousechristianpublishing.com

Eleanor Rowe

THE RUNAWAY

DEDICATION

Many years ago, the following poem was given to me:

"He knows, He loves, He cares.
Nothing this truth can dim.
He gives the very best to those
Who leave the choice with HIM."

When the Lord took my dear mother to Glory, I never thought He could give me someone else who would love me, care for me, pray for me, and give her talents and knowledge so bountifully to me. But in 1960, He gave me a friend who has not only been dear and precious, but who has spent months reading, rereading, rewriting and editing everything I have written.

It is with sincere love and gratitude, therefore, that I dedicate this book to my friend and my joy,

MARJORIE A. COLLINS

THE RUNAWAY is far more hers than mine.

CHAPTER 1

As Jonathan walked slowly toward the window, sleet was beating on the pane. It was 5:00 p.m. on the 25th of November, and he had to obey his heart. Without thought to the cold, he pulled on an old pair of jeans, a sweat shirt, and old sneakers. He threw a gray jacket over his shoulders and headed to the cemetery.

Two days before, his beloved wife and unborn son had been laid to rest in a mahogany casket covered with red and white roses. He had left with his mother and father after the Chaplain had prayed. He held his dad's arm, and fell into the back seat of their car.

Now, alone, he had to go back. With his hands stuffed in his jacket pockets and his head down to protect him from the icy sleet, he went to the closed grave. He knelt in the dirt and laid his head on top of the soil.

The day she died was their first wedding anniversary. And it was just one month before their son was to have been born. Deep in thought, his breath came in short groans. Tears froze on his face. His blue eyes turned gray. His body was wracked with pain. Taking a handful of dirt and holding it to his heart, he cried out, "Oh, God, why? You not only took the most precious one in all the world, but our son, too! WHY? People say You are a God of LOVE! What kind of love is this? Have you no heart? Don't You care about anyone? At the funeral I was told You had a purpose in all you do. Taking life? Robbing a man of all he holds dear? Oh God, I want to dig her up, hold her in my arms, and tell her I love her with all my heart. You have ruined it all. I have no life left and nowhere to go. Every dream has been dashed into sorrow and bitterness. You call this LOVE? With all my heart I hate You and hate all You have done to me and my family. If I could see You, if there IS a You, I'd fight back. I'd knock you into the ground and wait for You to stand up and look me in the eye and tell me You love me! If you are God, speak to me. Give me a reason for all You have done!"

Jonathan threw his entire body across the grave and wept uncontrollably. Soon, he realized he was frozen. He could not stay there any longer. Taking a little handful of dirt, he staggered away, falling next to a leafless oak tree - then stumbled to his feet and headed to his parents' home. Hair white with sleet and newly falling snow, clothes taut to his body, ankles and feet frostbitten, he opened the kitchen door. His mother caught him as he fell. Together, his parents took off his icy clothes, wrapped him in warm blankets, rubbed his hands and feet, and covered his head. When he opened his eyes, they gave him some warm milk, staying by him and holding him tightly. There were no words spoken. His parents knew where he had been, and his agony was theirs as well. Finally, his dad gave him a small glass of sherry and medicine. By noon, while his parents wept, Jonathan slept.

CHAPTER 2

Jonathan's parents were quiet New Englanders. His father had graduated from Yale University with an M.D. degree and was now a Neurosurgeon. His greatest enjoyment on weekends was fishing and sailing. His wife kept a spotless home, raised roses and gladiolas, and fried fresh-caught fish on Saturday nights. On Sundays, they sailed in and around the Cape Cod Canal and near the local beaches. After two years of marriage, Mrs. Allen had given birth to an 8 lb., brown-eyed, bald boy. The couple was elated. The third day, they took him home to his newly decorated nursery. The walls had ships and swimming fish painted on them. Blue sheets and blanket covered his crib, and the sun shone through the wide open window. They named their son, Peter Lynn after his grandfather. The house was filled with joy, as well as bottles, diapers and crying. After a week, the Pediatrician examined him and said he was fit and handsome. A week later, his crying could not be stopped. His temperature was normal, but his baby smile was gone. After a night of sleepless watching, and trying to comfort him, they took him back to the doctor. Blood tests, heart tests and finally a CT scan was done. The tests revealed that his hemoglobin was low, and his pulse was very slow, especially for a baby. After an I.V. was given and a small amount of blood, his cheeks colored and his crying stopped. The doctors could not find the source of the problem, and after two days, his frightened parents took him home.

John and Laura took turns staying with Peter every minute. John took time off from his practice. In three days, the baby was again crying, and whenever Laura picked him up, he screamed. Rushing him back to the hospital, the doctor found a small lump near his heart. He could not keep anything down, and just three days later, he had no pulse and no heartbeat. The devastated parents watched his life leave him. An autopsy revealed small cancer cells surrounding the heart and approaching the lungs.

A minister from a nearby church came to the home and prayed with John and Laura, but their grief could not be assuaged. Close friends, doctor colleagues, neighbors, and grandparents attended the funeral. Buried in a blue outfit, little Peter looked alive in his tiny casket. Even though it was June, the air was cold and clouds hung across the afternoon sun. No matter the flowers and the friends, comfort was not to be found. The family left the grave weeping and silent. Their home was full of food. Neighbors had fixed a lovely meal. Coffee and tea were ready. But there was a dreadful emptiness and few words were spoken. Death had defeated the family. Before they went to bed, they closed their son's door. It would not be opened for many weeks.

Two years after losing their firstborn son, Dr. and Mrs. Allen were told the best thing for them to do was to have another child. They wanted to think about it, and went to the White Mountains in New Hampshire for two weeks. It was six weeks later that Laura came home and bounded into the arms of her husband. She was pregnant! They were both scared and thrilled. The following March, Jonathan was born. He was healthy and handsome, and a real bundle of joy. Growing normally in every way, he soon became a bounding, mischievous little boy. Life was good again for the family.

As the years sped by, he sailed miniature boats, wore snazzy boots, broke two windows playing football, enjoyed school and made friends easily. When he was a senior in high school, he not only looked like his dad, but he told his parents he wanted to follow in his dad's footsteps. They were so proud of him!

An application was made to Yale and mailed in, even though his closest buddy wanted him to go to Harvard. Acceptance came quickly, and a special party was given. Jonathan's graduation present was a green Mercedes with yellow trim. And before leaving for Yale, the family planned to take a trip to England.

CHAPTER 3

Judith Sanders came from a long line of Bostonians. The family lived in a lovely home on Beacon Hill. Her dad was a well-known lawyer.

When Judith was two, she saw her mother's tummy getting bigger. But she thought older people always got fat. She asked her mother if she was hungry all the time.

"No, Judith. You are going to have a little sister, and I know you'll love her. Feel my tummy. Do you feel her move?"

Judith took her tiny fingers, and to her surprise, felt her mother's tummy jump around.

"When will I have my sister?" she asked.

"In just a few more weeks. We'll bring her home from the hospital, and you can hold her, and even help me feed her."

Judith thought it would be nice, but would her mother and father still love her? She found her dad in the living room, crawled up in his lap and asked, "Daddy, when my little sister comes, will you still love me?"

He squeezed her and told her they would always love her. And with that, she got down from his lap and ran to her room. Her bed was full of dolls, but her favorite was a pink, stuffed, one-eyed, small one who always looked alone.   Judith picked her up and hugged here. Then she looked at all the rest and thought maybe that would be like having a sister. One would always be the favorite - and she hoped she would be the one.

When her parents brought Brittany home from the hospital, Judith held her with her father's help. She was so tiny and mostly covered in blankets. She had blue eyes, but no hair. She was happy about that, for she had long brown hair and people always said it was beautiful.

"Mommy, will my sister ever have hair and teeth and be able to walk and talk?"

"Of course, but many babies are born with no hair, and after some time, they walk and talk. You don't remember, but you looked almost like your sister when we brought you home from the hospital. She'll grow up to be a beautiful girl."

"As pretty as I am?"

"She won't be just like you, but I am sure she'll be very pretty, and you'll be able to play with her, and you'll love her. You can teach her lots of things as she gets older."

When Judith started school, she loved it. Every day when she came home, she took her sister for a little walk in the house and told her all about school. It wasn't long before she knew her sister didn't understand a word she said, so she stopped doing that. She met kids who lived nearby and played with them after school and then did her homework.

Their early years were spent in their own worlds. Their personalities were very different. Judith was quiet with a winsome shyness. She loved making friends and was full of fun ideas and her schoolmates enjoyed being with her. She had dark skin, dark brown eyes, long, wavy hair, and a dimple in her left cheek. Clothes meant little to her, and she blended in very well with the tan walls at school. Her mind was quick and studies came easily. The books she read were about doctors and nurses, especially those which had an Operating Room setting.

Brittany watched her sister and somehow wanted to be quite different. She didn't have to try hard, for she was already outspoken, quick-tempered, and dressed so everyone would notice her. She was a blue-eyed blonde with short, wavy hair. At least once a week, she and her mother went shopping for the latest in new dresses and shoes. She loved anything green, especially if it was trimmed in yellow. She waltzed around the halls at school and students ooh'd and aah'd as she danced by singing and laughing.

Brittany dreamed of music and longed for the day she could take voice lessons. When she was six, her parents had arranged lessons with the finest teacher they could find, and Brittany began singing. While high, sour notes filled the living room, Judith was in her bedroom, cutting open her dolls - first the head, and then the arms came off. Her little closet became an autopsy room, and she was forever asking her mother for more dolls! She wanted someday to enter the medical field!

The Sanders' three-story home overlooked Boston Common and both girls loved taking paddle boat rides around the little lake, or chasing each other through the tall pines and oaks. After running hard, they would flop on an iron bench if they could find one not already filled with tired workers on their way to the subway station beneath the park. At noon, they would often hear chimes from Park Street Church across from the Common.

The girls loved to go home and smell the aroma of freshly baked cookies their mother would cook for them. Fridays was always brownie day. And on Saturdays, the whole family was free, and since their dad loved the water, sailing was fun for all of them. They'd pack a super lunch, wear old clothes and sneakers, and take along blankets and swim suits (though it was often far too cold to swim), and head for Sandwich. They enjoyed that little old town on Cape Cod, filled with piers and all kinds or sailboats, motor boats, canoes and yachts. Sometimes they sailed toward Plymouth Harbor. Other times they headed toward Provincetown. As the western sky was turning pink, yellow, red and orange, they would drive back home to Boston, often stopping to buy live lobsters - claws tied and safe for handling - arrive home, heat up the lobster pot, and boil up a wonderful feast.

The Boston Globe hit the front porch early Sunday morning. Bill read the financial section while Martha turned to the Society page. The girls grabbed muffins and milk, and were off to shop, visit school pals, or just goof off. This was a "do as you please day," and each one did just that.

CHAPTER 4

Judith had a close friend at school. One weekend, in their Sophomore year, Mary Beth invited her to spend three days at a cottage her parents rented for a month each summer. They left after school on Friday. It was a hazy, breezy New England day at the end of May. As always, weekend traffic was heavy. Halfway to the Cape, they stopped for a frappe and some chips. Crossing the Bourne Bridge, a small freighter was fighting the strong current in the Canal. It suddenly felt damp, the wind had changed and a small cloud of fog followed them across the Bridge.

The little cottage faced the bay, and they carried in their bags, the sailboats looked almost becalmed and the darkened sky and sea sent small crafts toward shore. It was dark when Judith and Mary Beth hurried into a small crab shack. Fried clams with French fries and cold slaw hit the spot. Mary Beth's parents were not able to be at the cottage since they were caring for her aging grandmother.

As the clouds rolled, jackets felt good. Blowing sand pricked their faces. After a short time, cots felt warm and cozy. The only noise was the howling of a

Great Dane, wanting to get off his leash, while a little black and white terrier returned his barking. But sleep overpowered the noise. This would be a lovely weekend for boating, sunning and shopping on Saturday.

Terrifying screams, metal scraping on metal, awakened them, and without even donning robes, they ran to the front window. Three cars, a motorcycle and a bicycle were in a crumpled pile. People ran from every cottage. Someone yelled out to call 911.

Judith ran to the first car and without hesitancy, pulled a young child from the wreckage. Smoke was quickly clouding the scene. A man came out of nowhere with a blanket and wrapped it around the little girl. A woman, covered with glass, fell onto the pavement. Two men picked her up. Then Police sirens screeched, ambulances followed with flashing lights, and fire trucks flanked the little two-lane road. Someone grabbed the boy away from the bike, realizing his foot was pulling part of the metal with it. After what seemed like an eternity, the Police dispersed the crowd, and Judith handed the small girl to an EMT. Somewhere in the distance, a church bell tolled three times. Cape Cod Hospital was closest to the accident scene and ambulances rushed down the road, lights flashing wildly. No one moved from the places where the Police had ordered them to go. Judith shivered and suddenly realized the fog was mixed with the smell of ashes. Mary Beth ran and brought robes for both of them. After all the emergency vehicles had left, and the road was sealed with yellow ribbons, the shaken crowd silently fled into the darkness.

Returning to the cottage, the girls made coffee and drank it silently - still shivering and still frightened. Empty police cars were parked on the roadside. Strangers

were not allowed into the area. The air smelled putrid. Clouds covered the summer sun. It was much later they learned that it was a local Neurosurgeon, Dr. Allen, who saved the little
girl's life.

CHAPTER 5

Judith graduated with honors from high school and knew she would go to college. She had, of course, always hoped to attend a Medical College. Many of her friends were accepted at the University of Massachusetts, but Judith wanted to be "on her own." So she applied to the University of Connecticut in New Haven. Her dad was disappointed she had not chosen Yale, but both parents were happy she was going on with her education. She had dated several boys in high school, but wasn't serious with any of them. She was a Cheerleader her Junior year, and was involved in several school activities.

Her parents had promised each of the girls a trip to Europe when they graduated. For each, it would be special. So after Judith's graduation the following year, Brittany chose to work in a camp while the family went to England to celebrate Judith's milestone.

It had not always been a happy family. Bill Sanders was an excellent lawyer, but many times, his temper and determination to be right followed him from his office to his home, and both girls were aware that their mother bore the brunt of his problems.

One Spring day, before Judith graduated, she found her mother crying on the sofa in the living room. She sat beside her and tried to comfort her.

"Mommy, daddy doesn't mean to hurt you, but I know he does. What can I do, or what can either of us do to help?"

Mrs. Sanders dried her tears and hugged her daughter and told her it was just a bad day. She looked sad and hurt.

Then one night, a week before they were to leave for Europe, the girls heard loud noises coming from their parents' room. They crept quietly to the door, and realized their dad was really angry with their mother. Without too much thought, they knocked on the door. Their father opened it, then slammed it shut in their faces.

The next morning, Mrs. Sanders did not come to breakfast and, since their father had left early for court, they knocked on her door and went in. They saw the bruises on her face and her swollen eyes. She said she had hit her head on the door and had cried because it hurt. Neither daughter believed her. They got her tea and toast, and left for school, knowing they would be late for classes. On the way, they had the best sharing time they had ever had. They wondered how they could help their mother, and what to say to their father.

The night before Brittany left for camp, and two days before the rest of the family sailed for England, the girls sat beside their dad and told him how much they wanted him to have a great vacation, with lots of relaxation and enjoyment. It seemed to Judith he was going merely because he had promised her this reward.

As they finished their packing for the trip, Judith noticed her dad was taking several law books with him.

Before the suitcases were closed, she ran upstairs, took out the books, and hid them under the bed. She would wait for his anger when they returned home.

CHAPTER 6

The Ocean was smooth, the activities too numerous to enumerate. The ship was a floating palace. Sports, swimming, a choice of six dining rooms for dinner, and breakfasts on the 14th deck with a view of the whole wide world.   The fellows wanted to swim and dance with her. Her parents played bridge, sat on deck chairs, swam and were happy Judith was having a good time. Things seemed to be going well with the family. Yet, with all the activity, Judith was lonely - until the last night at sea, before the ship slipped into Southampton, when she met Jonathan. He was different. So gentle, handsome, warm and friendly. He danced, and she floated on air. They spent the entire evening together. When it was 2:00 a.m., she felt she must say goodnight.

"I'll give you my address," she shyly said. "Promise me you'll write when you get home. I know I'll miss you. Maybe we'll see each other in London, even for a minute or two." For a short moment their eyes met, and he kissed her goodbye, promising to write and see her as soon as they were both home.

Her lavender and yellow dress swirled around her as she danced to the Stateroom in Cloud 9 or above! Maybe she would tell her folks in the morning, but they would be busy with debarkation, immigration and customs. England was sunny, but cold - but her heart was warm and happy. This man - yes THIS man - she was going to marry!

Enjoying coffee and scones on the boat train, they were soon in London. Little black taxis were everywhere. The streets were buzzing with traffic seeming to be driving down the wrong side of the street. It was great, and even her parents were smiling and seemed happy. It was going to be a wonderful vacation! It just had to be.

"Oh, daddy, thank you for bringing me and making this so special. I love you for it."

He put his arm around her and held her gently.

Yes - it would be a memorable summer!

England was more beautiful than Judith had ever imagined. Roses, flower baskets, gardens galore, rainy misty nights, cool sunny days. She had been told about London all her life, but to see Westminster Abbey, the crown jewels, Buckingham Palace, the changing of the Guard, the winding Thames, Piccadilly Circus, and Hyde Park was a wonderful experience.   Then on to Oxford and Stratford on Avon and Shakespeare's Theater. Freshly baked blackberry buns with a cup of tea was her favorite afternoon snack.

Strangely enough, each place they went, she wondered if Jonathan might be in the crowd, or if they would see each other somewhere. She had never thought to ask him how long he would be in London, or where he was staying. Their time together on the ship had been so short. Why hadn't she asked him anything about his plans? Nor had he asked her the same questions. Why did he pop into her thoughts at every turn?

From England, the Sanders visited Wales where Judith's grandfather had been born and raised. They stayed in a lovely old home on the way and took day trips through the hills, took a tour through Cardiff and visited Gothic churches built in the 1600s. The cathedrals and quaint homes were centuries old.

Two cousins took Judith shopping. She had long wanted a real Cashmere sweater and she found exactly what she wanted. She had never worn boots, but her cousins insisted they were all the rage, so she bought a decorated black pair and wore them almost every day.

Their last trip was to Scotland where they visited the Moors, the castles, and Loch Lomond where they took a cruise on a bitter, rainy day. The waves slapped against her face. Her wet hair dripped on her new jacket and dampened her kilt skirt. As she looked across to another tourist boat, she caught her breath as she thought she saw Jonathan leaning against the railing. Could it be? Just on the chance that it might have been, she waved , and then quickly put her hand back in her pocket before anyone saw her.

After four days in Scotland, the family boarded the train for London, packed their bags reluctantly, took the coach to Heathrow, boarded a British Air plane, and soon were back at Logan International in Boston. It had been a glorious trip - but it was good to be home.

Brittany had worked hard at the camp in Pennsylvania and kept busy with the tasks of being a counselor. She also began dating a young fellow, enjoying her free time with him. Her parents had wanted her to take the trip with them, but she chose not to go. When they returned, however, she happily met them at the airport to take them to Beacon Hill. The July warmth had brought all the flowers to full bloom.

Mail was piled high on a table in the living room, and Judith dashed to it. After scanning bills, letters and greetings for her parents, she found a postcard from England. Jonathan had remembered, and mailed it from London. He mentioned he was on his way to the underground where he would head for Westminster Abbey, and he wished she could take the trip with him. Could it be that they were there on the same day? Unfortunately, the postmark was unclear, so she couldn't read the date. But he did write a P.S. stating that he would call her when he arrived back home the middle of July. It was already the 12th. How soon would he call? Better yet, how soon would she see him?

It was Friday, and Brittany stayed home for the weekend to hear all about their trip before returning to Pennsylvania. She shared that one of the fellows in the office dated her a couple of times, but the third time she refused. He was nice enough, but was too short and too young. She had very special ideas about the men she would spend time with. In fact, she had actually found someone who was extremely nice and with whom she had spent a great deal of time. His name was David and he had come from Illinois to be the chef at camp.

As they were finishing dinner Sunday afternoon, the phone rang. Mr. Sanders answered.

"Just a minute please, and I'll call her," he replied to a warm, friendly, masculine voice. "Judith, a gentleman by the name of Jonathan would like to speak with you." He smiled as he watched his daughter's face light up. Her heart skipped a beat as she uncurled her legs from the couch pillows and walked quickly to the phone.

Having just arrived back on the Cape from England, he had wasted no time in calling to ask when they could have dinner. They decided on Tuesday evening. He would pick her up at 7:00 p.m.

When she placed the receiver back in its cradle, she was shaking, suddenly realizing she had never mentioned his name to her parents. They were surprised, for both of the girls had always confided in their parents. But when she told them about meeting him only the last night aboard ship, they seemed content, as long as she would not stay out after midnight. She promised and also assured them they would meet him before they went out.

Brittany teased her, but was soon on her way back to camp. Judith unpacked and looked at every dress in her closet, trying to decide what to wear Tuesday night. After their long flight, the time change caught up. She put half her things away, showered and fell asleep dreaming of Jonathan's invitation, and mentally buying a whole new outfit.

CHAPTER 7

Jonathan was very excited as he donned his white suit. He was going to put on a black tie, but thinking better of it, he grabbed his favorite white one trimmed with a touch of silver. He combed his jet black hair three times and slicked it down so even a tornado couldn't move it. He rubbed shaving lotion on his face, then put on some more. After looking in the full-length mirror to make sure everything was just as he wanted, he ran down stairs, and waved goodbye to his mother. She knew a little about Judith - but there had been other beautiful girls.

Climbing into his green Mercedes, he sped off for the 50 mile trip to Boston. The sky was overcast, though the summer sun peeked out every little while. But who cared about the weather? Traffic was light, so he made good time. As he approached Boston the sky darkened. As he approached the Common, he heard a strange noise just as tiny raindrops began skidding across his windshield. Pulling up next to a DO NOT PARK sign, he hopped out of the car and checked his tires. Oh no! The right rear tire was as flat as a pancake. He grabbed his cell phone to call AAA, but in his rush of dressing, the card had been left behind. Then he called Judith to say he would be late and after hesitating, he asked if she would kindly call AAA for him.

But maybe he could start changing the tire to save time. Opening the trunk, he found the jack and yanked it out. The unused cover brushed across his leg and left a huge black mark on his white trousers. He tried to brush off the dirt, but then his hand was black. As he reached for a rag, his hand dragged across his other trouser leg. Could anything else happen? He was frazzled and angry with himself. A passerby offered to help and Jonathan gratefully took him up on his kind offer. The man was unkempt and dirt would certainly not hurt him. He took the jack, making sure the brake was on, gently lifted the car, took out the bolts and the old tire fell on the sidewalk. It seemed to Jonathan that the man was humming the whole time he worked. As he started to put on the spare, the rain teemed. Thunder shook the surrounding buildings, and lightning crossed the street in front of them. Soaked to the skin, the man finished the job just as the AAA truck pulled up.

Jonathan, soaked and dirty, grabbed his wallet and handed the man $50.00. Startled, the dripping man smiled, but refused the money.

"It was my joy to help you," he said. "I can't take money from you. You'll have to buy a new suit or get that one cleaned, so you'll need the money."

But Jonathan insisted on his taking it. He then shook the stranger's hand. As he started to get in his car, the man gave Jonathan a small piece of paper. Jonathan never looked at it, but he thanked the poorly clad man.

The clothing stores were closed, the hour was late and he knew he could not meet Judith and her family as he was. What could he do?

Finally, in desperation, he called and asked if he could come another night. He told Judith he had gotten into a mess helping change his tire and he was soaking wet. He apologized profusely.

But Judith quickly responded that he should come anyway, dry off and they could eat something at home rather than going out. Embarrassed and disgusted, yet wanting more than anything to see Judith, he drove up Beacon Hill and found a place to park near their home. Grabbing his umbrella, he tore to the front door and rang the bell. A smiling, beautifully dressed Judith opened the door and gave him a warm welcome. His hands were dry and fairly clean, so he shook her hand. Apology and disappointment was written all over his face.

Mr. and Mrs. Sanders were in the living room. Without commenting on his appearance, they greeted him warmly. And soon Mr. Sanders stated, "I think I have a suit that would fit you. If not, I certainly have a warm bathrobe." Even though their home was luxurious, and their wealth was easily recognizable, these people were far from being snobbish.

The men ascended the stairs and Judith and her mom decided to head for the kitchen to fix something to eat since the weather was far too terrible to think of going out.

When Jonathan took off his wet jacket, he came across the little piece of damp paper the man had given him on the street. He put it with his wallet, keys and comb. The paper was white with red and black marks across the front.

One of Mr. Sanders' suits fit perfectly, and Jonathan was grateful and happy. He rolled up his white suit and laid it on a table, put is wet shoes under it and followed Mr. Sanders to the living room.

The ladies had fixed a super taco salad, made coffee and put cheese toast in the microwave. Conversation was friendly, but a little after nine, the Sanders said goodnight and left Judith and Jonathan alone. A few minutes later, Mr. Sanders brought Jonathan's clothing down to him. Jonathan felt he was stupid for not having brought them down himself. Again he apologized, but Mr. Sanders assured him, "If that's the worst mistake you ever make, you'll be very welcome in our home!"

After an hour of getting to know each other better, Jonathan said he should leave. the weather had worsened and he knew it was best to go. He did make a date for the following Friday night for dinner. In the meantime, he would call her. Judith hated to have him leave, but it was a friendly goodnight.

The weather was dreadful. Police were everywhere. Ambulances rushed by him. Jonathan called his family to assure them he was all right. It was a little after 3:00 a.m. when his key unlocked the front door. The house was quiet. He took off his borrowed clothes, carefully laid them down, took the little piece of paper and put it with his wallet, and jumped into the shower. As he hit the bed, he hoped he could redeem himself on Friday night. And his last thought was that he should send flowers to Judith in the morning.

CHAPTER 8

Jonathan awoke with the feeling that his head was in a vice. He could hardly turn his neck. The clock was on the night table, but he couldn't even see it. He put his hand on his forehead. It felt like fire. He called, but no one answered. It was Wednesday, and his dad was, as always, at the hospital. His mother was getting her hair done, after which she was to have lunch with a friend in Hyannis.

After a few minutes, the floor swirled and everything Jonathan had eaten was on the sheets and the floor. His phone was on the desk by his computer - across the room. He rolled out of bed, crawled across the room, reached for the leg of the desk, but he couldn't pull himself up. After that, he remembered nothing.

Dr. Allen called home at noon to say he had emergency surgery to perform and would be late, but there was no answer. When Mrs. Allen got home, all was quiet. Something seemed very wrong. She hurried up the stairs and was shocked to see her son lying unconscious on the floor. His face was scarlet, his pulse weak.

Immediately she called 911 and within minutes, EVAC arrived. Sirens screamed and brakes screeched to a halt as they reached Cape Cod Hospital. Dr. Allen was paged as were several doctors whom Mrs. Allen knew.

Dr. Allen ran to his son's bedside. Blood work and a CT scan had already been begun. An I.V. was running. Neurological tests were being done in the Emergency Room. After nearly an hour of needles, tests, and medications, Jonathan opened his eyes wondering where he was and who all these people were who stood over him. His pulse was stronger. His fever was beginning to lessen, but his head was still throbbing. He recognized his family and nodded to them. His mother held his hand.

What had happened? Where was he, and why?

By evening, the diagnosis came back that he had food poisoning aggravated by pneumonia. His stomach was bloated, and his lungs made it difficult to catch his breath, but his fever had subsided somewhat. Oxygen was helping him breathe. Strong medicines were given. Around the clock nursing care was ordered. And a cot was set up in his room in I.C.U. so one or the other of his parents could be with him. He was asked everything about what he did on the evening before, and he told his dad all that had happened. His memory was normal. He had gotten soaked with the rain, but had not felt cold. And dinner was good. On the way home he hadn't even stopped for a drink.

His frightened parents were shaken, and one or the other stayed with him night and day until the danger was past and he was well on the road to recovery. Their minds raced back to the loss of their first son, and their imaginations went wild with worry. Was he really going to be well, they asked themselves over and over again.

Blessedly, after five days, he was home - weak and eating very little, but gaining strength. His head was feeling much better as well.

Then out of the blue, Jonathan remembered the date he had promised Judith. It was days past Friday, and he was too ill to have remembered this earlier. Questions flooded his mind. He thought Judith had his telephone number, or surely she could have looked it up or asked the operator for it. Did the food poisoning begin in their home? Were they ill as well?

Then he took the phone and called Judith's number. A strange voice answered. He asked for Judith, but the lady only told him that she and her parents were out of town. He was left speechless. Surely they had lost all faith in him. He would never be allowed to see her again - of that he was sure. He felt better physically, but his heart was crushed. He hadn't fully realized how much he cared.

That night before going to bed, he remembered the little piece of paper the poor man had given him in Boston. He took it from the dresser and read the title: "Does Jesus Care?" The only times in his life he had heard that name was in swearing. What could it mean? He read it and re-read it. It told of a God who loved and cared. Jonathan was not a man who cried easily. But that night, in his weakness and loneliness, the tears fell gently down his manly cheeks. Where could he find this ONE who cared? He would certainly begin to look when he was well. But where was Judith? Would he ever find her again? His mind, body, and spirit were extremely weary. Then he turned off the light and slept.

CHAPTER 9

By 7:00 p.m. on Friday evening, Judith was beside herself. She had tried calling Jonathan at his home, but there was no answer. She did not have his cell phone number. Her mother tried to console her, saying since it was Friday night, the traffic would be very heavy on Route 3, but he would soon be there.

By 8:00 p.m., there was still no answer on his phone. Judith's new, dusty rose dress was wet with tears, and her father was angry.

"Last time, it was a flat tire, and he was very late. Now this." And he told his daughter she was better off not even going with a man who did the same thing twice.

Judith's mother finally cooked a light meal, but Judith ate nothing. It was much too late to go anywhere, even the movies. Besides, Judith wanted to stay by the phone - just in case.

While Judith stayed in the living room, her parents went upstairs and decided they should drive to the North Shore, or the mountains on Saturday, and maybe that would help their daughter forget about this Jonathan.

After midnight, the family went to bed, but Judith just tossed and turned. About 3:00 a.m., she called his number again, but still there was only silence.

At breakfast, few words were spoken. Then Judith headed for the phone, but her father told her it was a waste of time. Jonathan was not worth bothering with.

Their trip to the Lake Region was a silent one. Nothing that her parents said made Judith feel any better. She realized that she really loved Jonathan, and for most of the trip, she sniffled and blew her small, pink nose. They had planned on staying overnight, but when nothing seemed to help, her father turned back and headed home.

It was late when they parked in the garage. But there was singing and laughter coming from the Common. There were hundreds of young people sitting on blankets and chairs under the floodlights. Even with all the regular traffic noise, the singing was loud. But the only words Judith could make out as she stood on their front steps were, "Awesome God." She thought it sounded nice, but the two words were very strange to her.

Judith awoke Sunday to a pouring rain. She planned to call the Police Department in Sandwich to see if there might have been an accident, but her father, who had become very stern over the entire situation, told her she should not do that. So she went for a walk in the rain. Finding a public phone booth two blocks away, she called the Police, but they had had no report of an accident on Friday. There had been one early Sunday morning, but no one had been seriously injured. She gave them Jonathan's name and asked if there was any word concerning him or his family. There was none. She hung up the wet phone, dried her tears, and walked through the Common. The sun had finally begun to peek through, and she kept walking - trying to force herself to believe that Jonathan didn't care and he had really stood her up.

Against her parents wishes, she insisted on driving to Sandwich on Monday. She would find out where Jonathan lives. That was the only ray of hope she had. She would NOT give up!

Monday morning, she ate half a bowl of cereal and headed for the cape. Today - yes today - she would learn the truth about the man she had come to love.

CHAPTER 10

When Jonathan was finally awake and his mind was clear enough to think, his heart sank. What about Judith? His illness hit him hard and for a few days he knew nothing. Now he began to remember. The first thing he needed to do was to contact Judith. It suddenly struck him. On their first date he had had that flat tire and arrived filthy dirty in soaking wet clothes. Now he had completely missed their second date, and no one had called Judith to explain. He grabbed the phone by his bed, got her number from his cell phone, and dialed. After three rings, a man answered. Jonathan asked to speak to Judith - but the angry voice on the other end asked if this was Jonathan. When he said it was, without another word, there was the slamming down of the receiver and the phone went dead.

Jonathan was still far too weak to think of driving to Boston, so he called his mother. But she had just left the hospital for a little rest at home. When she answered, she sounded frightened. He assured her he was fine and then told her what had happened.

"Could you please call and ask for either Judith or her mother, and explain what happened?"

Mrs. Allen was unaware of how much her son cared for Judith. After all, he had only seen her once on the ship, and once on a rainy night in Boston. But she agreed to call and explain her son's illness. At the moment, it didn't seem that the call was that vital or urgent. But she was willing to grant his wish. As she was dialing the number her son had given her, the doorbell rang. She put the phone down and saw that the mailman was leaving a special package that would not fit in the mailbox. Opening the door, she picked up the package, opened it and found a gorgeous flower-trimmed hat she had purchased the week before to wear to a wedding. She grabbed the hat, took it upstairs and tried it on. It was lovely. Of course, her hair needed coloring and curling, but with her new orchid-colored dress, it would make a superlative outfit. Her hubby would be proud and she could hear the guests now remark about her exquisite taste in clothing.

Dr. Allen called and asked if he could bring a colleague home for dinner. She put her hat on the bed, went to the kitchen and grabbed some steak from the fridge. That along with baked potatoes and a salad would be fine. So she started to fix that and, in between, set the table. Their dining room overlooked a small lake. There were pink and yellow roses blooming in the garden. It made a lovely setting for dinner.

After finishing preparations for dinner, except the cooking, she drove to the hospital to make sure Jonathan was doing better. As she turned in to the Visitor's Parking lot, she remembered his request. Oh, dear! She had neither the number of the girl, or her cell phone with her. But her son would understand and she would call as soon as she got home.

Jonathan's face paled when she told him she had not phoned Judith. Immediately Mrs. Allen realized her mistake was not a little one. She stayed with him about 10 minutes and then went home to make the call. As she arrived in the driveway, her husband and his friend were pulling in behind her. She embraced him and asked that they sit on the porch and have a drink while she finished getting dinner.

When the steak was in the broiler and the potatoes in the microwave, she ran to the phone and dialed Judith's number. The line was busy.   She placed the salads on the table as well as the ice water in crystal glasses. Then she dialed Boston again. Busy. Busy. Oh dear!

Since everything was ready, she called the men to the table, filled their china cups with coffee and sat down with them. Their big concern was Jonathan and much of the conversation around the table concerned him and his sudden illness. Quietly, while the men were talking, Mrs. Allen excused herself, went to the phone in the kitchen and called Boston again. She let it ring 6 times. With no answer, she finally gave up and hurried back to the table.

After finishing their apple pie and French vanilla ice-cream, the men went to the porch, taking their coffee with them. It was a lovely cool evening. Soon the men were engaged in a deep medical discussion. So Mrs. Allen went to the phone again. But there was still no answer.   Her conscience felt better, but she knew Jonathan would be very upset.

Meanwhile, from the hospital, Jonathan used his cell phone to call Judith. First it was busy. Then there was no answer. When his doctor came in about 8:00

p.m., he asked if he could be discharged in the morning. The answer was a very stern "NO." He had hoped he could get out and drive to Boston. But all hopes evaporated. In desperation, he asked the nurse if he could have a piece of paper and an envelope. He told her it was really important. She found a yellowish looking pad and a hospital envelope. At least he could write to the girl who was beginning to be more than life to him.

When his parents arrived after their guest had driven off, his mother told of her many attempts to call Judith. He understood and thanked her. His dad did all the looking and poking that a doctor/father would do. He seemed pleased at his son's progress.

It was late when they left the hospital - relieved and encouraged that their son was doing so well. He looked so much better outwardly - but little did they know the condition of his heart.

After the nurse took his temperature and blood pressure and fluffed his messy pillow, she left the door ajar and said good night.

"Be sure to call if you need anything. Remember, the call bell is right by your pillow."

Jonathan thanked her, sat up, and started to write. It was long after midnight, and after two nurses had come to check on him he finally put the letter in an envelope, closed it, laid it on the night stand, pushed the button that shut off his light, turned over and finally slept.

Would tomorrow be a better day, he wondered. Would Judith finally be home, and could he really speak with her? His mind and heart were a jumble of confused thoughts and hopes. It couldn't get any worse.

CHAPTER 11

The R.N. who worked from 7:00 p.m. to 7:00 a.m. came at 6 o'clock the next morning, took Jonathan's vital signs, gave him a basin of coolish water and a wash cloth, and told him he looked really good after being so ill. She told him she would soon be leaving and hoped he'd have a good day.

As the door closed, he pushed the over bed table far away, walked to the bathroom, brushed his teeth and slowly stepped into the shower, though he felt weak. He dried himself quickly and carefully began to put on the clothes he had arrived in. Then it suddenly dawned on him that he had arrived by ambulance and he had no transportation for his fast, vital trip to Boston.

He grabbed the phone book and looked up "Rental Cars." Avis was at the top of the list. Luckily they had an office and lot in Hyannis not far from the Cape Cod Hospital. He dialed the number and they assured him there would be a car ready in about 20 minutes. He grabbed his wallet and checked to see if he still had all his credit cards. He was relieved to find them.

He didn't know his way out of the hospital, but in street clothes, maybe someone other than his nurse, would think he was a visitor and guide him to the lobby. Just as he left his room, he ran into an Orderly and followed him until he was away from the Nurse's Station. Then he asked about the lobby. The elevator was pointed out to him and he was told to push "M", not "1", for main floor. He thanked the man. When he entered the elevator, he leaned against the door, slowly descending to the lobby. He hadn't remembered to close his hospital room door, but was too weak and in too much of a hurry to go back. They would discover him gone soon enough, and would call his folks.

The Avis, blue Subaru was at the door. He thanked the driver, drove him back to his office, and headed for Route 6. After a few miles, he knew he needed food. He felt so weak. A Friendly's Restaurant was on his right. He parked and walked in slowly, choosing a corner booth. The waiter smiled, and took is order. The coffee, toast and eggs tasted good to him. Hospital food never had much flavor.

Quickly, he was on his way, and although traffic was picking up on this route that took so many workers to Boston, he made fairly good time. Once over the Bourne Bridge, he headed straight for his destination. It was a warm morning. His brow was soaking wet. And he knew that to get to Judith's, he needed to slow down and realize this was his first day out of bed since the ambulance had picked him up five days earlier.

Jonathan's mind turned to his parents and knew they would be upset at his sudden "disappearance." It would be cruel to hurt them when they had been so good to him. To assuage his guilt, he pulled off the highway at a rest stop and called his dad on his cell phone. When his usually quiet father answered, he was anything but! What on earth was his son thinking of and why couldn't he have let his mom and dad know what he was doing?

Jonathan tried to explain as best he could, but his father was stern and demanded that he return and have his physician check him out. Jonathan told his dad he was really fine and it was urgent that he see Judith.

John Allen told his wife what their son had done. She tried to calm her husband. She told him about the phone call she had promised to make for Jonathan the night they had company, and after a short while, John quieted down. He remember when, years ago, he had felt that way about Laura and some of the foolish things he had done then to hold on to her. At that very moment, he would still do anything to keep her. After all seemed quiet, he took her in his arms and everything seemed better. He called the Hospital to tell the nurses about Jonathan. They had been searching frantically for him and were ready to call Dr. Allen when his call reached them.

Jonathan had forgotten that every morning, Route 3 was the world's longest, largest parking lot. Traffic moved at a snail's pace. When he finally turned off the main highway and headed for Boston Common, the roads were crowded and streets filled with business men and women on their way to work. He rounded the Common and parked in front of Judith's home. Totally spent, he put his head back for a quick breather and in seconds fell asleep.

A knock on the window awakened Jonathan with a start. The policeman asked if he was all right. In total shock, he assured the man in uniform that he was fine. Then he exited the car and climbed the steps to 608. He rang the bell and a lady, dressed in white, opened the door. He asked for Judith. The lady said she had left early in the morning, and both parents were out.

"May I leave a message?" he inquired, as he wrote down his name and cell phone number.

"How soon do you expect any of the family to return?" She said she had no idea, but one of them would call him as soon as possible.

As he was leaving, after thanking the lady, he remembered that he had no stamp for the letter he had written Judith. He fumbled in his pocket and took out the crumpled envelope and asked her to give it to her when she returned. She smiled and assured him that she would.

Downhearted, weak and discouraged, he stepped into his rental car. Strange - there was a paper under the windshield wiper. He got out and opened it. A ticket! NO PARKING FROM 10:00 a.m. TO 5:00 p.m. He slowly pulled away from the parking spot and headed for home. He didn't have the strength to stay there all day. Maybe someone was right when they said, "Put brain in gear, before putting car in motion." Or maybe it was the other way around. But he drove off anyway wondering if other people had days like this!

CHAPTER 12

There had been no sleeping after 4:00 a.m. for Judith. At 5 o'clock, she quietly showered, dressed in an especially pretty summer outfit, descended the stairs quickly and wrote a short note saying she was going to the Cape for the day. Leaving it on the dining room table, she cut off the alarm system, opened the heavy door, hurried down the steps and opened the garage door with her key, knowing the door opener would have made too much noise. She drove out on Boylston Street, winding her way to Route 3, headed for Cape Cod. The hot summer sun was creeping over the horizon. Pink and pale yellow tinted the clouds. Since most of the traffic was headed toward Boston, traveling south was easy.

Leaving Boston, and turning East in Braintree, she realized she hadn't eaten since the little she had had the night before. Years before, the Pewter Pot had lots of places to eat with yummy coffee and sweet rolls - but they were now out of business, so she stopped at a little place with a sign, "Breakfast, Lunch and Dinner All Day." A blueberry muffin and a cup of coffee tasted good, but she didn't linger, and soon was on her way.

With almost no cars or semis heading south, she quickly passed Plymouth and onto the Bourne Bridge.

The Canal was blue, but no boats were out yet. She turned on 6A and headed for Sandwich. She knew any Post office or Police Station could direct her to the Allen's home. There was a long line of people mailing packages and buying stamps, but she waited impatiently, finally getting to a friendly clerk. She told him she was a stranger in the town, but knew the Allens and needed directions to their home. Even in a little village in New England, people are private and slow to give information to strangers without knowing details. So he told Judith where there was a phone booth. There would be a phone book there and she could look up the address or call their number. Surely the family would be happy to tell her how to get to their home. She thanked him and went back to her car.

She had, of course, had the number all the time, but that was not her problem. She was afraid to call again. She wanted to go to his home and find Jonathan. She drove to a gas station, took the phone book and found their address: 100 Willow Lane. She checked the phone number, and it was the one she had.

Going inside the station, she asked the woman at the counter if she could direct her to the address. After a moment the lady called to a man who was putting Coke on the shelves.

"Bill, I'm not from here. Can you help this lady find an address?"

Bill came out from under his load of bottles and told Judith to go two red lights, two stop signs, turn left and go half a mile. It would be a large home on the right. The man had already returned to the shelves. People were pushing from behind in a hurry to get to work or wherever, and she didn't want to ask again. So she went to her car, wrote down everything that she could remember and started on her way.

She had arrived at the first light when the school patrolmen were slowing traffic. She went on to the next light. While it was red, she looked at her scratching, and was sure she must turn right there. After going two streets, there was a sign, "Dead End." Going back to the light and finding it green, she went straight ahead. It was a lovely winding road. On either side were large homes, gardens, and bed and breakfast signs. She finally came to a very narrow road. At the end there was an arrow directing her to turn either right or left. She took the road to the right. Not too far along, dogs were barking and a lady was standing in the middle of the road, waving her arms. Judith stopped and realized a large tree, that looked like a large pine, was lying across the road. There were two cars and a dump truck behind her, so she couldn't turn back. Neither could she move forward.

After some time, the truck turned into a driveway as did the two cars. Judith backed up and turned around. She was totally lost, discouraged, embarrassed and disgusted. The driver of the truck was getting out, so she lowered her window and asked him if he knew how to get to 100 Willow Lane. He was in a hurry, but told her she should go to a gas station and ask, for he was from out-of-town. She went back to the traffic light and asked one of the lady patrolmen if she knew the address.

"Oh yes, that's the Allen's home. You go back to the light and …" Judith had heard it all before and done the wrong thing. But she finally found the stop signs, the turns, and came to the most beautiful home she had ever seen, Parking in the driveway, she hurried to the front door. A beautifully dressed lady answered the doorbell, and Judith asked if Jonathan was home.

The lady asked who she might be, and Judith blushed with embarrassment that she had not so much as given her name. Then the lady said she was Mrs. Allen's sister, and none of the family was home. Dr. Allen was at the hospital, and she had no idea where Jonathan was, but she thought he was still in the hospital. Mrs. Allen had gone shopping in Hyannis.

"In the hospital," Judy inquired. "Is he ill?"

Afraid she had already said too much to this stranger, Mrs. Allen's sister suggested that she should go to the hospital and talk to Dr. Allen.

Judith thanked the kind lady, ran to the car, then realized she had no earthly idea how to get to the hospital or what hospital she was looking for. She ran back and asked directions. This time, she carefully wrote down every word that was said. Judith thanked her graciously. It was 11 o'clock already!

Returning to Route 6, she went East to the exit for Hyannis and, following the directions she had been given, she reached Cape Cod Hospital. Her heart was pounding and she was both worried and scared. Parking in Visitor's Parking, she went to the Front Desk and asked for either Dr. Allen or Jonathan. The Pink Lady said she couldn't page Dr. Allen, but Jonathan was in room 302. The elevator was just behind the desk, and Judith ran, quickly pushed the button for the 3rd floor, and found the room. The door was almost open, so she peeked in. The bed was made and the room was empty.

She walked slowly to the Nurse's Station, and asked for Jonathan Allen. The nurse hesitated, cleared her throat, and finally said, "He left this morning." Judith asked if he was all right, and the nurse nodded her head and tried not to show any emotion or give anything away. Judith asked if she could see Dr. Allen. The nurse informed her that he was a surgeon and would be in the Operating Room all morning. Then seeing the concerned look on Judith's face, the nurse told her she could wait if she wanted.

At the end of the hallway were two chairs. Judith walked back and sank into one of them. She was exhausted, bewildered, frightened and lost. In a strange place and without anyone to talk to, she felt alone and forlorn. The world had forsaken her. The man she loved was somewhere, but where? His father was in Surgery and he didn't even know her. She couldn't go back to the house, and wouldn't be able to find it anyway. What in the world could she do?

She had remembered seeing a Gift Shop in the lobby. She went in and bought some note cards. She wrote a quick note to Jonathan, then found the cafeteria where she had a salad, Pepsi and a few crackers. She was churning inside and out. It was a long trip back to Boston. There was nothing to tell her parents. But there was nowhere else to go.

After sitting in her car, shaking, and silently wishing she were drowning in Cape Cod Bay, she headed home. Maybe if all her good luck followed her, the car would fall off the Bridge as she crossed the canal!

Route 3 was quiet, and she calmed down a bit until she heard sirens behind her. She pulled over as they whizzed past. Lights and sirens were blaring. In the median was a car turned on its side. All traffic was stopped on both sides. She pulled over and looked across the road. A man with blood on his face staggered and fell. She looked again - and screamed! It was Jonathan. She ran in front of everyone including police and firemen. She almost knocked down a Highway Patrolman in her rush. She reached for Jonathan. He looked up, blood flowing from his head, grabbed her and cried, "Judith." And then completely spent, he fainted in her arms.

CHAPTER 13

The EVAC driver was running toward the injured man and yelling to the Highway Patrol Officer, "Liquor? Drugs? Know what happened? Did you see the crash?

"Just arrived moments ago when some motorist called 911. Only saw what you are seeing. Haven't touched anything. My buddy is taking care of the traffic problem."

Judith held Jonathan tightly in her arms. The Officer approached and asked for their names. She gave him both. Then the ambulance driver pushed her aside and knelt beside the injured man.

"Lady, do you know if he drinks alcohol or uses drugs?" Judith didn't really know the truth, but she shook her head and said, "I'm sure he doesn't drink, and he certainly would never take drugs. His father is a doctor."

Jonathan's pulse was strong, and his eyes flickered. The stretcher was placed beside him and the men lifted him up very carefully.

"Where do you want him to go, lady?"

"He lives in Sandwich on the Cape," she replied.

"Best take him to Plymouth. It's closest."

The ambulance door closed and the motor was still on. The red and white vehicle sped down the highway, leaving Judith with those who gathered around, but very much alone.

Judith had no idea how to get to the hospital in Plymouth. But she quickly asked the Patrol Officer and he gave her directions. "If you know his family, you better call them. Do you have a cell phone?"

She ran back to her car which was holding up traffic, pulled open the door, grabbed her purse and pulled out her phone. The Officer was telling her to move the car. She knew she had to make that call. Shaken and petrified, she dialed the number. Trying to drive, pushing buttons and trembling didn't mix, and after a short distance, she pulled off on the grass and stopped the car. She dialed the number. It rang three times before a man's voice answered, "Hello." Judith gave her name in a half-crying manner. "This is Judith and I'm trying to call either Dr. or Mrs. Allen."

"I'm Dr. Allen. You sound ill. Are you all right?"

"Yes, I'm fine, but your son has been in an accident and they are taking him by ambulance to a hospital in Plymouth."

In a shaking voice, Dr. Allen asked, "What happened? Was he badly hurt? Where are you?"

Judith told him as much as she knew and then said she was on her way to the hospital. He told her he would be there as quickly as possible. "I'll call the hospital right away to see how my son is."

Judith swayed as she put the cell back in her purse, then looked for the next exit to turn off on the road to Plymouth. It wasn't far, but it seemed an eternity before she saw the sign for the town. She drove down the half-empty narrow street and soon was facing the water. Somewhere she had forgotten to turn onto Main Street. She turned around, went back and finally found what seemed like the center of the little town. Cars were going slow and pulling in and out of parking places. She went through two lights and then gratefully saw the sign for Jordan Hospital. She drove up the hill and parked in the Visitor's lot.

She grabbed her jacket and purse, slammed the door, forgetting to lock the car, and ran toward the front entrance. Before entering, she put on her jacket to cover most of the blood that had gotten on her clothes from holding Jonathan.

In the lobby, she found a lady sitting at a round desk. "Could you please tell me where I could find Jonathan Allen?"

The lady took a long sheet of white paper and began looking for names. After going through the list twice, she said, "I'm sorry, Miss, There is no one listed by that name here in the hospital."

Judith stared in unbelief. Still trembling she asked weakly, "Is this the only hospital in Plymouth?"

The lady assured her it was the only one.

The ambulance must have just arrived. Could you please check to see if he's in the Emergency Room?

The lady picked up the phone and dialed a number. She said something into the phone that Judith did not understand. Then she looked up. "Yes, he's in the ER. You will have to wait here for a little while." She hesitated and then said, "Of course, if you are a family member, you can go back to the ER."

Judith didn't want to lie, but she shook her head up and down, and then saw the large sign behind the desk: EMERGENCY. There was an arrow pointing to the left. Judith thanked the lady and hurried off.

The heavy doors to the ER were shut and there was a large sign, "No Admittance." However, there was a little thing that looked like a bell beside the door. Judith pushed it and in a few moments, a nurse opened the door. Relieved, Judith said, "May I please see Jonathan Allen?"

The hurried-looking nurse shook her head and said she would have to wait as the ambulance had just brought him in.. Judith's big, tear-filled eyes pled to enter. "It won't be long, child, the nurse said. Sit there, and I'll call you as soon as I can."

Sinking slowly onto the hardest chair, she suddenly looked at her watch. It couldn't be! It was 3:00 p.m. Her parents would be worried. She grabbed her phone and dialed home. Her mother answered.

"Mom, this is Judith. I am SO sorry. It's late. I'm fine, but Jonathan was in an accident and I'm waiting at the hospital in Plymouth. I went to the Cape early this morning. Please don't scold me. I'll explain everything when I get home. I'll call you just as soon as I know how he is. And if it's not too late, I'll drive home."

Her mother waited a moment and then replied, "Judith, the next time you leave, please let us know where you are going and why. We know you are old enough to do things alone, but we love you and care where you are. Naturally, when we heard nothing all day, we were afraid something had happened to you. Is your friend hurt badly?"

I'm so sorry I didn't call. It's been an awful day. I don't know Jonathan's condition. They won't let me in the ER. I'll call you as soon as I know anything. If it's very late, do you want me to stay in a Motel here, or drive home?"

"Please don't drive late, dear. Let me know how he is as soon as you know. "

After about an hour, a tall, handsome man came running toward the ER door. He looked down at Judith and said, "Are you Judith? I'm Dr. Allen."

She stood up and almost hugged this man she had never seen before, but he looked kind and called her by name. He pressed the button and an R.N. came. He told her who he was and she immediately let him in. He put his arm around Judith and took her with him.

At Jonathan's side, blue eyes were looking up at both of them. "I'm not hurt much. Just a fractured right arm. I think I'll be able to go home in the morning. Oh, Dad. Oh, Judith! We never planned it this way, but at least you have met one another."

A nurse appeared and gave a pile of papers to Dr. Allen. He held his son's hand and sighed with little tears falling down his cheeks. Judith took his hand and thanked him for being so kind.

"I don't know any details, but my son left a hospital bed early this morning, and I'm sure it was to go to see you. You look as though you must have left wherever you live to see him. This is not the best place for an introduction, but for both your sakes, I'm glad he will be all right. My wife said she thought you lived in Boston. Do you?"

"Yes," Judith answered. "I am so sorry for everything. I am sure you must be angry with me."

"Oh no, on the contrary. I am just grateful everything turned out with both of you being safe. I think it would be best if you came home to us tonight, and not try to get back to Boston. You look as though you have been dragged through a lawnmower and a washing machine. You need some food and some rest. We'll get this stuff signed, I'll call my wife, you call your folks, and we'll drive back to Sandwich. How does that sound?"

Her smile through her tears gave him her answer. No wonder Jonathan was so wonderful - with a dad like that!

They said goodnight to Jonathan with the promise of being back in the morning and the assurance that Judith would be with them that night.

Jonathan held Judith's hand, smiled and said to his dad, "You're the greatest!"

CHAPTER 14

The court case had been long and had not gone well. Mr. Sanders flung his brief case in the back seat of his maroon Cadillac, turned on the motor, but the car was silent. He put the gear in park and started again, but nothing happened. Grabbing his wallet, he found the number for AAA Roadside Emergency. The lady took down all the information, but said they were backed up, but she would send someone as soon as possible and they should be there within an hour.

Exasperated, he called home. Brittany answered. She sounded excited to hear her dad's voice, but he sounded angry. She didn't understand and asked what was wrong. He told her about the car - then told her he'd be home as soon as possible. There was a click as he closed his cell phone.

Brittany's mother walked through the front door and hugged her daughter. It had been a long summer with Brittany working out of the city.

"How are you, dear?" Please tell me all about your summer and everything you didn't have time to write in your notes or tell me in your phone calls."

Brittany returned the hug warmly, then said, "Daddy just called and sounded upset. Something is wrong with his car and he's called AAA. He promised to call when he was able to start home."

"Don't feel bad," her mother replied. He probably had a hard day in court and is upset that the car wouldn't start. Let's work on dinner while you tell me about your summer."

They walked arm in arm to the kitchen and began gathering things from the fridge and the cabinets.

"Oh, mom, I've met a wonderful fellow, and he wants to come and meet you, and then take me out. He was the Chef at the Camp and gave his whole summer so the kids could have wonderful food. We saw each other after the kids were in bed. Sometimes we'd just stay in the dining room. He's tall, blonde, has a great smile and loves people. He wants to work with kids and feels it should be in Asia. His parents are missionaries in Pakistan and he wants to go back there. His mother is in Idaho right now to care for her ill mother. She hopes to be home this month when they put his grandmother in a nursing home." She continued, "Oh mom, I know you'll love him."

She had talked to fast and was so excited that her mother only heard parts of all Brittany had shared. But the words that pierced her soul were "missionary" and "Pakistan." She had never heard of missionaries, and barely knew where Pakistan was.

"Oh Brit, how well do you really know what's his name?"

"David. David Whitmore. And I spent a lot of time with him at camp, and on Sundays, when we were free, we went to church together."

The phone rang and it was Bill Sanders saying they had put a new battery in his car and he would be home in 15 minutes. Martha said to her daughter, "Don't worry about your dad and how he sounded on the phone when you answered. He'll be fine now. I'd wait a little while, though, and let him talk before you tell about your summer and David."

Brittany nodded her agreement.

When Mr. Sanders walked in, he kissed his daughter and told her how glad he was that she was home. She hugged him and said it was good to be back.

"Something smells good, and I'm famished," Bill said. "What's cooking?"

He soon found his place at the table and began a long story about the trial. "I hate it when everything I say gets turned around, but that Judge just isn't fair and some day I'm going to tell him so."

They had apple pie with ice cream and coffee in the living room after dinner. Then Bill turned on the TV and his mind wandered away from his family. Then all of a sudden he exclaimed, "Martha, where is Judith. Why isn't she here?"

Martha told the whole story about Jonathan, his accident, the hospital - and because it was so late, Jonathan's kind father had taken Judith to their home in Sandwich for the night.

"I want to know every detail about that family! I don't want my daughter going off to some strange place on the Cape with someone we don't know. Why didn't you insist she come home?"

"It was so late, dear, and she was exhausted from the long day and the accident, so I thought it best not to have her drive back to Boston so late at night. You can call her if you wish. I have the Allen's home phone number right here, and you have Judith's cell number.

Bill dialed the cell phone and Judith answered, sounding happy. "Are you sure you're all right and that the people you are staying with will take good care of you?"

Before she could answer, her dad said, "First thing in the morning, I want you to come home, young lady. Do you understand?"

Judith, weary from the hard, frightening day, tried to explain to her father she wanted to see Jonathan at the hospital in the morning.

"Young lady, you are going to learn to obey me. You are to come home first thing tomorrow."

"All right, father, I'll be home sometime tomorrow."

Mr. Sanders turned off the TV, and threw the financial pages of the Boston Globe on the floor. He said he was tired, so kissing his wife and waving to his daughter, he headed toward the stairs. Brittany was close to tears, but her mother sat beside her and said, "Your dad gets very upset about his cases and his law business - so much so that he forgets everything else. I know you feel bad about him not asking the details of your summer, but tomorrow things will be better. Besides, you and I are going to enjoy the day together while you tell me all about your David. Then I'll know more what to say to your father. I don't want him to get upset with you. And you haven't heard anything about Judith, so I'll share that with you while we have a day all to ourselves. How does that sound?"

Frustrated, tired, lonely, and afraid of her dad, Brittany hugged her mother and said it would be great to have a day just for the two of them. Then she quietly went up to her room, closed the door and planned to call David on his cell phone. She knew talking to him would make everything all right. She unpacked a few things, and under one dress, she saw the burgundy covered Book - the Bible - that David had given her. He had asked her to read some part of it every day. After she called him, she would read. He had repeatedly told her that God loved her and wanted her to love Him. She wasn't sure what that meant, but looking at David's life, it must be better than anything she had ever known.

She crawled into bed, curled up and rang David's number. After trying three times, without an answer, she gave up. Surely tomorrow would be better. She picked up the Bible, opened it to where David had marked the place, and started reading the Gospel of John. She didn't understand a word she read, so she put it down, turned off the light, pulled up the sheet and put her head in her pillow. Tears streamed down her face. It was a long while before she finally slept.

CHAPTER 15

Judith was relieved to have Dr. Allen take her home that night. It had not been an easy day for any of them, and he seemed to understand she needed rest in a safe place.

When they arrived in Sandwich, she began to fear that she may have done the wrong thing. Mrs. Allen was just coming in the back door and they all met in the kitchen. Dr. Allen said, "Laura, I want you to meet Judith. She saw the accident and made sure the ambulance took Jonathan to the hospital. He's all right, but they need to keep him over night, and since it's a long way to her home in Boston, I thought it best to bring her here."

Laura Allen smiled. "I'm so glad you did that, dear. It's been a rough day for all of us. Are you sure Jonathan is all right?

"They checked him with x-rays, CT scans and found all was well. He hurt his arm as it hit the door. But he didn't hit his head. We left after they had given him a tranquilizer and he was almost asleep. We'll go back early in the morning, and I'll phone the hospital later tonight."

Dinner quickly appeared on the table, and though no one ate much, they had coffee and cake for dessert. Mrs. Allen took Judith to the guest room, gave her a lingerie set, showed her the bathroom and said, "I'm so glad to finally meet you. Have a good night's sleep, and call if you need anything. Our bedroom is just down the hall."

Judith took Mrs. Allen's hand. "Thank you for taking me in and being so kind. It means so much. I just want to take a shower and call my folks on my cell phone so they'll know I am safe and in caring hands. Good night - and thank you again." Mrs. Allen embraced her.

Judith called home and told them all was well and how wonderful and caring the Allens were. She promised to call in the morning, and after stopping at the Hospital, she would be on her way home. Her mother was very gentle and kind on the phone and told her to get a good rest.

Dawn came early for Judith. She could hear the birds chirping. The sky was clear. She dressed quickly and took the sheets from the bed, folding them up with the used towels to make less work for Mrs. Allen. She walked quietly and slowly down the stairs. She tiptoed into the kitchen and found the Allens already there.

They had cereal and strawberries with heavy cream, and the coffee was as delicious as it smelled. Dr. Allen said, "I called the hospital last night and spoke to the nurse on Jonathan's floor. She said he was sleeping and all his vital signs were fine. He had never complained and she was quite sure the doctor would discharge him when he came in."

Having finished breakfast, Judith again thanked the Allens for how much it meant to her to be with them. She hoped she had not given them any trouble.

Because Judith had left her car in Plymouth, she and Dr. Allen started back to the hospital. "I'll go see Jonathan for just a few minutes, and then head back to Boston. I don't want to interfere. I've caused enough trouble already," she said sheepishly.

"You've not caused any trouble and we are very happy to have had a little time with you. We hope to see you again in the near future." Mrs. Allen waved as they left.

They went straight to Jonathan's floor. Arriving at the nurse's station, they were told to wait a few minutes. "The doctor is with him now, and I'm sure you can see him shortly. He slept all night and only complained of a headache when he awoke."

Judith and Dr. Allen waited outside Jonathan's room. Her fears rose by the minute. What could possibly be wrong and what would the doctor say?

In a few minutes, the doctor came out. "Is Jonathan all right?" asked Dr. Allen.

"He complains of a headache, so we're gong to do some more testing to make sure if it's just a result of the accident yesterday." His voice was calm and he didn't seem outwardly concerned. Judith asked if she might see Jonathan and was told she could stay for a few minutes.

Quickly Judith went to the bedside with Dr. Allen closely behind. He held her hand and she put her other hand on his forehead. He smiled weakly.

"Does it hurt bad?" she asked.

Jonathan held her hand and just nodded without saying a word. She stood by the bed for a minute or two when the nurse came in and asked her to step outside for they were going to take the patient for tests.

Judith was shaking. Dr. Allen took her hand. The nurse sympathetically said, "I'm sure he'll be all right. He's trying to get over an accident and from the little he told me last night, he has been through a lot lately. There's a Coffee Shop downstairs. Why don't you get a cup and come back up. The test will not take long." Judith was grateful for a caring R.N.

Dr. Allen went with the patient as he went for the test. In his heart, he felt the headache was probably a result of all the stress of the accident. But they certainly wanted to make sure.

The Coffee Shop was crowded with both visitors and staff, but Judith got a cup of coffee and sat in a little booth in the corner, waiting. Surely, she tried to reassure herself, nothing could be seriously wrong. She tried to tell her heart to slow down, and hoped the coffee would ease her nerves. That was not what doctors said about coffee! But it cleared her mind enough to call Mrs. Allen to report what was happening.

After an endless 20 minutes, she paid the cashier and went back to Jonathan's room. The hallway was empty for the moment, so she tiptoed to his door and opened it. The bed was empty! It couldn't be! The nurse had said the test would not take long. What had happened and what was wrong with the man she knew she loved?

As she stepped outside the bare room, Mrs. Allen was coming down the hall. She looked at Judith's ashen face and asked what had happened.

"All I know is that the nurse said the test would not take long, and yet he isn't back. I don't see anyone to ask."

Then a nurse came toward them. "The test is taking longer than we thought, but he should be back shortly. Please take a seat in the waiting room. I'll call you when he returns. His father is still with him."

The two women sat side by side, holding each other's icy cold hands - and waited.

As the two women sat nervously in the waiting room, Judith looked out the East window. The typical New England fog was blanketing the area and even the tree tops were no longer visible.

"Shall I get you a cup of coffee?" Judith asked Mrs. Allen.

"Thank you dear, but I don't think I can even swallow. Do you want one?"

"No thank you," came Judith's weak, shaky voice.

It seemed like an eternity, yet the clock had moved forward only 30 minutes, when the waiting room door opened and two men with heads down, approached the women. Dr. Allen's face was whiter than a hospital sheet as he came over and tenderly took his wife's hands. No one spoke, and the silence was like that at a graveside.

Finally he said, "Laura, they did an MRI, and both the neurologists looked at the results. Jonathan has a small tumor at the base of his skull. They believe it will be operable, but right now he is under heavy sedation with medicine to reduce the swelling. When we left his room, he was in a deep sleep."

Laura grabbed her husband's arm and pulled him beside her on the small bench-like sofa. Judith simply stared in unbelief and then tears and trembling took over her whole body. Laura gently placed her arm on Judith's, and somehow, from the opening of the door, fog rolled into the waiting room.

No one knew better than Dr. Allen what all this meant, since he, too, was a neurologist. The other physician walked away quietly, promising to return within a few minutes. Shock and fear permeated the waiting room along with cooler air. All three shivered in their disbelief.

Finally Judith spoke almost in a whisper, "Dr. Allen, will he be all right? I mean, can they operate so the tumor will be gone and he will be well?"

"I don't know how to give you the answer we all so desperately want to hear. I only know that everything that medical science knows to do will be done. As soon as he is able, he will be transferred to Massachusetts General Hospital. The finest Harvard men are there and the best neurosurgeons in the country practice there."

After a long pause by the three who were so closely joined together by one very ill young man, Judith said, "For the first time in my life, I wish there was a God who could help us."

Silence reigned.

After a moment or two, a volunteer came with hot coffee and some little cakes and pastry. Not because of hunger, but for the need of something to do, and to help each one think, they each took a cup of hot coffee and a cinnamon roll.

After some time, Judith said, "I promised my father I would come home today. I must call my parents and explain what has happened. I'll stay here in Plymouth until they transfer Jonathan to Boston."

"No, my dear," said Mrs. Allen. "You will stay with us. We have already come to think of you as one of the family. If your parents have any questions, please let me speak to one or both of them. You WILL stay with us."

Overwhelmed by what she heard, Judith could only reach for her phone. Her eyes were too filled with tears of gratitude to see the dial. Drying her eyes with her sleeve, she called her home number.

"Hello!" It was the voice of Judith's mother.

"Mother, I promised I would call, but I can't come home today. Jonathan is very ill and I am going to stay here until they transfer him to Mass General. The Allens have been so kind and want me to stay with them. Oh please, please try to understand."

Judith's shaky voice and begging words made her mother ask, "What has happened that you need to stay? What about Jonathan?"

"I'm going to let you talk with his father, who is a doctor, so you will understand how critical all this is." And with that, she handed the phone to Dr. Allen.

After introducing himself and explaining that he was a neurologist, he told Mrs. Sanders what had happened and about the situation with their son. He tried to be professional, but kind, wanting to convey the need for Judith to stay. "We do want your daughter to stay with us. We have come to think a great deal of her, and we know she cares deeply for our son. I do hope you can understand."

Martha Sanders was a compassionate lady, and even though these people were strangers, she felt they were being very kind in an extremely difficult situation. "I know how terrible you must feel. I know if it were one of my daughters, I would be petrified. I understand your willingness to take care of our daughter, and I'm grateful. Please keep me posted on Jonathan's progress - and could I speak with Judith again? Thank you so much for your kindnesses to her."

"Judith, I'm sure everything will be just fine. Please call again when you can. Don't worry about your father. I'll explain and I am sure he will not be upset. Eat and take care of yourself, and please thank the Allens again for me. Goodbye dear. We'll talk later. Thank you for calling me."

Judith put the cell phone in her lap and put her head back against the couch. "Please know how grateful I am for your talking with my mother. Now she will better understand the whole situation."

In about an hour, the doctor entered the room and said that Jonathan had roused a little and one of his parents could see him. Both parents jumped up and Dr. Green, the neurosurgeon, walked toward the elevator with the family.

Mrs. Allen entered the darkened room, walked quietly to her son's bedside and put her cold fingers on Jonathan's hand. "Jonathan, how are you feeling?"

He slowly opened his eyes, then squeezed her hand. "I'm better, mom, and my head doesn't hurt much now."

With that, he closed his eyes again. His mother left the room so her husband could go in. He just stood by the bed, and laid a gentle finger on Jonathan's head.

The room was silent. Judith, who had followed the Allens to his room, tiptoed in, touched his forehead gently and said, "I love you Jonathan." And without a sound, she left the room.

The hospital physician suggested they all go out and get a good meal. After writing down the number of

Dr. Allen's cell phone, he assured them all if there was any change he would call them.

       The fog and chill kept them close as they walked to the Allens car. They drove to the center of Plymouth and found a Friendly's Restaurant. Inside, it was warm and there were few people there. At they sat in a booth, their eyes met in a frightened silence. Yet even though no one spoke, their hearts and thoughts were in tune like a wonderful musical masterpiece.

CHAPTER 16

Bill Sanders was a freshman at Yale, and soon tired of college fare. Since he had some money, he began eating at quiet, reasonably priced restaurants. He finally found a small family-owned place and began eating there every Friday night. A new waitress came to his table one evening, and took his order. She was pretty, quick, and the food was always hot. And best of all, his coffee was poured before he even asked.

The next week, Bill learned the name of the waitress was Martha, and after dinner he asked if he could take her to the movies. She declined. She didn't get off duty until after 10:00 p.m., and that was too late for dating. So he asked when she had a day off.

"I work Monday, Tuesday and all weekend. I'm saving money for college, and really don't have time to go out."

"Do you live at home?"

"My father is very ill and when I'm not working, I care for him to relieve my mother. Thank you for asking, though."

As the weeks went by, Bill tried over and over again to get Martha to go out with him, but she always refused.

A month later, on a Wednesday, Yale had a special holiday. Bill asked Martha, because it was her day off, if she would have time for either lunch or dinner.

"I guess I could take time for dinner, since my mother will be home that evening."

Bill was thrilled, and said he would pick her up at home.

"I live about six blocks from campus in an old white house at 200 East Street."

Bill took her to a lovely, quiet place overlooking the harbor. They relaxed, laughed and shared a little about themselves. And as he left her back home, he asked, "Could you find another time when we could go out, even for a picnic, or even just a walk about campus? It's beautiful there."

Soon Martha was seeing Bill more often. When he met her mother, he understood why she was so shy and beautiful. He also met her father - but he was too ill to say much. Yet with a feeble handshake, he smiled and thanked him for coming.

Before Bill finished his first year at Yale, he knew Martha was to be his wife. And one moonlit starry night, sitting on a campus bench under a weeping willow tree, he asked her to marry him.

"Oh, Bill, as much as I like you, I'm not ready for marriage. I have to care for my father, work, and try to get into college this Fall. I like being with you, and you have been so good to me. But I can't promise anything right now."

Bill was silent. Then he said, "Maybe over the summer you will miss me a little?"

She smiled, showing her deep dimples, and said, "I'll miss being with you."

During the summer months, Bill worked in Boston and one weekend he went to visit Martha. She was glad to see him. They had dinner and went to an old movie. "I'm glad you came," she said, "but maybe you shouldn't come again until classes start in the Fall.

August came slowly, and as Bill drove to Yale, he was excited and nervous. Maybe, just maybe, Martha would have thought of him and would be glad to see him again.

When he called her, she told him her father had died in July, and she would be working until she left for college. "I love children and want to teach. I'll be majoring in Education at the University of Connecticut. I can live at home to save money."

Bill was thrilled that she would be so close and perhaps he could see her often. Maybe he could even help her financially in some way, since she had such meager funds. But whenever he called, she was studying or working, or away from the phone. She had little time for personal interests.

Martha's birthday was November 10th. The week before, he called. "Could you have dinner with me on your birthday so we can celebrate? We can even make a whole day of it if you get the time."

Martha agreed to dinner.

The wind was wild and raindrops hit the roof of Bill's Mazda as he drove up to her home. His umbrella turned inside out as he ran for the door, holding flowers in his hand. He rang the bell and Martha came out dressed like a Princess! And even the rain and the wind didn't seem to bother them.

During the scrumptious steak dinner, Bill looked into Martha's sparkling eyes, and then blurted out, "I won't take NO for an answer, so don't even try. I want to marry you this Christmas." And from his pocket, he took a little velvet box with a satin ribbon tied around it, and handed it to her.

When she opened it up, her blue eyes filled with joyous tears. She never hesitated when he put the ring on her finger.

"But . . ."

"There are no buts. This Christmas! We can live in an apartment off campus and continue with college. You know you love me, Martha, don't you?"

"Oh yes, I love you - and have ever since you first came to my table last year. But I'll still have to work."

"No, you won't have to work. I have enough money, and more, for both of us, and can afford a nice place near both schools."

Back in the car, with the rain still pelting down, they kissed and held each other for a long time. It was hard to say goodnight, and when Martha went inside, she wondered what her mother would say about this turn of events.

"I've liked Bill ever since you first bought him home, and you have my blessing. Now you can be treated as you should be." And she hugged her soon-to-be son-in-law, and told him how happy she was for both of them.

The December 28th wedding was beautiful in its simplicity. The Yale Chapel was a perfect place. The Chaplain of the University married them. Bill's parents were happy for them and gave them a week-long honeymoon trip to the Bahamas as their wedding gift. Mr. and Mrs. Sanders enjoyed a week of dancing, swimming, loving, shopping, sunning, and much of the time being in each other's arms.

College was busy, and the more courses Bill took, the harder he had to study. Much of his homework had to be done in the library, and soon the newly-married couple had less and less time for doing things together. Martha found Childhood Education a new world and she loved her studies. Everything came easy for her. She kept their apartment spotless, shopped, cooked, and often waited dinner until 10 or 11 o'clock. By the time Bill hit the bed, he was asleep, often with one leg hanging off the side. Martha would tenderly tuck him in.

Graduation from Yale was news all over the area. Martha sat with Bill's parents as he received the coveted parchment.

"Imagine! My husband is a lawyer, and you must be so proud of your son, graduating with honors."

Martha had another whole year of college, but Bill had already accepted a position as a Junior partner in a prestigious Law Firm.

But Bill and Martha argued severely. She wanted to finish college. He was moving to Boston. They could see each other on weekends, or maybe more often. "Of course, I will keep the apartment and pay all the bills, but I can't give up this opportunity that may not come again. It will not be that long, and we'll have long weekends and holidays together."

"Then when I move to Boston, I'll be teaching in an Elementary school. That will be great. It's something I've dreamed of since I was a young child."

But her enthusiasm ended when Bill said, "I'm sorry, Martha, but you'll be far too busy entertaining my lawyer friends to even think of teaching."

She held her tongue, but her heart was wounded.

Bill moved to a large apartment in Boston, and Martha stayed in New Haven. They were both busy - too busy. Every night they talked on the phone, but soon, Bill would be out with a client, or at a business meeting, so phone calls became less frequent. He drove down over Labor Day weekend, and Martha was pleased, but all he could talk about was the firm, his beautiful office, his work."

"Bill, aren't you interested in anything I am doing?"

"Well of course I am, but my work is so exciting."

Thanksgiving holiday weekend, the University was closed, so Martha boarded a train to Boston as a surprise for Bill. The taxi driver in Boston chatted the whole way, but she was so excited, she didn't hear a word he said. She paid him, grabbed her suitcase and flew up the apartment steps. She rang the bell, but there was no answer. She called his office, but the message on the answering machine told her the office was closed for the holiday weekend. She was cold and hungry, so found a small store a few doors away, and came out with a doughnut and a cup of coffee just as Bill was opening his door.

"Darling! I'm here for the weekend! Oh, it's so good to see you." She ran up to him. He hugged her quickly and kissed her cheek. "Why didn't you let me know you were coming? I've made plans to go to New Hampshire with one of my partners. It's for men only. I'm so sorry, but we leave in an hour. I'll be back Saturday night. Here's the key to the apartment. Have a good time, and remember, I love you."

Martha took the evening train back to new Haven, sobbing all the way. She spent the weekend with her mother. On Saturday, they took the train to New York City, saw a play and ate at Stouffer's. At least she had a good day with her mom.

The following week, Martha's thoughts ran to Christmas, and she called to ask Bill, "What will we be doing over the Christmas holidays and for our anniversary?"

"I have a surprise for you. The company is taking all of us and our wives to the Poconos for Christmas. They promise us a great time!" Martha's disappointment was so deep that she could only agree to go with him, knowing she would otherwise be alone.

A month after the endless holiday week, Martha was finishing her studies. But she was feeling ill. For two days, she just wasn't herself. So she finally told her mother.

"My dear, do you think maybe you are going to have a baby?"

The following day, the doctor confirmed her mother's thoughts. Martha called Bill and he was absolutely ecstatic.

"A son -- a son! I'll be down tomorrow!"

They spent a glorious day together and happiness returned to the Sanders home.

74

CHAPTER 17

Dr. Allen rode in the ambulance with his son to Mass General in Boston. With blaring lights and screaming sirens, there was little conversation. Jonathan had been given a tranquilizer before they left Plymouth so he would be quiet and have some relief from his headache.

Judith and Mrs. Allen drove as fast as possible toward Boston, but the traffic was heavy and it took them what seemed an eternity before they were parked by the ER. They rushed through the double doors and asked for Dr. Allen and his son. They were taken to a small cubicle. Two doctors were already in the tiny area, so the family waited outside. A few minutes later, Jonathan was transferred to a private room. Anxious and frightening questions were non-verbal, but obvious, to the medical team caring for the newly-arrived patient.

The Head of the Neurology Department met with the family. He and his group felt it best to operate immediately since the tumor was pressing on Jonathan's spinal cord and the longer there was pressure, the more dangerous the procedure would become.

Dr. Allen longed to be in the OR, but knew that was impossible since Jonathan was his son. So dad, mom and Judith kissed the patient tenderly as he was being rolled toward the surgical unit. Returning to the waiting room, they noted it was 3:00 p.m. No one had told the family how long the operation might be. At times like this, the clock seems not to move and the world becomes a tyranny of emptiness.

A volunteer kindly brought them coffee and something sweet. Dr. Allen paced the white tile floor. The women sat holding each other's trembling hands. Then a middle-aged gentleman in a dark suit came to the family asking if he could pray for Jonathan. They thought it a strange request, but without hesitation they nodded willingly. With bowed heads, the man, whose silver name tag simply read, "Hospital Chaplain," prayed.

"Dear Lord. You know the aching hearts of this dear family. And we are aware of how much You care for each of them. I ask that you will give wisdom to the doctors and nurses, give peace and comfort to the family, and put Your healing hand upon this one so dear to You and to them. In Jesus' Name. Amen."

He asked if there was anything he could do for them, and they remained silent. Then Mrs. Allen said, "Thank you so much for your prayer. It meant a lot to us."

"I've been in the Ministry for many years, and know that at times like this, the only One who can comfort and give peace is the Lord. I'll be back in a little while to see how you are and how your son is. God bless you." And with that, he walked quietly down the corridor.

At the end of the waiting room was a large window. Judith walked to it and looked at the sky. It was teal blue with thin, floating white clouds. She looked up as far as she could. "Is there really a God who cares and hears prayers? " she asked herself. She remembered one Easter when she wanted to go to church, and her father said she could not, since it was just a place where they take your money and tell you a lot of stuff that's not true.

All of a sudden it struck her. She had not called her family since early morning and she had turned her cell phone off per hospital protocol, and they could not reach her. She walked back to tell the Allens she was going outside to call.

Fortunately, her mother answered.   Judith explained all that had happened, where she was, and said she would be there until the surgery was over and then, depending on Jonathan's condition, the three of them would get something to eat. "I promise to call as soon as Jonathan is out of surgery, and will give you a full report. I may be very late, but I will come home tonight."

"Your father is already very upset about your being away. Please come home as early as you can. I don't understand all of why you are doing what you are, but I will try to understand. I just don't want you to be hurt by your father."

Judith assured her she would call when she could, and would be home as soon as possible.

When she returned to the Surgical waiting room, she noticed the clock on the wall. It was 7:00 p.m. How much longer? Oh, how much longer?

An hour later, one of the Assisting Physicians came out and the family rushed to the door.

"Your son will soon be in the Recovery Room in the ICU Suite, and you can go in. The surgery went well. The tumor was removed and the spinal cord was not touched or injured in any way. The result of the biopsy should be back within a short time, but the surgeons do not believe it was malignant."

Tense, strained, frightened bodies suddenly felt weak and shaky. Tears filled their eyes. No one spoke as the doctor gave the information. Three pairs of eyes, six hands, three bodies met in a moment of united relief. Quickly they headed toward the ICU. The RN answered the bell and told them it would be a few minutes more before they could enter, one at a time, and only for five minutes each. "I will come and get you as soon as your son is settled. I'm sure you understand. She smiled, and closed the door.

The three sat down quietly. It was decided Dr. Allen should go in first, and then, of course, Mrs. Allen. Judith understood perfectly, although she longed to see Jonathan's face and to know he was really all right.

Dr. Allen pushed his shoulders back and stretched. The aching was beginning to lessen. It seemed he had been tense for longer than he could imagine.

At 8:45, the nurse came out and took Dr. Allen into ICU. The five minutes became an eternity for the two women waiting, wondering how Jonathan really was and what the Chief of Neuro had to say.

When Dr. Allen emerged, his face was almost glowing. He smiled and took his wife in his arms. "He's going to be fine, dear. He's not awake because of the anesthesia, but the doctors assured me that the tumor was removed and there is no sign of malignancy!"

Mrs. Allen hurried to the double door and Dr. Allen put his arm around Judith. "You can see him in a few minutes. You can begin to relax now, my dear."

The pent-up hours finally lifted in unabated tears. Her sobbing soaked Dr. Allen's coat, but he just held her. He would cry, too, if he could.

When Mrs. Allen came out, Judith hurriedly wiped her red eyes, ran her hand through her long hair, and went to the room that had been calling her for these many hours. She stood by Jonathan's bed and touched his hand. His eyes were closed, but when she squeezed his hand, he opened them for just a second. His face was flushed, but the nurses assured her that he was doing well and would sleep. Her five minutes lasted as a moment in time, and she returned to the Allens. It was time for joy, but the stress and strain were still a part of each one.

Finally Dr. Allen said, "We are all spent, but relieved. We need to get some food and be very thankful that Jonathan is doing so well."

As they left the ICU area, the gentle Chaplain was coming toward them.

"How is your son?" he asked ever so kindly and concernedly.

Dr. Allen told him all he knew.

"Now you will believe that God hears and answers prayers. He loves you and He loves your son. Don't ever forget that as long as you live. May God bless you and keep you." And with that, he shook Dr. Allen's hand, then slipped away.

Before they ate their dinner at a nearby restaurant, Mrs. Allen said, "I don't know what to say or how to say it, but I think we should thank God for caring for our son. So with heads bowed they spoke their thanks in silence. Refreshed and renewed in body and spirit, the Allens said they would find a motel. But Judith said, "Oh no, you must come home with me. We have plenty of room and my family will be glad to have you. We'll even find something for you to wear to sleep. After all your care of me, you must come home with me."

The trio got into Judith's car after Dr. Allen drove his car to Visitor's Parking. It was only 12 minutes until they drove into the Sanders' driveway. It had been an endless day, but the stars were shining and Boston Common never looked so beautiful under the light of the full moon.

CHAPTER 18

The front door opened slowly. Brittany stood there in her bathrobe and bare feet.

"Judith, am I ever glad to see you! I'm dying to tell you all about David right now."

"Brittany, please open the door wider. I have friends with me. I want you to meet Dr. and Mrs. Allen. They are going to be our guests tonight. Where's mother?"

"Oh, she and daddy went to some kind of concert and they won't be in until late."

Judith tried to explain who the Allens were and why they were staying overnight Then she said, "Please fix us some coffee and muffins or doughnuts while I take them upstairs to the guest room."

Brittany then put out her hand and shook the outstretched hand of the couple who were trying to get through the door.

"Sis, I'll explain everything to you later, but the Allens are tired and need to get some rest. I'll take them upstairs and come right back down. I want to find something for them to wear tonight. I know either you or mother will have something for Mrs. Allen, and I'm sure dad will have pajamas to fit Dr. Allen. I'll find toothbrushes and things like that and get them settled."

Together, the three of them climbed the stairs where they were ushered into a large, beautiful room. There were oil paintings on the ecru walls, satin curtains matched the luxurious bedspread. Judith excused herself in order to find things that would make them comfortable. She found a lingerie set of her own and a matching robe and pajamas that her dad had never worn. The large bathroom had plenty of shower gel, lotion, towels and other essentials.

"Please get comfortable, and I'll bring you some hot coffee and some doughnuts. That way, you won't have to go downstairs. And after you eat, you can close the door and rest. The phone is on the night table if you wish to call the hospital or anyone."

The Allens thanked Judith. Then she left them, arriving five minutes later with coffee and crullers on a silver tray with a lace cloth and napkins. Judith told them to sleep as long as they wished, and they could meet her parents in the morning. She thanked them for their kindness to her, and they returned the thanks. And with a quick hug, she left the room, closing the door behind her.

Brittany was in the living room, sprawled across the couch, waiting for her sister. "Tell me who they are and why they are here for the night. Then I have to tell you about my David. Oh Judith, he is marvelous and I know you will love him. Mom and dad don't know it, but we plan to marry this fall. Don't say anything, promise?"

Judith promised - then spent a few minutes explaining about Jonathan and his surgery and why his parents were there.

"Mom and dad won't be happy when they get home and find out what you've done," said Brittany.

"I can't help that. They have been wonderful to me and they live on the Cape and they need to be near Mass General where their son is just getting over serious surgery. I'll explain that to them when they come home. I've been up a long time and I'm very tired, so for just a minute, I'll rest, if you'll let me."

In less than a minute, Judith's eyes were closed and she was asleep. The next thing she heard was a key in the front door.

She got up quickly and went to meet her parents. They were dressed in evening clothes and both looked very handsome. She kissed each one, and before she could say anything, Brittany blurted out, "You won't believe it, but my sister has brought strangers home and they are sleeping in the guest room, wearing our family night clothes!"

Judith stood in silence while her parents looked shocked. "What is the meaning of this, Judith?" her father roared.

Quietly and calmly, Judith explained about the Allens and the fact that their son, Jonathan, had had brain surgery at Mass General. And since it was a long trip back and forth to Sandwich, she insisted that they stay with them - a thoughtful, caring gesture.

Before her father said more, her mother spoke to him, "Dear, you know I have told you about Jonathan and his serious illness and his coming to Boston. You were at the office when everything else happened, and I didn't want to interrupt you there. The Allens must be lovely people, and certainly it was good of Judith to bring them here instead of having them stay in a hotel. I'm sure they will leave early for the hospital, but we can certainly give them breakfast."

"Judith, I want to see you alone, right now in the den," boomed her father's voice.

Judith followed her father, entered the den before him and heard him close the door. "Young lady, you have not been honest with me. You have never told me about this family you brought here. I only know you have a crush on their son and that does not give you the right to burst in here with them and expect me to accept and understand. I've provided this home for you, and while you live here, you will obey me and keep me informed of who you are seeing and what you are doing. Is that understood?"

Tears of weariness and heartache slipped down the sides of Judith's cheeks. She looked at her angry father and wondered how long she could put up with his cruelty. Brittany could do no wrong, but Judith had never done anything to please him. Maybe, after all, she didn't need to live under his roof, and he could take his millions and spend it elsewhere.

"Yes, father, I understand. I am very tired. May I please go to my room?"

"Not until you have said you are sorry!"

Judith had no idea for what she should be sorry except for not telling him every detail. But she blurted out, "I am sorry, Father, for all I have done to upset you. Please try to forgive me." Her voice quivered and she was openly shaken.

"Go to your room, then. I expect to meet these intruders in the morning."

Judith rose without a word and left the den. Her mother was waiting for her in the living room. "I'm so sorry you're hurt. Now do go to bed and get some rest. You have had a weary, difficult day. And dear, tell me how Jonathan is doing after his surgery."

"I saw him for five minutes in ICU and the doctors said he was doing well. They thought the brain tumor was malignant, but it wasn't, and he should, in time, make a full recover. I'm sure he will be fine. Oh, Mom, he is so dear. I know when you get to know him, you'll find him as wonderful as I do. I know I'm young, but I care very much about him, and I know he cares for me. Please don't tell any of this to daddy. He's already angry and I don't want him to be unkind to the Allens when he meets them in the morning. They are wonderful, loving people, and have been as kind to me as though I were a member of their family. Thank you for understanding and loving me. I couldn't stand to stay here if you didn't really love me. Good night, mom."

They kissed good night and Judith slipped quietly into her room and closed the door. She was grateful Brittany did not try to enter. She was too tired to listen to anyone, and had to get some sleep. Her heart was at peace knowing that Jonathan would be all right. She couldn't forget what the Chaplain had said, "Now you will believe that God hears and answers prayer." As her head touched the pillow, tears of gratitude, and exhaustion, dampened the pillowcase.

"Maybe I should thank God before I go to sleep," she muttered to herself. "Thank you, God, for . . ." and immediately her weary body fell into a deep sleep.

CHAPTER 19

As the ICU Head Nurse walked into Jonathan's room, he was reaching for his call bell.

"What can I do for you?" she asked.

"My legs feel so funny, as if I couldn't move them."

She removed the sheet and put her hands on his right leg. It felt cool, but nothing strange. "Do you feel my hand?"

"No, I don't feel anything. I've tried to move my toes and they don't feel like they always used to."

As she was turning around to get the surgeon who was making rounds in ICU, he walked in the door.

"How are you this morning?" he asked in a friendly tone.

"I can't feel anything in my legs. What does that mean?" Jonathan's voice was full of fear and his eyes stared wildly at his surgeon.

The doctor took Jonathan's foot and rubbed his hand across the sole. Then he took the right leg and bent it up and let it go gently. The leg fell back to the bed while the surgeon held his hand underneath, but without touching it.

"Sometimes after heavy anesthesia, there will be a loss of feeling." As he was speaking, he was reading the patient's chart. Nothing was noted as to lack of feeling when the surgery was completed, or when he was moved from the OR to Recovery. His toes had been moving and there was no sign of a problem.

We'll do some tests immediately to seek out the cause, but I think when the anesthesia is completely worn off, you will move as you always have."

The doctor left the room, but the nurse stayed and tried to reassure her patient that he would be fine.

Dr. Allen had left the Sanders' number in case he needed to be contacted. Immediately upon leaving Jonathan's room, the surgeon called the number.

The phone rang in the living room and kitchen. Mrs. Sanders left the breakfast table, and returned saying, "It's for you, Dr. Allen. I believe it's the hospital calling."

John Allen jumped to his feel and grabbed the phone. He nodded his head, placed the phone back and said, "They want me to come to the hospital right now. Laura will you come with me?"

Laura was already standing, as was Judith. "May I go, too?" Judith asked with ashen face and quivering lips.

Before leaving, Dr. Allen said, "You have been very kind to us, and when we come back, we'll thank you properly. I'll pay for the clothes we wore. Please accept our apologies for running out. I am sure you would do the same if it were one of your daughters."

Mrs. Sanders took Mrs. Allen's arm and squeezed it, hugged Judith, and the three left.

Short of running red lights, they drove rashly through traffic, arriving in just 10 minutes. The slow elevator finally came, and when they reached ICU, they were breathless. It suddenly occurred to them they had not spoken since leaving the house.

After pushing the button, the ICU door opened and Dr. Allen went in. The surgeon was standing by Jonathan's door. After a brief explanation, they entered the room. Jonathan's face wore a mask of sheer terror as he reached for his father's hand and held it tightly and would not let it go. In a moment, an orderly entered to take the patient to X-ray. An MRI and CT scan were also ordered. Both men went with Jonathan while the women were left standing by the ICU door waiting for some word from Dr. Allen, but in all the rush and fear, he had neglected to go back to them and explain.

Finally, Mrs. Allen pushed the button and was allowed in to speak with the nurse. "I'm so sorry we didn't get back to you. They have taken your son for an MRI and CT scan. He seems to have no feeling in his legs. The surgeon feels it may be a delayed reaction to anesthesia. I'll let you know the minute they return from the tests."

A shaken, frightened mother went out to share what she knew with Judith. The two sat in silence, each rubbing her own hands and trying to calm their fear and anguish.

Finally, after what seemed an eternity, Judith said, "What do you think has happened? Could it just be something temporary? I don't know anything about anesthesia. Does it ever act this way?" The words were blurted out quickly, and somehow she knew not even the doctor's wife knew the answers.

Mrs. Allen took Judith's hand and said, "I know little about the medical field, but my husband has told me of cases where feeling is delayed. I don't know the cause, though."

An hour passed, and then another before the two men emerged.

"I'm so sorry for not coming back to tell you what was happening. Please forgive me. The MRI shows no damage, and as the heavy plates fell, Jonathan began to show signs of movement in his toes. The Scan revealed nothing, and now that he's back in bed, he says he can feel his right leg and there is some feeling in the left. Naturally, he is still frightened, but the color is back in his cheeks, and he wants to see both of you. My good doctor friend had given permission for both of you to go in but stay no longer than 10 minutes."

A smile greeted both of them as they entered his room. His mother kissed him and Judith held his hand with a firm grip.

"Sorry I scared you to death, but I was really afraid. Never thought I'd feel nothing. It was eerie and all I could think of was that I would be paralyzed for life. It was awful."

They chatted a few minutes and then realized Jonathan needed rest.

As they returned to the waiting room, sitting next to Dr. Allen was the Chaplain. He stood up and said, "I came by earlier and prayed with your son. My heart was heavy last night when I left, and my heart hurt for you. I hope you don't mind my coming by to pray."

"Thank you so much for what you have done, Chaplain. I've never believed in prayer, and don't know anything about it, but I'm sure your prayers have done something for our son to be better," Mrs. Allen said. "You had told us yesterday that God loves us and answers prayer, and now I'm beginning to believe you. Where did you learn that, may I ask?"

When I was a young man, my father was near death from an auto accident. We lived in a small town, and the only minister we knew came to see my dad. He came every day for two weeks, and one day told us he knew God would heal my father. He said, 'Dear Ones, the Bible tells us that God loves us enough that he sent His only Son to die for us. But he not only died - he rose again and He lives today. If we believe, He will answer prayer - maybe not always the way we want, but He knows best and always answers.' And that day I asked Christ to come into my life and save me. He changed my life. I learned that when everything fails, He never does. When all seems wrong and the world has lost all hope, He gives hope. He healed my father. When I was older, I went to Bible College and became a pastor. Christ has been my life ever since, and my greatest joy is to help others in their time of fear and sorrow. My prayer is that you will come to love Him, too, and KNOW that He loves you and truly answers prayer."

He bowed his head and prayed for Jonathan and the family, then smiled and walked quietly away.

To each one, it felt like the weight of the world had been lifted. Dr. Allen went in and found his son asleep, so they took the elevator down and went to get a much-needed breakfast. For the first time in a long while, they felt hungry.

CHAPTER 20

After Bill Sanders had gone through several briefs and court papers, he called home. His wife answered. He wanted to know what had happened to the Allen family, and more especially, to his daughter.

"They got a call from the hospital, and it must have been an emergency, for they left after only a bite of breakfast. I don't know the details, but I'm sure Judith will call when she can. It was a hard night for all of them and the family was most apologetic for coming here unannounced, and even offered to pay for the clothes they had used. They said they would return as soon as possible and thank us properly. They are really a lovely couple, and they surely think a lot of our daughter."

"I don't care what they think of our daughter! Strangers don't just barge into our home for the night with little explanation, and then leave the same way. I'll have a talk with Judith when she gets home and put an end to all this, and she'll not be going back to the hospital every minute, either."

"Oh Bill, please try to understand that no one was unkind, and they were terribly worried about their son, and obviously, Judith cares for him, too. You have to realize she is no longer a little girl, and you can't control her forever. She loves you and has always tried to please you."

Bill slammed the receiver down. With one leg propped up on his desk, and a word to his secretary that he was not to be disturbed, his mind raced back to the years when he was such a different man. His father was a Bostonian and a good father, a great provider - but a man the family saw very seldom. When Bill went to Yale, his parents were proud, but his father always reminded him that it was because he worked hard and saved his money that Bill was able to go to College.

When he met Laura, everything changed. She was gentle, kind and loving. For the first time in his life, he felt someone really cared. When they were expecting their first baby, he knew it would be a boy. Then he would have someone to follow in his steps and a kid he could enjoy, take to Red Sox baseball games, Patriot football games, and do all kinds of "man" things.

When Judith was born, he was happy. She was beautiful and normal, but the initial excitement left him. He was sure their second child would be a boy. Brittany was a sweet baby, but in no way was she like a boy. Then, instead of loving his girls and caring for them, his life turned to making money and trying to buy their love with gifts, trips and things. He became strict and demanding, and the older he got, the less he was at home, and the farther his family was removed from him.

Laura begged him to spend time with the girls. "Dear, please take off weekends when we can go to the Cape or the Lake - time when we can be together. Your daughters want to know you and spend time with you."

"You don't understand how vital my law practice is and how demanding. They are your girls and you have lots of time with them. They should be happy that I give them more than they will ever want or need."

"Bill, that is not the same as being with them and enjoying them. They will soon be old enough for college and then maybe marriage and we won't see them that much. You need to enjoy them now while you can."

He had every reason to be proud of both girls. In their own areas, they did well, and in school, they held top honors. Inside his gut, he had to admit he wanted to be with them, but he resented them. They were popular, good looking, and to him, he wasn't needed in their lives. After work, it was easy to slip into a bar on the way home. It often made dinner late, and the girls had left for a special practice at school, a date, or shopping. He and Laura ate alone many nights. He shared some of his practice with her, but not a great deal.

His anger with himself turned to bitterness, and he began lashing out at either girl, but especially Judith. Many of his colleagues had a good home life and loved their families, and he was jealous because he did not have this kind of happy home.

Judith was to obey him while she lived in his home. Now she had suddenly met someone who was taking his place, and he resented it. Obedience would force her back and she would soon forget the young man who had been in and out of hospitals, and had come into his home wet and messy with an unbelievably strange excuse. Then when he made a special date to take his daughter out, he never showed up and never even called. This was not the man he wanted for his daughter. When he had an opportunity, he would tell him so and would not allow him to see his daughter again. Neither were his parents to barge into his home, without even a call to ask

permission, use their clothing and food, and treat his home as a first class hotel. He would see that there would be an end to all that!
94

CHAPTER 21

Judith's body was totally weary, her heart hurting, her concern for her father's anger heavy, her longing to be with Jonathan unbelievable. Yet with all these forces within her, her mind was crystal clear. She was determined to do three things in priority order:

First, she would see her father and face whatever was behind his feelings for her.

Second, she would tell Jonathan that she loved him.

Third, she would find the Chaplain and listen to his words of wisdom and try to understand how to make his kind of faith real in her life.

The Allens were leaving Boston for the Cape. Before they left, flowers had been sent to the Sanders to say thank you, and a quick note had been written with an apology for barging into their home and leaving without adequate explaining. After caring for his patients, paying bills and spending time with his wife, who was in need of loving quiet and peaceful assurance that their son would be all right, they would return to Boston.

"Judith, we can never thank you enough for your kindnesses to us and for keeping us at your home," said

Dr. Allen. Through all that had taken place, they found in this beautiful lady a strength and genuiness they had not seen before. Indeed, she had won their hearts.

"I'm deeply grateful to you for making me feel almost like one of the family and allowing me to be with you through these unending days of turmoil, tragedy and testing. You must know by now that your son is very dear to me."

It was a warm and loving parting.

After a hot bath and a cold glass of soda, she dressed in a pretty yellow dress, threw her small purse over her shoulder, ran down the steps and took a taxi to her father's office. She left a note for her mother who had gone to the beauty salon.

Her father's secretary smiled and told Judith her dad would be free in just a few minutes after one of his partners left.

"Do have a seat. I'm sure your father will be happy to see you. It seems like a long time since you were last here," the friendly secretary said.

The door opened, and a tall, well-tailored man walked quickly past Judith. His face looked much older than his years.

The secretary entered Mr. Allen's office and returned hurriedly. "Your father will see you now."

The mauve carpet, the brown drapes, and the leather furniture seemed to echo the mood of Judith's trembling heart.

"Well, it's about time you came to see me. You should have called to see if my calendar was free. My next appointment has been cancelled, so you came at a good time. You need to give an account of your actions and insubordination of the last few days." His tone was cold and calculating.

"Dad, I've come to ask your forgiveness for my lack of an explanation, and I beg of you to try to understand what I have gone through. You have often said you love me, but this week you have been completely indifferent. I do want us to understand each other. I've never meant to hurt you. I hoped you would try to understand. I have never wanted to disobey you."

The phone rang twice. Mr. Sanders picked up the receiver. "Oh, Jeb, I forgot all about the meeting. Shall I meet you for lunch, or when would be best?"

After a long silence, he said, "Well, if you're talking about that much money, we should meet as soon a possible. Lunch would be fine. Yes, the Yale Club at one will be great. Thanks for the call and I'll see you shortly."

"I'll have to leave in about 10 minutes. We can continue this discussion at a later date. Make an appointment with my secretary."

"Dad, is money and business always going to come before your family? Will you always push us aside and never have time for us here or at home? Is this what you call loving me and your family?"

Judith's voice broke and tears welled in her eyes.

"Listen here, young lady. Haven't I provided a beautiful home, given you the best of everything, taken you on vacations or given you money ? What other father you know has done that much for his family? Don't you call that love?"

"No, daddy. We don't want your money. We want YOU. We want your love and your time and to be first before law or money. We all long for your visible affection, not for more clothes or a bigger house. Don't you realize a house is not a home?"

"Our beautiful house is the very best one money can buy. The cars we have are the largest Cadillacs on the road. Most daughters would be proud of their father. You are not grateful, nor do you show me any kind of respect. You can leave now. I need to get over to the Club for lunch."

Judith rose from the dark sofa, held her cold hands together and went toward her father to say goodbye. He turned toward a large mirror in the corner of his office, looked at his suit and his hair, and felt his cheeks to see if he needed a shave. After turning completely around, he looked at his Rolex and headed for the door.

"Please say goodbye, dad. Please let . . ." Before her words were in the air, her father had vanished through the door.

After drying her tears, she walked quietly to the secretary's desk and asked for an appointment to see her father.

"Well, let me look at his calendar. Next week he will be at a Law Convention in Chicago. The week after that he will be in court all day every day. Why don't you call me in about three weeks and we'll squeeze you in. Will that be all right?"

"Thank you. I'll call. Perhaps I will have some time with him at home and it won't be necessary for me to come here."

Tears blinded her eyes as she walked across the marble floor to the elevator. As the door opened, she stepped in, and the man who had left her father's office was standing toward the back, his arms full of books and a briefcase between his feet. His face was drawn and his pale lips made her wonder if her father had just made the gentleman leave the firm of SANDERS & SANDERS. On the first floor, she offered to help the man with his books. He thanked her, but said he could manage.

"This is only the first of many loads, I'm afraid."

And without thinking Judith blurted out, "There are many other excellent law firms." And amazed at what she had said, she rushed through the revolving door.

Around the corner was a little Fish and Chips place. She sat down on a wooden seat and decided priority number one was a waste of time. Priority #2 would go better!

CHAPTER 22

Mass General was always busy. It was known far and wide for great doctors and excellent nursing care. Judith hurried to the elevator and quickly found her way to Jonathan's room. Her heart stopped when she saw the bed empty and made up for a new patient. She leaned against the door. When she tried to speak, nothing came out. Finally, she ran to the Nurses' Station and asked for Jonathan.

"Oh, you'll be happy to know he has been moved to a private room on East 4. He's doing just fine. You're his wife, aren't you dear?"

"Thank you so much. I'll go right down. No, I'm not his wife, but I hope to be."

"He must think the world of you. He asks so often if you have come in yet. His call bell is a bit of a bother, but he's such a great man, you can't get angry at him. Run along now and see him, or he'll be pestering some other nurse to ask when you are coming."

Judith wanted to hug the very large, warm-hearted, white-uniformed nurse, but she simply smiled, thanked her and ran for the elevator.

Finding East 4, Judith asked the Ward Clerk for Jonathan's room number.

"402. Glad you're finally here. What took you so long? Your hubby will be eyeing someone else if you stay away so long." The lady in blue smiled broadly.

Dashing in to Room 402, Judith found Jonathan sitting on the side of the bed trying to force down some horrible hospital food. He immediately pushed the overbed table aside and held out his arms. After a long and lingering oneness, he asked, "What on earth took you so long? I've been looking for you since 5:00 a.m.!"

The short explanation didn't really matter because she went on to say, "There's something I have to tell you and it won't wait another minute!"

Jonathan looked into her smiling eyes and said, "Bet I'll beat you to it. I love you and want to marry you!"

The nurses's station heard no more from Room 402 for a long time. Two hearts, two lives were going to be one. Jonathan had already told his parents and they were in total agreement and couldn't say enough wonderful things about Judith becoming part of their family.

For about three hours, they talked of wedding plans, his college education, her willingness to work, where they would live - and a hundred other little things. Finally Judith said, "But we have one barrier. My father will not approve and we need to talk about what we can do about that. If he knew you, he would love you. But right now, he's only interested in making money and being a famous attorney. His family seems to come second."

"Even if he doesn't approve, will you marry me anyway?"

"You know I will, even if we have to run away."

"Oh no, my love. We will have a beautiful wedding - and I'm sure your mother and sister will be there with all our friends."

There was a gentle knock on the door and an Aide came in to take his uneaten tray of food, and to scold him for not eating. She took his vital signs, and with a wry smile said, "She finally came, I see." She closed the door behind her.

Judith offered, "Since you are on a regular diet, I'll go to the Coffee Shop and bring you something you'd like - maybe a hamburger and a milk shake?

"That sounds perfect! While you're gone - please don't be gone long - I'll call my folks. They'll be thrilled."

As Judith was leaving she said, "I wish my dad was like your dad. He's so wonderful and loves his family so much." Then she kissed him and Jonathan pulled her back and they kissed again - and again, and again - before he let her head for the door.

The Allens were overjoyed when Jonathan called. They said they would be there the next day and after his dad talked with the M.D., they could take their son home. And since it was Friday, maybe Judith could go and spend the weekend. "What a glorious idea," responded Jonathan, hardly able to contain his enthusiasm.

As Judith hurried to the Coffee Shop, she could only think of her father and what he would say when she told him of their wedding plans. If only he would spend some time with her sweetheart, he would know what a tremendous gentleman he was. But how could that be managed when he didn't even have time for his own flesh and blood!

A hamburger and two milkshakes later, sitting on the side of the hospital bed, Judith remembered she had never called her mother. Using Jonathan's cell phone, she nervously dialed the number and her mother answered.

"Oh, Mom, I'm so sorry I didn't call before, but I went to see dad and he was so unhappy with me. I left there, had a bite to eat, and came straight to the hospital to see Jonathan. Please forgive me. I didn't mean to worry you."

"My dear, I'm so glad you called. I have been out longer than I thought. I called home and left a message for you so you would know I had errands to do. So we were both busy. But tell me, how is Jonathan?"

" Mom, he's fine - and I am the happiest girl in the world, for he has asked me to marry him - and I've said YES with all my heart. His parents know and are very pleased. I want you to be happy, too, knowing we love each other so very much.

"Dear, I'm very happy for you if you're really sure you know what you are doing. Remember that you haven't known him that long or that well. Are you entirely certain that you love him and want to be his wife? It's a life-long commitment, you know."

"Oh yes! I love him and have loved him ever since he was so ill and I thought we would lose him, and if we had, I wouldn't have even wanted to live longer. He loves me as I love him - and I'll tell you more tonight. I'll be home for dinner."

"You know your father will be here, and you'll have to tell him. He may not be happy about it, but if you are really and truly sure, then you must quietly stand your ground. He does love you, you know, but has difficulty showing how he feels."

"Yes, mom, I know. And I will tell him, and hope he will get to know my sweetheart as he really is. I'll be home before long. Love you!"

Jonathan and Judith sat side by side on the bed for a long time, dreaming of their life to come, and just being content together.

"Darling, I don't even have a ring for you!"

"Well surely you could have found one in the OR or in Recovery! Silly boy - all I want is you. The ring can wait. Your love means more than a million rings. Don't you know that?"

It was about 5 o'clock when Judith kissed him goodbye, promising to come back early the next morning. In the meantime, she couldn't hide her happiness - nor the black cloud of telling her father. Surely priority #2 had been more wonderful than she could have possibly dreamed. And within a few days, she would make #3 a vital part of her life.

It rained as the taxi drove her up by the front steps - but behind the little drops, way in the distance, the sun was peeking through, and as it did, she looked over her shoulder where a rainbow crossed from Boston Common to the ends of the earth! As she turned back toward the steps, a little girl passed her on the sidewalk. "Look, Mommy. God's promise is there in the sky. He makes everything beautiful, doesn't He, Mommy?"

As she opened the door, Judith found herself within the warm embrace of her loving mother.

CHAPTER 23

As Judith entered the dining room, she couldn't remember when it had looked so very special. The light blue candles were tenderly lit. The yellow roses were still touched with drops of dew. The dishes were sparkling next to the crystal glasses. And the aroma from somewhere filled the room with beauty. It was not a special season or day, but somehow her mother wanted everything to be as perfect as possible for the evening meal.

The front door closed, and Judith's father threw his briefcase on the sofa and entered the dining room as Brittany and her mother came from the hallway. They greeted one another, and Mr. Sanders sauntered into the kitchen to wash his hands. The silence was contagious. Finally, Martha asked her husband about his day. His comments were short. Then he asked his wife why everything looked so special and she replied, I just wanted the dinner and the evening to mean something to all of us. It's so good for the family to be together and I've been thinking that we are only given one day at a time, and I wanted this day to be a good day."

She smiled, and after they had begun to eat their favorite beef au jus, Brittany said, "Oh Dad, you haven't heard the wonderful news about Judith! We found out today that she is engaged to marry Jonathan Allen."

His fork hit the plate, the napkin landed on the carpet, and with rage in every word, her father screamed, "Engaged? To that man she doesn't even know? The one who barged into our home and gave us the make-believe story about a flat tire? The one who was dripping wet and left marks all over our carpet? That man! Why was I never consulted? Why was I told nothing? You seem to think I'm only here to pay the bills and give you presents. I'm the head of this household and what respect do I get? NONE! Judith, give an account of yourself and remember - you are not to see that young man until I have said you might. And I doubt that will ever happen!"

Dinner was cold and the roses seemed to droop as Mr. Sanders finalized his tirade. He stood up, and without another word, left the room. The only sound they heard was the slamming of the front door.

After time enough for the three ladies to find words and stop quivering, Martha spoke. "I'm so sorry for all this, and especially for you, Judith. But given time, your father will calm down and you will be able to talk with him. Don't give up. And know that I understand and will always stand beside you."

"I went to dad's office today and tried talking with him," said Judith between tears. "But after just a few minutes, he left to meet a business partner. He never listened to anything I tried to say. He even told me to make an appointment with his secretary to see him later. I tried doing that, but he had no time for three weeks. So I said nothing, and just left. I feel as if we really don't have a father anymore. His only concern seems to be making money, and he doesn't even try to spend time with any of us. I know, Mom, you must be more hurt than we are. Is there any way we can find a father again, or will life always be money first and last? I've tried so hard to talk with him, but he won't listen and I don't know what to do. I can't give up Jonathan because I love him - and he loves me, and his family are dear and caring and loving. I long for a dad like Dr. Allen. Oh, Mom, please tell me what to do."

The room had taken on an eerie coldness, and before any words were uttered, they all sipped coffee and tried nibbling on homemade apple pie. Nothing tasted good, but the coffee was warm and felt good inside. They left the dining room and went to the sofas in the large green and gold living room. It was warm and seemed to soothe the broken hearts.

The telephone rang and Brittany answered it. "It's for you, Judith. It must be Jonathan."

A shaking voice put her lips to the receiver and said tentatively, "Hello."

"What's wrong, my dear?" the tender voice asked.

"I'll call you back later, if that's all right, love. I really can't talk just now."

"Don't hang up, Judith. Please say something so I'll know you're not ill, and that nothing is wrong. Have I done anything to hurt you?"

"No, dear. You have done nothing wrong, and I will explain everything later. I love you and will talk with you tonight. I'm fine, so don't worry. Everything will be all right."

"'Til later, then. And I'm longing to hear from you. Before I hang up, you know we are expecting you here for the weekend. Dad and mom are really looking forward to getting to know their new daughter-in-love better. I can come for you or, if it's easier for you, you can drive down. I can't wait to be with you. We MUST set the date for our wedding!"

Judith hung up. "Mom, the Allens want me to come for the weekend. Unless you object, I'll go early tomorrow and come back Sunday evening. I can't face dad with any of this, even if he comes home. Please try to understand."

"Of course you can go, and have a wonderful time. I don't know what I will say to your father when he returns, but I will try my best to explain that you are a young lady and have a life to live. You should no longer be treated as a child, even though you live here. Many times I have had to go away for long weekends, just to get away, so I do understand. I'm anxious to get to know the Allens and maybe soon we can get together somewhere between Boston and the Cape, and spend some time together. I know Dr. Allen is a busy physician, but I do want to meet with him and his wife and trust they will find us a friendly and loving family. It's getting late, so maybe we all need to get some rest. Please don't leave in the morning without saying goodbye to me and to Brittany. When we have more time and are not so upset, she and I will share some of what she is facing. And she longs to tell you about David - the new and very important man in her life."

"Oh, Brit - I'm so sorry not to have spent time with you. Lately, everything seems to have revolved around me. I do love you and want to hear everything about your special friend. I'll see each of you in the morning and will call over the weekend so you'll know I'm all right. I love you both dearly and am so grateful for your love and understanding."

Judith rose up from the sofa, kissed her mother and sister and left for her bedroom. She couldn't tell Jonathan anything unkind about her father, but somehow she had to be truthful to the man who was to be her husband. She packed her bag, washed her wavy brown hair, remembered to pack her bathing suit, looked at her swollen eyes, and hoped morning would make a difference. She fluffed the pillow and slid between the satin sheets.

Sleep came slowly - and then she remembered her third priority. Maybe the one person in the world who could help all of them would be the Chaplain. She knew where to find him, and find him she must. She and her family had experienced much of life with bitterness and heartache, and she had long since learned that money and things were not the answer to life's problems. She had heard the prayers of the Chaplain, seen the peace on his face, and felt the joy in his presence. No matter what else, she would find him and listen to his words. Her beloved must come with her so they would hear it together. She knew that his prayers were answered, even though Jonathan was too ill to be aware of any of it. But his parents had heard every word. They were the kind of people who would listen, she was sure.

The music alarm brought her upright. It was still early, but she dressed, slipped to the kitchen, took a mug of coffee, tiptoed to her mother's side of the bed and kissed her lovingly - then said goodbye to her sleepy sister, and headed for the garage. All of a sudden she realized she had never called Jonathan back as she had promised. As she got on Route 3, headed for the Cape, she called him on her cell phone.

"Oh, darling, I wanted to call you last night, but when you didn't call, I knew there must be a reason. I had to believe you were all right. Drive carefully. We'll have breakfast ready when you get here. I miss you and love you. What a wonderful weekend we'll all have. You are now family and we all want you to be with us. Mom said last night that she couldn't wait to make you a real daughter, and I think dad wants you as his special gal. See you soon, and don't run off with anyone else before you are in my arms!"

They laughed together over the phone. Oh to be part of a family like that!

Traffic was light and soon she crossed the Sagamore Bridge, quickly heading for the Allen home. As she entered the driveway, the three of them were there to greet her. Hugs all around made her know there was still love in the world that she really never knew. How wonderful to have her heart joyous and her spirits lifted.

"Daughter," said Dr. Allen, "we welcome you into our home and into our hearts. If we had searched the world for a wife for Jonathan, we never could have found anyone
as wonderful as you. WELCOME HOME!"

CHAPTER 24

Brittany was a quiet, obedient girl who seldom expressed her feelings, even to her sister whom she loved and admired. - and about whom she may have felt a tinge of jealousy. From early childhood, she had been taught that fathers were right and not to be questioned. She loved school and had made many friends, but shared little with them. The fellows liked her and often dated her, but when she said little about herself or her family, they felt it difficult to really get to know her. As a child she remembered her father playing with her and doing special things for her. But as she grew, she saw less and less of him and felt she was in the way. In her youthful wisdom, she knew the same was true of Judith, but neither discussed their feelings.

When her family allowed her to be a Counselor at camp, she was excited and wanted to help the kids who came and show them the love she, herself, had missed for so long. It wasn't too long before David, another Counselor, invited her for walks on the camp grounds in the evenings. Soon he was telling her of his family, his growing up in Pakistan, and sharing what it was like to be an M.K. (She learned this stood for Missionary Kid.), and what it was like going to school away from home. She listened for hours as he told her of the country, the people, the strange foods, the different clothing the people wore, and the difficult language they all had to learn.

"Brittany, you would love the Pakistanis, but more than that, you would be thrilled when you could share Jesus with one of them. When I was home for holidays, I spent a lot of time talking with the Pakistani kids, and many of them came to love Jesus as their Savior. Then my mom and dad would get to know their families and invite them to our home or to our little church. We lived way up in the mountains, and in the summer we had a children's camp. At night we sat on huge rocks and watched the sun set over the mountains. Many times it would snow in the distance. I have lots of videos of the country and where I lived, if you'd like to see them."

"Wow - it all sounds so wonderful. But didn't you miss all the food and beautiful clothes and cars and everything like that? Yet, you sound so happy. Maybe those things didn't matter out there where you saw only poor people and you could help them in so many ways. I'd love to see all your pictures. I guess I don't understand why your folks went there, or why it's important to tell the people about Jesus. They must have their own gods and beliefs. Why is YOUR way better than theirs?"

"Yes, they do have their own beliefs, and their own god. But when you ask them if their god loves them, they don't even understand. To them, god is far away and only to be obeyed. Five times a day they bow and pray, saying the same thing over and over again in Arabic - a language they don't even understand. But it gives them no peace, no joy, and nothing to hope for. I have a God who is real and alive and Who loves me and gave His life for me. He rose from the dead and lives to pray for me. I have a Bible that is true, and in it there are words of love, peace, joy, comfort and so much more. It is because of my belief and that of my family that we went to tell these dear people of the Christ Who loves them and gave His life so they could have their sins forgiven and receive eternal life. No one made my family go there. We went because we believed God called us to share the Good News with the people of Pakistan."

David made it all sound so real to Brittany. Yet, she had never heard all this before. In her heart she wanted to believe what she had heard, but how did she know it was true? The only Bible she had ever seen was in their library at home. It was carefully dusted each week along with all the books of Shakespeare, Milton, poetry and many paperbacks her family had collected. All the other books were about Law and Justice. Many of these her father had kept since he had been a student at Harvard.

"David, I want to believe you and all you've said, but I have to think about it. It's so new and different. Please be patient with me."

Camp life was busy, and Brittany had many duties, so she didn't really spend time with David for almost a week. Then on Saturday, after the bonfire, they took a walk before going back to their cabins. It was a crystal clear evening, and there was a full moon - just right for walking down to the little lake and sitting on the rocks overlooking the sparkling water.

"Brittany, I want to share my heart with you. I'm sure I'm falling in love with you, and I think you care about me. I want us to see each other after camp is over, and I want you to meet my parents, and I want to meet yours. But before our relationship goes any further, I need to know how you feel about the Christ I love and serve."

Brittany slid her hand on his and with a pounding heart said, "Oh yes, David. I do care deeply. I want us to be together, but I still don't understand all about your Christ. When I go home, I want to tell my family all about you, but I don't know what they will say about your religion and your wanting to return to Pakistan after College. I guess I'm scared and feel pulled in two directions. Our time at camp has been short but wonderful, and yet after two weeks we have to leave. You're going back to Illinois, and I'll be going back to Boston. Can you help me understand more about your God? I want to believe because you do. Maybe that's the wrong reason. I know how much you mean to me, but will your beliefs separate us? Somehow I can't let that happen, and yet I don't know what to do."

David took her in his arms and gently held her. Finally he said, "Brit, I want to be with you and someday I hope to marry you. I'll be happy to share with you everything I know about the Lord. Maybe, when you believe, it will give you an opportunity to share your faith with your family, and your whole relationship with them will be so much better. I've sensed by your silence that you are not close to your parents. This could make all the difference!"

"It might make a difference if they believed - if I believed - but it could also mean . . .Oh, David, you don't know my father. He's smart and gives us everything, but neither I nor my sister have felt his love since we were little girls. We have both become afraid of him. Mother tries to help us, but she can't say very much either. I know you must pray, so would you pray to your God and ask Him to help me know what to do? I want to believe, but I am sure with believing there comes a price. I'm not sure I know how to pay that price."

"I will pray for you as I have every day since I first met you, Brit. Only now I will know better what to ask the Lord, In His Word He has said, 'Call unto Me and I will answer you and show you great and mighty things you know not of.' He will answer and show us the way. It's late and we have to get back to the cabins. But maybe after everything is finished tomorrow night, we can have a little time together."

Slowly they walked back to the cabins and parted quickly, each going to their assigned abode. Brittany quieted the kids in her cabin, kissed each one and crawled into her bunk. It had been a long day, and although she was tired, her mind raced through David's words, her father's attitude, her return home, her separation from the man she loved. Surely something good could come from it all, but what? Perhaps David's God would give the answer. When she finally fell asleep, the birds were chirping and the sun was breaking across the Eastern sky.

David went back to his cabin, said goodnight to all the boys and told them he would be gone for just a few minutes. He was very stern when he told them there was to be no more talking. Then he quickly ran to the main camp building and found the telephone. He dialed his parents' home.

"Dad, sorry to call so late, but I have a real prayer request for you and mom. I really love Brittany, but she doesn't know the Lord. Please pray for her and for me.

We only have two more weeks of camp, and I long for her to come to Him before we leave. I know I can count on you. I must run. Love you both. Good night and God bless."

Like typical kids, the boys were still chattering when David returned to the cabin. But quickly, all was quiet except for David's heart. He knelt by his bunk and prayed for several hours. Sleepy and tired, his head hit the pillow. By his window, a tiny bird was singing in the early morning sunrise.

CHAPTER 25

Bill Sanders sat in a leather chair while his wife told him about Judith going to the Cape for the weekend. Martha was quiet, and finally, as she watched her husband's face, she grew frightened.

"Martha, I told Judith that she was not to see that young man again. She has disobeyed me time and time again. I shall not only stop her allowance and refuse any money for her college or other schooling, but she can find somewhere else to live until she comes and asks my forgiveness and is willing to obey me!"

"Bill, when the girls were small, you held them, kissed them, tucked them in at night and read them stories. You took them on special trips. You even went to the circus and we all went camping and had a great time in Maine. But now you no longer show any love for them - nor for me. We have all been hurt and have tried to go on saying little - but the girls have wept over losing a father. The more you refuse to listen to them or be with them - the more you drive them away. Your business, your law practice, your newly acquired fame as a superior lawyer, your money - all have taken your time and interest and nothing is left for your family. You are not only going to lose the girls. You are going to lose me as well, if all this keeps up. In the 22 years we've been married, I've done everything I know to make you happy.

I have obviously failed. I have a beautiful home, gorgeous clothes, a huge auto and am the envy of all my friends. But the things that really matter are no longer found here. It's not a home. It's a house - cold, empty and lonely. You can rant and rave, stand up and glare at me, pace the carpeted floors - but I will no longer take your verbal abuse or your lack of love.!

As Martha finished, her hands were icy and her body shaking. But she had told the truth and would wait for the answer.

After Bill stomped around the room a few times, he threw his expensive jacket on the floor, hit the table with his fist - then sat down. His face was ashen. He breathed deeply several times. He opened his mouth, but nothing came out.

Finally he said, "Martha, next week I'm going to Denver for the Annual Law Convention. I'll be away another week after that visiting my brother in Oregon. When I return, we'll discuss all this. In the meantime, go and do what you please. If for any reason you should need me - and I certainly can't imagine you would - my phone numbers will be on the night stand. You have my cell number. Now goodnight!"

Bill grabbed his jacket and headed for the stairs, leaving his crushed wife sipping cold coffee left over from dinner. When she went upstairs, their bed was unopened. His clothes hung in the bathroom. A small piece of paper lay outside the guest room door.

As she stood by their bed, the phone rang. "Hi, mom. We're all sitting by the pool eating popcorn and laughing. Jonathan just threw a piece to me and it blew into the water. How are you and dad?"

"It's wonderful to hear your voice, dear. I'm glad you're having such a good time. And by the way, I've been wanting to get to know the Allens for a long time. If I drive down tomorrow, would they mind? Please be sure it's all right before you tell me to come. And I'll need directions as well."

"Oh mom, they would be thrilled. Time after time they've said they want to get to know you, so please come. They are all nodding their heads and grinning. Before I hang up, I'll give you directions. I'm so excited! Will dad be away, or will he be playing golf or something?"

Your dad will be busy tomorrow and I'm not sure what he's planning. But I do want to do come. Thank you for letting me do that. Just give me the directions."

After Martha hung up, her spirits lifted and she took out her clothes for the next day. It would be wonderful to meet a loving, caring family. How good that Judith had met Jonathan.

As she showered, her reddened eyes cleared, and she was so grateful for each of her daughters. She hadn't heard much about Brit's David, but he must be a great fellow, too. She had much to be thankful for, in spite of all that had taken place earlier. And maybe the two weeks Bill would be away would soften his heart and give him time to realize what was really happening to his family.

As she lay in bed, the radio music was especially lovely. The announcer was saying that he had just had a special request. A listener had asked him to play, "Nearer my God to Thee." The music was soft and gentle and the words slipped quietly into Martha's troubled heart.

CHAPTER 26

The early morning flights were just rising over southeastern Massachusetts as Martha's car headed down Route 3 toward the Cape. She had left a quiet house, taken a mug of coffee, and driven down Beacon Hill. For the first time in a long while, she was excited.

Sugar topped cinnamon buns were ready for the oven. The aroma of coffee filled the dining room. And Mrs. Allen busied herself with setting the table while Judith ran to the garden and picked yellow roses and purple snapdragons for the centerpiece.

John dressed casually and Laura put the last touch of perfume behind her ears when they heard a car enter the driveway. The whole family rushed out to greet Martha Sanders. Smiles and handshakes and a big hug from Judith made her feel at home already. The conversation included everything from the family dog to the trip to Sandwich, and finally Jonathan said, "You have no idea how much it means to my family and me to have you here. We've heard so much about you from Judith, and we were thrilled when we heard you were coming. We're sorry your hubby couldn't come, but he must have made other plans before the weekend. We spent yesterday swimming and throwing Frisbees, roasting hot dogs and drinking soda - and even went for an evening walk. We want you to have a relaxing, fun-filled day. My dad might have to go to the hospital for a little while. Otherwise, we have the whole day to enjoy one another. And believe me when I say again, thank you for coming!"

The home cooked breakfast was delicious. Afterward they took their coffee and sat by the pool. Jonathan had a good friend who was away for the weekend, so he inherited Foxy, a tiny pug, as his special charge.

Laura took Martha for a tour of their home, and even though it was so lovely, it was also such a warm and happy place. She envied the closeness of the Allen family, and was so delighted that Judith and Jonathan were so loving toward each other.

Just before dinner, Jonathan said, "Mrs. Sanders, we would like to discuss wedding plans with you. Judith and I want to be married at Christmas. It will be the first break I have from Yale, and we think it would be a beautiful time for the ceremony. Please feel free to discuss any ideas or thoughts you have. Since we're all here together, we can share everything so that all are happy and in agreement. We certainly didn't want to do anything until we spent time with you. Please share your thoughts with us."

After taking a deep breath, Martha said, "It sounds like a perfect time. Where will the ceremony be held? Of course, I'll want Bill's ideas on it as well as mine."

"Mom, we wondered if you would rather have the wedding in Boston, or here in Sandwich. When I first thought of having it near home, I wondered if Park Street Church would be the best place. I've only been in it when

I was a bridesmaid, and it was beautiful. But neither of us wants a large ceremony, so we thought of a small Chapel here in Sandwich. Yet because dad has so many colleagues in the legal arena and Dr. Allen so many medical friends, maybe the wedding wouldn't be that small after all. I only want Brittany for my Maid of Honor and Jonathan only wants his cousin as Best Man. That would make the wedding party small, but the Allens and you and dad might want to have a large number of guests. What do you think?"

All of a sudden, Martha's mind raced to her husband and she wondered what to say. She could not betray him nor express her true feelings. Yet she knew they wanted her to share her desires with them.

A few moments of quiet sounded like an eternity to Judith and Jonathan, but a barking dog and the ring of a cell phone broke the silence.

Judith knew that her mother must be thinking about her dad and after all he had said to her, she was sure he would not consent to any of it. However, she was determined that no matter how he felt, the wedding would go on.

She broke the silence. "Since we are going to be a family and be truthful with each other, I think it's time for me to say what's in my heart. My father is not in favor of my even seeing Jonathan and he has told me I should never see him again. He has been very cold to all of us, even my mother. Since I am almost 19, I believe I have to make decisions, even if they don't please my dad. Perhaps when he knows we are going ahead with the wedding with or without him, he may change and agree to be part of the ceremony. I didn't want to say all this, but I cannot go on pretending everything is fine when it is not. I love the Allen family and always want to be honest with them about everything. If I have betrayed you, mom, I'm sorry. But it had to be said."

Laura Allen put her hand on Martha's arm and said, "Although Judith has said nothing to us about her dad, we surmised that things were not as happy as they might be at your home. We have been concerned for you and her sister, but have not wanted to pry. I can understand much of what you are going through for my father locked my brother and me in a closet and left us there day after day when our mother was in the hospital. After she came home, she was so good to us, but her cancer took her when we were just 11 and 13. My father drank and finally left home without a word, and so our grandmother raised us. When I met John, I couldn't believe anyone could love me, and it took me a long while to accept his love. But after nearly 28 years of marriage, I have known a love that is beyond all explanation. Jonathan is not perfect, but he is very much like his father, and we know he loves your daughter. She will find in him all the love she has longed for all these years.

About the wedding, we are willing to plan it as you wish. We will wait to make any decisions until you have talked with your husband, or if you want it otherwise, we will plan it as you wish. You can be assured we want to be supportive and understanding and will do all we can to help in any way."

Martha put her head on Laura's shoulder and let the tears, so long withheld, flow gently down until all was quiet and hearts felt at peace.

Nothing further was said about the wedding. Judith and Jonathan took a dip in the pool before lunch and splashed each other until they dripped all the way to the back door.

Dinner discussion was all about Yale, and Dr. Allen told many tales of things he and his room-mate did when they were students. He told that one winter night when it was really freezing, he and his roomy went outside and screamed, "FIRE!" All the men had to run out in their jammies, barefoot and shaking, until one of the officials was told it was a false alarm. They were never caught, but they never tried it again.

It was an afternoon of warm hospitality and the aroma of love was so real you could actually reach up and touch it.

It was about 5 o'clock when Martha said she wanted to start for Boston and Judith said they could go together. She would drive and leave her car with the Allens. Jonathan and his love spent a few quiet moments together and then Martha and Judith took their leave. The Allens all came to Martha and hugged her and told her to come anytime, day or night. It could be her second home.

All the way to Boston, mother and daughter discussed the wedding and how Mr. Sanders would react when he was told about the tentative plans. Martha said, "Your dad will not be home, and he is going to a convention, and then spend a week with his brother, so we can do little, unless we talk with him by phone. Maybe it would be easier that way."

The living room lights were shining brightly when they walked in and Mr. Sanders was sitting in his favorite chair, reading the Boston Globe. Judith went over and kissed him, and Martha took his hand and said she was glad he was home.

"Brittany called and asked for you, Martha. She left her number, so maybe you should call her back. She said she would be at that number after 8:00 p.m."

It was almost that time, so Martha went in the den and called her daughter. She listened intently to her excited daughter, finally hearing she was really in love and was bringing her David home in two weeks when camp was out, if that was all right. Two shocks in one day!

Martha said, "Of course, dear, do bring him home and let us know when you will be arriving. How long does David plan to stay? Maybe we can show him some of Bean Town if he's never been here before.

I'll call you in a couple of days with details. David has a car so I won't have to come by train. I think he'll plan on spending the weekend. He has to get home to get ready to return to college and to help his family. They are going back to Pakistan and will be leaving very soon now. I'm so glad you want him to come here. It may be his only home in the States once his family leaves. His younger brother is going back with them. His grandmother died recently, so he really has no family here. But he has lots of friends. You will love him, mom. He's kind and loving and can't wait to meet you. Thanks so much for letting him come. Talk with you soon. Love you."

Martha walked back into the living room and sank into the softest chair. Judith brought some coffee and little cakes for a snack. For the moment, it was just what Martha needed. She was grateful she only had two daughters!

Everyone ate a little and then Bill said he was going out and would see them in the morning before he left for the convention.

Judith moved over to the sofa by her mother and wanted to know if Brittany was all right.

"Yes, dear, she's fine. Now I have two daughters in love, and her sweetheart is coming to visit in a couple of weeks. Should we have a double wedding?" And they both laughed.

"Maybe because of dad, we should both run away to a small island to say I do!"

It had been a good day and a happy one. Sleep overtook them both before the chimes rang 10.

CHAPTER 27

The Allens were not a perfect family, but they were loving and kind. They had been through some deep waters when Laura had full charge of the home and Jonathan. Dr. Allen often worked late, was called early, and sometimes spent entire nights at the hospital, but he tried to make it up to his family. He and Martha had quarrels about his putting his work first. Yet she knew, deep in her heart, this was not true. Some days were long and nights even longer. But she had made friends in the area and when Jonathan went to school, she became involved with volunteering at the hospital and for the Heart Association.

Dr. and Mrs. Allen had taken trips alone and they had been times of deepening their love and enjoyment of being together. Many times, Laura had wanted her husband to take six months or a year off, but with a short staff and few neurosurgeons, he never felt he could leave for that long.

When Jonathan became a teenager, they shared much with him about family life and love and loyalty in marriage. He had seen his parents love for one another in many ways, and he wanted to pattern his married life after theirs. When things became serious with Judith, he spent a long time with his folks talking about his feelings and hers, and also his fear that Judith's family was not a happy one, and how best they could become friends with her father. He desperately wanted to ask Mr. Sanders for his blessing on their wedding. He well remembered how bad his first impression had been when he had that flat tire, was late arriving at their home, and then dripped water all over their beautiful carpet. His worst side was Mr. Sanders' first and lasting impression.

During their great weekend, Judith told Jonathan that her dad was leaving for a law convention. Jonathan wanted to talk with her father before he left. Somehow, things had to be made right.

The night before Mr. Sanders was to leave, Jonathan appeared at the door. No one had expected him, but Judith was delighted, and so was her mother. Jonathan was told that Mr. Sanders had gone upstairs, so he asked his sweetheart if she could go up and ask him to come down for just a short time. Mrs. Sanders said, "Maybe it would be best if I go up and ask him. He often has coffee before bedtime, and we can have something to drink with pie and ice-cream."

She left the room quietly and ascended the steps. Judith and Jonathan held each other tightly - then sat down on the couch until they heard the Sanders approaching.

Jonathan stood up and walked toward the couple. He smiled and thanked Mr. Sanders for coming down. Neither the smile nor the warmth were returned. Judith went to her dad and hugged him.

"Well, to what do I owe this intrusion so late at night? Or do you always barge in uninvited, Mr. Allen?

"I'm so sorry if you feel I have come too late. I wanted so much to talk with you for just a few minutes, and your daughter said you would be leaving in the morning for a law convention. Please forgive me," Jonathan pleaded. "I had not meant to disturb or annoy you."

"Well, what do you want to say in these few short minutes?"

Jonathan drew a deep breath and stated, "I'm sure your daughter has told you that we are very much in love, and I wanted to ask you for your blessing upon our marriage, which we hope will be very soon."

The long pause, the cold face and the empty silence made Jonathan tremble inside. He so longed to feel he could belong in the family, and that Judith's dad would understand and show that he cared - especially for the sake of his daughter.

After what seemed like an eternity, Mr. Sanders put his hands on his hips, raised his chin, threw back his beautiful, wavy, brown hair, and said, "From the first time I met you, I never trusted or liked you. I hoped you would never enter this house again. The last thing I wanted was your interest in my daughter. I realize she is old enough to do what she wants, and I cannot stop her. I had wanted her to marry someone strong like me - and not a young whippersnapper just headed for college. I will NEVER give my blessing to your marriage and I certainly will not be present at the ceremony should you go ahead without my permission , nor will I . . ."

As he started to finish the sentence, Mr. Sanders grabbed his heart with his right hand, and without warning, hit the floor and yelled, "Call 911."

All three ran to him. Then Martha ran for the phone and dialed. In seconds, they could hear the sirens. Jonathan tried to lift him up and hold him, and Judith ran for some cold water. He did not speak, but began to gasp, and his face whitened. Perspiration was pouring across his cheeks, falling on his fancy shirt.

In less than five minutes, there was a loud knock at the door. Martha rushed to open it. The EVAC men ran toward the man on the floor. They opened their bags, pulled out I.V.'s, opened syringes, tore open his shirt and placed cables on Bill's chest. Firemen raced through the room while lights flashed across Beacon Street. Martha and Judith stood back, silent and petrified. Jonathan then held Judith as tightly as he could, whispering in her ear that everything would be all right.

The men kept yelling, "ALL CLEAR" over and over again. One man stood up and said that the patient's heart was beating, but he was in serious condition. A stretcher was carried through the door. Five men lifted Bill up and placed him on it, covered him with a sheet and blanket and tightened the straps around him. His hands were at his sides with I.V. fluids running into both. They soon left and with lights blazing and sirens screeching, they headed for Mass General. Martha and Judith grabbed jackets and ran to Jonathan's car, leaving the door ajar and the lights on. His hand firmly on the horn, he drove as fast as he could, racing to the Emergency Room. Parking in a spot marked "Clergy Only," they left the car and ran in. Jonathan grabbed his cell phone and called his parents while Martha called her sister in Seattle.

After a minute or two, Judith called Brittany and tried to break the news as gently as possible, but explaining that she needed to come as quickly as possible, regardless of any previous plans.

Brittany hung up, sobbing into David's arms. They headed for the nearest airport some 75 miles away. Surely there would be flights to Boston that night. Driving would take far too many hours.

The Allens left everything and drove beyond the speed limit toward Boston, passing everything on the road including a blue and white car which was soon flashing its lights. They had to stop. The Officer listened, and since Dr. Allen was an M.D., the Officer told him to follow his police car and he would take them to the edge of Boston. Their fear held them speechless as they followed hard behind the Officer.

After several minutes had gone by, Martha asked if she could see her husband, but the nurse said she would have to wait, though the doctors would be out in a few minutes.

Was he still alive? Would he make it? Would he be well again? Each one was asking the same questions, but they asked them in silence. As they waited, the ER became a whirlwind of activity. Many families were waiting with the same panic on their faces. Sobs were heard in every corner of the large room.

It was almost an hour before a tall, young physician came toward Martha. His face was tense, but his words were kind. "Your husband is in critical condition and the CT Scan shows he will have to have by-pass surgery as soon as he is stable. We've placed him under sedation, are giving him several medicines, and we hope to be able to operate by tomorrow morning at the latest. You may see him for just a moment, but he is in a deep sleep. As soon as possible, he will be moved to the

Cardiac Unit. We will let you know when. There is a waiting room there and we will keep you informed as much as possible. By the way, has your husband ever had heart trouble before - or any other illnesses?"

No," Martha stammered. "He has always been in good health"

After giving the kind doctor necessary answers to his questions, he said, "You and your family can go to the 5th floor." The doctor squeezed her hand reassuringly. Then he returned through the awesome and frightening double doors.

At 10 o'clock, John and Laura parked in Doctor's Parking and ran into the Emergency Room. At least 30 people were standing, sitting, lying down, crying - but within seconds, they found Martha, Judith and their son. Laura held Martha and Dr. Allen put his arms around his son and Judith. After explanations were given, they all headed for the lobby. Dr. Allen spotted the coffee shop and quickly filled a tray with coffee, sandwiches and cookies. The line at the Admission Desk was long, so the family sat on a couch and chair and were grateful for the quiet and the nourishment.

After a minute or two, Martha put her head in her hands and sobbed. It was best to let her get some of her fear out in the open. Then Dr. Allen told the four of them he would try to get in to see the men treating her husband. And he left the room.

The admitting procedure was over, questions answered, and the family headed for the Cardiac Waiting Room. When they arrived, Dr. Allen was there with the news that Bill's vital signs had improved and the doctors hoped to take him to surgery within the next two or three hours. It was the best news they had had, and Dr. Allen assured them he would keep in touch with the surgeons. It was late and Laura held Martha, and Jonathan did not let go of Judith. They all sat in silence as the large clock on the wall slowly ticked off the minutes.

It was at 2:00 a.m. that they took Bill into the O.R. It had been a long night and each mind and heart raced with dread and anticipation. But no one spoke a word.

CHAPTER 28

The austerity of the O.R., the scurrying of uniformed medical personnel, the bright lights - all spoke of the urgency of the surgery at hand. The doors swung widely open and the stretcher was rolled to the operating table. The patient was lifted quickly, the numerous wires and tubing were secured, and the head surgeon held a scalpel. Three Harvard surgeons stood by as a vanguard. They quickly opened the chest. Serious as this was, the well-trained, experienced men moved carefully through the operation as the patient's blood pressure rose and fell. They had to give two pints of blood - but after nearly five hours, Bill Sanders was lifted into the bed prepared for him and nurses wheeled him to the Cardiac Intensive Care Unit.

The waiting room was cold and stark. It held families whose only common bonds were their fears and their empty coffee cups. They paced from one end of the room to the other quietly speaking to other anxious souls. Whoever had decorated the room knew only sterility and lifelessness - utilizing white walls, dark carpet, brown chairs, dark-colored tables - and no windows. It reminded some of a prison cell in which they all longed for an approaching footstep, an open door, a word of hope. One doctor came in and spoke to a couple. The words were hushed, but the expression on their faces was grim and hopeless.

Finally Bill Sanders' surgeon walked through the swinging doors, and pulled off his mask. His facial expression told a thousand words. Bill had made it thus far. His condition remained critical, but the family was assured that everything possible was being done, and the next few hours would be the most serious. A triple bypass had been performed, and had it not been for the quick action of getting him to the Hospital, his life might not have been saved. Martha was told she could see him as soon as he was awake. She thanked the doctor, sank back in her chair, and let the tears of relief fall unashamedly down her cheeks. Jonathan and Judith then took her to the coffee shop and they all had something to eat, even though nothing really tasted good.

Dr. and Mrs. Allen had waited near the family, and joined them for coffee. John Allen was not only well known in his field, but he was President of the Massachusetts Medical Society. He told Martha he would talk personally with the surgeon. That gave her hope and gratitude. He left his wife with the family and took the elevator to the 5th floor. He had tried, without success, to see the Cardiologist before the surgery. But he felt sure he would have a minute or two with one of the men who performed it now.

As he stepped away from the elevator, the Chief of Cardiology approached him. "Bill, I didn't know you were the M.D. who wanted information before the surgery. I'm so sorry that in the rush, names seem to have been lost."

"Please don't apologize. I didn't mean to intrude and I knew how critical the situation was. Can you tell me how Mr. Sanders is doing?"

"Considering it was a very serious coronary with extensive damage, he is doing well. The recovery will be slow and long, but I think he'll make it. Let me give you my card so you can call if I fail to see the family. I have another serious case waiting at Beth Israel. Have to rush." And with that, he was on his way.

John Allen lost no time in going back to the coffee shop to share the encouraging news with the family. He assured Martha he would keep in touch with the surgeon.

Dawn had broken, and with much persuasion, Martha agreed to go home and try to rest. As they walked to the Allen's car, Martha begged them to stay at her home where they could all get some sleep. As exhausted as they all were, the invitation was gladly accepted.

Martha called Brittany. She was at the airport in Philadelphia with David. A plane was leaving for Boston at 10:00 a.m. Her mother gave her the latest information about her dad. Jonathan said he would pick her up at Logan Airport at 11:15 a.m.

Each of them took a quick shower. Sleep came readily to all but Martha. Her mind could not be turned off. She thought of the anger of her husband before the attack. Could things have been handled differently? Should she have waited to talk with him until after the convention? Her fears and questions had no answers.

Never would that day be forgotten!

In mid-morning, the nurses saw Mr. Sanders open his eyes. Then he asked where he was. "You're in the Intensive Care Unit at Mass General and you are doing fine. His forehead wrinkled, but his eyes closed. The monitors registered normal. The I.V. beeped and a new I.V. replaced the empty one. The nurse sighed with relief. Color began to return to his face.

Back in Pennsylvania, David was driving a distraught Brittany toward the airport in Philadelphia. He held her hand and drove as speedily as he could with the other. He tried to give words of comfort and support. Because of his strong belief in his Lord, he tried gently, but firmly, to explain how much God loves and cares for her - and her father as well. She had heard him share his trust in the Lord and how he had come to believe, but at that moment her heart and mind could only think of her dad and mother. Then after stopping for a soda and peanut butter crackers, David suggested that they have prayer. Holding both her hands in his, he prayed, "Dear Lord, You know the whole situation and You love and care for Mr. Sanders. We ask that You will be with the surgeons and medical team, that he may come through the operation and will heal in Your time. We especially pray that while he is in the hospital someone who knows and loves You, will have an opportunity to share the Gospel with him and with his family. We long to see him come to know You and to love You. We ask for your will to be done for your glory. Amen."

"How do you know God has heard and will answer your prayer, David?" Brittany asked.

"My God is a prayer-hearing and prayer-answering God, and all through the Bible we are told to pray and believe and trust Him for the answer. For years, I've seen Him answer prayers, and God has brought many to Himself because people have prayed. I ask Him many times a day that YOU will come to love Him and serve

Him. We love each other, Brit, but we can never have a real relationship until you accept Christ as your Savior."

Brittany was silent. Yet she knew in her heart that if she and David were ever going to be more than friends, and think of marriage, she had to trust Jesus.

Philadelphia traffic was slow and slower. They were on the opposite side of the city from the airport. It had taken longer than they thought to be on time for her flight. Every emotion possible ran across their hearts and minds. Finally, the terminal building rose above the runways and they parked in Short Term. David grabbed her bags and they ran through the terminal. Just before going through "Charley Check Point," David held her in his arms as tightly as possible, kissed her - and the last words she heard as she headed down the concourse were, "Brit, I'll be praying for you, and I love you."

David's guilt was overwhelming, for he longed to go with her. But he knew he had to help his family with many details as they were soon leaving for Pakistan, and he had to get ready for Bible College.

Back in his car, before starting the motor, David bowed his head and prayed for Brit and her father and the whole family. Then, with peace in his heart, he headed home. As soon as he was out of the city, he called his family to let them know he was on his way. Since it had been almost 24 hours since he had slept, his mother begged him to stop at a motel and get some sleep. He promised her he would.

As he drove, he kept repeating, "Call unto Me, and I will answer you and show you great and mighty things that you do not know." He longed for the answer. He knew His God would hear and answer. But he never dreamed of the way He would work.

CHAPTER 29

Most hospitals have an amazing staff hidden in the shadows. Some are seldom seen because they work in the laundry, paint walls at night, or cut up lettuce and veggies for a good lunch for staff and visitors. These are the little people who are willing to do things without any glory, and often with little remuneration. Many are volunteers who answer the telephones, sell gifts in the shop, give out coffee to hurting people outside Recovery Rooms, or bring pets for little children to touch. But one of the most important people is the Chaplain. He visits, reads Scripture, prays with patients and family, and puts place cards of comfort on dinner trays. He sacrifices a great deal of time to bring cheer and comfort to those in need. Although his name may be engraved on a metal pin, it may not be remembered. Yet almost always, his face and his words are never forgotten.

After Bill Sanders was moved from ICU to a regular room, his family came often and stayed long hours to encourage him and let him know they loved him.

One evening after the Sanders had left, the door was ajar and a little knock was heard. A friendly face peeked in and asked if he might come for a few minutes.

Bill was delighted to have company, especially since he was in a private room. The gentleman smiled and introduced himself as the hospital Chaplain.

"I have spoken to your family briefly, and know you have been a very ill man, but you are gaining every day and that is wonderful news. I wonder if you would let me read you some encouraging words?"

"That would be very nice. Please have a seat and stay a while."

"The Chaplain sat in the nearby chair, and pulled a little brown book from his jacket pocket.

"The Lord is my Shepherd, I shall not want. He leads me beside still waters and in green pastures. He comforts me and promises to be with me." I wonder if you have heard these words before? Perhaps you read them daily from your Bible?"

Bill looked into the chaplain's eyes and said, "I am not a religious man and I don't go to church or read a Bible. I don't even own one. It's kind of you to read this to me, but I'd rather watch the Red Sox game on TV. But thank you for coming."

The chaplain stood up and pushed back the chair. Then he said, "Would you mind if I prayed for you before I leave?"

"I don't believe in prayer nor any god, but you can pray for me if it will make you feel better."

The chaplain laid his hand upon Bill's and prayed, "Father, we come to you tonight thanking you for making Mr. Sanders so much better. We thank You that you love him and care about him. We praise You that you hear and answer prayer, and we ask that this dear man may one day soon come to know You, love You, and follow You. May

You bless him and give him a good night's rest. In Jesus' Name. Amen."

"Thank you for coming. You certainly sound as though you believe there is a God who loves and cares. I've never heard that before. I'm sorry I was so abrupt. Perhaps you could stop in another evening and tell me why you believe what you have read and said."

"I'll be more than happy to come by any evening. Would tomorrow night be too soon?"

"No, that will be fine. My family usually leaves right after I have supper. It's a long day for them to be here with me. Thank you again for coming. Good night."

"Good night, and God bless you. I'll see you tomorrow evening."

Bill Sanders liked this gentleman, though he didn't believe anything he said. Then he mused to himself, "I wonder if there is any truth to what he says? Surely no one in my family has prayed for me. It was good of him to come. I often think of things my mother said and one of them was, never close your mind, even if you don't believe a word of it. My mother told my dad she would never marry him if he was the last man on earth because she hated a beard. I wonder if she remembered those words after 44 years of happy marriage?

That night, Bill took no sleeping pills and he had the best night's rest since he had been in the hospital - almost two weeks. Maybe? Maybe? Oh Bill, you know it had nothing to do with the chaplain's prayer. You have more sense than to believe that!

When Brittany came the next morning to see her dad, he told her about the chaplain and what he had said and prayed.

"Oh, dad, that is what David has been telling me all along. And I know David and his family pray for you many times a day. I'm beginning to believe God loves us and wants us to love Him. David says when he found Christ as his Savior, it changed his whole life. Many times lately, I have begun to read the New Testament he gave me, and each time I read the Gospel of John, it means more and more. Maybe you would let me read some to you. I always carry it with me now."

"Brit, for so many years, things have not been right in our family. Do you think God can change any of that?"

"Oh Daddy, I want so much for us to be a loving family and to care about each other. Mom feels the same way and I know Judith has been so hurt because you do not accept Jonathan. Maybe - just maybe - God could change that. What do you think?"

As her dad was ready to speak, a nurse and his surgeon came in and both were surprised and pleased with how much better he looked and acted. "You must have dunked under the Fountain of Youth during the night! I'm beginning to think you will soon go to Rehab and then home. How does that sound?"

"Great! It's been a long siege, but I'm so glad things are looking up. My family will be as excited as I am. Thank you for all you've done. I'm sure I could never thank you enough, but maybe my paid bill will say thanks." They all laughed.

The doctor and nurse left and Judith and her mother arrived and were enjoying the good news from the doctor. Bill didn't say any more about the chaplain or his discussion with Brittany. That would come another day.

Maybe tonight he would learn more and have something to tell them the next day.

For a special treat, the family had lunch together in his room, and there was a warmth none of them had felt for many years. It made Bill wonder, and he gave thanks in his heart.

CHAPTER 30

Now that her dad seemed so much better, Judith wanted to spend some time with her sweetheart. In only two weeks he would be headed for Yale and there seemed to be so little time. She wasn't sure what to tell her father, knowing how he felt about her relationship. But she explained she had a lot to do herself, so might not visit for a couple of days. Her dad surprised her by saying, "I know you have been here day and night and that has meant more to me than you will ever know, so do get some rest, and do things you have had to put off." His voice was tender and kind, and Judith smiled and thanked him.

She drove home quickly, called Jonathan to see if she could see him for a couple of days, packed her bag, threw some clothes in the trunk and headed for the Cape. She promised Brittany that when she was back home, they would have a long heart to heart talk. She certainly wanted to know more about David and how her sister really felt about him. Their time together had been short between hospital visits. They had both tried to relieve their mother, for she was physically and emotionally drained ever since before their father's heart attack.

In less than two hours, Jonathan was squeezing his beloved, and the Allens were hugging her. She told them the good news about her father. They were already such a family that no matter the issue or problem, they all felt free to share cares and concerns.

The lovers sat under the willow tree in the back yard, and Jonathan said, "We must make some wedding plans. Now that nothing seems to be stopping us, could all four of us make some decisions together?

"We had discussed a Christmas wedding and that sounds perfect to me. Mother thinks it would be fine. As you know, I don't know about dad. He was kinder to me today than I can ever remember. Maybe I'm dreaming, but I want so much for him to know you and understand how we feel. He has never given us a chance, but I haven't given up."

Iced tea and crumb cake was followed by a few hours of wedding plans. Dr. Allen had to leave for the hospital, and assured them that anything they decided would be fine with him. He had several serious cases and had been at the hospital from early that morning and now it was time to go back. Neuro men were on call day and night, and Laura was used to hearing her hubby leave before dawn, taking a mug of coffee with him, and often not returning until dinner time or later.

After considering several dates and times for the wedding, they decided on Saturday, December 22nd at 2:00 p.m. Even though both families were well known, neither Judith nor Jonathan wanted a large wedding. Brittany would be the Maid of Honor and Paul Martin the Best Man. He had been a buddy of Jonathan's since they were in Middle School. Jonathan would schedule a flight on the 23rd from Boston to Miami, where they would take a 7-day cruise to the Eastern Caribbean. They would be back to have almost a week to get everything together to move to New Haven.

"I can't wait to tell my family!" Judith waved her arms in excitement. She knew Jonathan loved red, and since it would be a Christmas wedding, every one and all the decorations would be in red and white. Jonathan's mother grinned and said, "I'll start right away to find just the right red dress. I know you'll want us to wear long gowns, won't you dear?"

"Oh yes. And you'll look gorgeous and so will my mother. Maybe the men could wear red ties with their tuxedos!

Judith had planned for years to go to Swarthmore, or UConn, and had been accepted by both - but now that so much had changed, she really wanted to be a wife and homemaker, and work some to help with expenses. Even though both families would give them money, they wanted to do as much as possible on their own.

At dinner time, the phone rang. It was Judith's mom.

"Hello, dear. Just wanted you to know that the doctor is discharging your father tomorrow. He will be going to New England Rehab for at least two weeks. Everything has been done, so don't feel you have to rush home. You've had so little time with Jonathan. But don't get in the Allens' way! David called and wanted Brit to go up there to meet his parents. Her dad said that would fine, so she will be flying to Chicago tomorrow. I'll be fine, and have some time to rest and relax, so don't be concerned for me. It seems like a long time since everything has been this quiet. We'll all take advantage of it. Call me in the morning and then you can talk to your sister as well. She is out now shopping at the mall. Have a great time. My very best to the Allens."

Before Judith had a chance to say anything, her mom hung up. All eyes were upon her as she returned to the table.

"Oh, you can't believe that for the first time in so long, all is quiet. She repeated what her mother had said as she slipped, with a sigh of relief, into her chair. It didn't seem possible, after all these weeks, that calm reigned. It was as if the butterflies were gone from each one, and a white dove flew into each heart, bringing peace.

It was early to bed for them all - perhaps due to the tiredness in each - and sleep came quickly. As Judith was closing her eyes, she remembered the third piece of her agenda that had been left in the background. Before returning home, she would make an appointment to talk with the Chaplain in Boston.

CHAPTER 31

As was his custom, the Chaplain checked with Admissions for the names of new patients and those who had been discharged that day. The doctors' orders did not always reach this office, but the Chaplain made sure to see the patients he believed wanted a visit. Uppermost on his mind was Mr. Sanders, whom he had promised to see that evening. After visiting many others, he stopped to pray before entering the room of this patient who had been so much on his heart and mind.

"Good evening, and how are you tonight?" he inquired.

"Great! They're letting me out of this prison tomorrow and I'm going to New England Rehab. Isn't that wonderful?"

"Surely this is an answer to prayer, and I'm sure your family is rejoicing at your good recovery. You've been on my mind ever since our last conversation and, if you have a few minutes, maybe we could share with one another tonight."

"We have lots of time, and I especially want to hear about your religion."

The Chaplain hoped Mr. Sanders hadn't seen his mouth drop open! Nevertheless he began.

"Well, let's start at the beginning. My mother was a fine woman. Our family was poor, but happy. Dad died when I was only four, so my older brothers did all they could to help out with odd jobs, and my mother took in sewing. After several years, she married again. This man was a real father to all of us. He worked in construction, so all of us were able to finish high school, and one of my brothers and I went to college. My roommate had just returned from nearly 17 years in West Africa, and was preparing to return. He didn't ever preach to me, but as I watched his life, I saw something remarkably different about him that I did not see in my other classmates. Every morning and evening, he read his Bible and knelt beside his bed in prayer. After only a few weeks, I had heard amazing stories of African life and what it was like being a Missionary Kid (MK). He loved sports and we both played on the basketball team. Students and faculty alike respected him. One Saturday night, he asked me if I would like to go to a Youth for Christ meeting with him. I had never even heard of that, but went along to please him. The speaker was vibrant, with a great sense of humor - and when he opened the Bible, it came alive. He told us that all of us are sinners and that God could not look on sin. Christ gave his life so we could be forgiven. He took our sins in his own body and died on the cross to give us eternal life and to be our very own Savior. When the invitation was given, it took only seconds before I went forward and asked Christ into my heart. That very moment, I became a child of God and life took on a whole new meaning. I was sure God loved me, and I have loved

Him ever since. He gave me a clean heart and a purpose for living."

Mr. Sanders closed his eyes in thought. Then spoke slowly, "I've always tried to live a good life and give to the poor and care for my family. Isn't that all God wants of me? Why do I need to ask Christ to do anything for me? I have a beautiful home, lovely family, and a great position as a lawyer. And I've done it all myself. Why isn't that good enough for God?"

The Chaplain smiled. Moving his chair closer to the bed, he took Mr. Sanders' hand in his strong one. "The Word of God tells us there is not one good - no, not one. No matter how much we have done or given, there is still sin inside our heart. Have you ever had evil thoughts, hurt someone, done what you wanted? Have you ever wondered why Christ died if it was not for you and for me? Have you never taken the Name of the Lord in vain? Never told a lie, or taken anything that was not yours - perhaps not money, but maybe taken their ideas and used them as your own?"

Mr. Sanders was quiet and looked toward the dark shades covering the window. Finally he said, "Yes, I suppose I have done all those things, but I believe I have done more good things than bad. Doesn't that stand for anything with God?"

"I understand what you are saying, friend, but I remember what Billy Graham said the night I came to Christ. 'Every one of you is a sinner in God's eyes. No matter who you are or what you have done, no matter your fame or fortune, God's Word tells us we will never have peace - real peace - until we ask Jesus to cleanse our heart and take away our sin. Then, and only then, will we have real joy and true peace, and then. He will lead us and love us all our days. And one day he will take us to Heaven to be with Him forever.' Are you sure, Mr. Sanders, that your heart is completely at peace? Can you put your head on your pillow tonight and know His hand is holding yours? Are you absolutely sure?"

Mr. Sanders looked into the Chaplain's eyes and said, "No, I do not have that peace, joy and assurance. But I would like to have it. Will you pray for me? Help me to pray so I can ask Christ into my life."

With tears of joy, the Chaplain took both the patient's hands in his, bowed his head and said, "I will pray, and then you can pray aloud with me, or silently, as you wish."

"Dear Lord, I thank you for loving us and giving your Son to die for us. Right now I ask that you will open the door of my dear friend's heart, come into his life and save him."

Mr. Sanders, with tears slowly falling on the sheet, bowed his head and very simply, but earnestly, asked the Lord to come into his heart. And when he raised his head, the Chaplain said, "Now we are brothers in Christ and sons of God, and He has given you the same wonderful life that He has given to me and all believers. I have many Bibles, so I will leave mine with you. In the morning, as the sun comes up, do start reading. I will open the book to the Gospel of John. You may not understand all you read, but keep reading. The Spirit of God will help you to understand. Now good night, dear brother. I will come early tomorrow to see you before you are discharged."

They shook hands. Mr. Sanders' eyes were bright and joyful as he said, "I can never thank you enough. Tomorrow I will share all this with my wife and daughters as soon as I see them. Thank you again, and may God bless you."

The Chaplain left the room with a song in his heart. His steps were light and his face was aglow with joy for all that the Lord had done.

When the nurse entered the room about 9:30 p.m., to see if Mr. Sanders wanted anything and if he had had his sleeping pill, she saw the book open on his chest and his eyes were closed. Not wanting to disturb him, she quietly walked away, leaving the door ajar. After almost an hour, she went back to give him fresh water, fluff his pillow and see if he wanted his sleeping pill. She pushed open the door and saw her patient just as he had been before. She called his name, and ran to the bed. She grabbed both hands. They were already cold. She felt for his pulse and screamed for a Crash Cart. In seconds, the room was filled with doctors, nurses, machines and needles - but Mr. Sanders was safely in the arms of Jesus.

The phone rang loudly. Mrs. Sanders picked up the receiver. Then she heard the dreaded words, "Your husband seems to have taken a turn for the worse. Could you please come to the hospital immediately?"

Brittany and her mother drove wildly through the dark Boston streets, leaving the car by the front entrance, entering the elevator and running to the room. Two doctors and a nurse were still by the bedside. The Cardiologist took Mrs. Sanders and her daughter out of the room and told them Mr. Sanders apparently had had another heart attack, and this time it took him.

The shock seemed more than they could bear. Mrs. Sanders collapsed and Brittany held her mother.

They brought water, and a doctor stood by them until both sat alone on the couch.

The rear door to the hospital made a strange noise as the Chaplain pushed it open. He stopped. His heart was telling him to head quickly back upstairs it was there he found the broken family. He knelt beside them, took their icy hands in his, and bowed his head. He asked what had happened.

"My dad died a few minutes ago. He was doing fine. We don't know what happened."

Sobbing, the child held his hand. The Chaplain's tears flowed gently, but his heart rejoiced - for his new brother in Christ was safely HOME.

CHAPTER 32

When the initial shock had passed, each mind went in a different direction. Papers for the funeral home were somewhere at home with Bill's legal materials. Judith had to be notified. David had to be called. Bill's brother in Seattle needed to know.

The hospital staff members were kind and gave no pressure. After some time, the cardiologist approached Martha to gently ask if the family wanted an autopsy performed. The only constant for Martha and her daughter was confusion.

"Mrs. Sanders," a quiet voice asked, "Is there any way I can be of help?" I spent some time with your dear husband last night, and whatever I can do, please let me do it."

Martha looked into the kind eyes of the man in dark blue and recognized he was the Hospital Chaplain. There was so very much to do, and this man was a stranger to her. But he had offered to help.

"Thank you for offering. I must go home to get telephone numbers and information that the hospital needs, but I know you must stay here, so I just can't think of anything right now. Perhaps when I return . . ."

"I don't have to be here now, and would be glad to take you home and help with any details, if that would take any of the burden off the two of you."

Without saying anything, he gently took Martha's arm as well as Brittany's, and the three headed for the elevator. But before reaching the door, Martha remembered she had said nothing to the doctor about what really took Bill.

"Brit, dear, could you go back to the Nurse's Station and tell them to let the doctor know that an autopsy would be appreciated. And tell them I'll call as soon as I get home to let them know what Funeral Home to call." So Brittany retraced her steps.

The car was still near the front entrance - with a red tag on the windshield. The chaplain took the tag and helped the ladies into the back seat. Martha handed him the keys and gave directions to their home on Beacon Hill.

"Oh, Brit - all the folks at the law firm must be notified. Your aunt must be called. All of this is so overwhelming. I'm so glad you're with me."

The phone was ringing when they entered the living room. The clock was chiming midnight.

"Brit, why haven't you answered either the home phone or your cell phone? I've been trying to get you for three hours. Where have you been?" Judith voiced genuine concern.

"Oh, Judy. . ." and the tears gushed down her face so she could not speak. "Oh, Judy - Daddy died in the hospital tonight. His heart gave out, Please come home right away. We need you!"

All Brit could hear was a scream and then sobs followed by Jonathan's voice. "Tell me what has happened. Judith can't even speak. What is it?" Brittany answered quickly, and still crying, put the phone down.

"I have to call David, Mom. What shall I tell him? My flight for tomorrow has to be cancelled, too."

Rev. Garrett, the Chaplain, broke in. "I'll make any calls you wish. Just let me know."

Brittany fumbled in her black purse for David's number. "Could you call him for me? He's my sweetheart. Lives in Chicago. His parents are soon going back to Pakistan as missionaries. I was to fly out this morning to meet them."

"I'll call David. And if you tell me the name of the airline you are booked on, I'll cancel your reservation. When either of you know the name of the funeral home, I'll call them as well as the hospital."

Martha found the papers and the Chaplain called in the information and explained they would let the funeral home know soon when the service would be held.

The man at the funeral home kindly asked when someone would be there to pick out the casket, make the arrangements, help prepare the announcement for the Boston Globe, what cemetery was to be notified." Rev. Garrett told them the circumstances and asked them to wait until after the body was picked up, and the family would be there as soon as possible.

Then he dialed David's number, and gaining a bit of strength, Brittany took the phone.

David answered sleepily, surprised to hear Brittany's voice in the middle of the night. "Oh David, Daddy died at the hospital tonight. I can't come to be with you. We don't know when the funeral will be.

Maybe you could be here for that? When do your parents leave? Oh, David, I need you so much." Then broken hearted, Brittany burst into sobbing and the chaplain took the phone.

"I'm the hospital chaplain and am here to help in any way I can. Your parents are leaving for Pakistan soon? And you are a believer? Let me share with you that last night, Mr. Sanders asked Christ into his life. He is safe now in the arms of the Lord. The family here knows nothing of what I have just shared with you. Can you come? I know it's a hard time for you, but Brittany needs your love, your strength and your Savior."

"I'm still in shock, but my family will understand. They leave in two weeks, but they would want me to be there. Please tell Brittany I will fly out as soon as I can get a flight, get packed and tell my family. Please tell her I love her. Thank you, too, for all you are doing. You are surely God's messenger to them right now."

Brittany had left the room to help her mother start making a list of all that needed to be done. Will Garrett found the kitchen and made coffee and heated some rolls. Since his wife had been called Home, he had cooked for himself and could find his way around a kitchen. When Martha and Brittany returned, they had all the papers Bill had so carefully filed away with details concerning the cemetery, the type of casket to be ordered, the names and addresses of his law partners and colleagues.

Martha took two Aspirin and gave two to her daughter. Will brought the coffee and rolls in to them. For a few short minutes the room was quiet - and then the doorbell rang. Who on earth - at this time of night?

The chaplain went to the door and through the window he saw the face of Bill's cardiologist. Entering in, he said he wanted to make sure the family was all right, and he had brought some medicine to calm them and help them sleep.

"You will want to know, Mrs. Sanders, that your husband had a massive heart attack that caused his death. I'm so sorry to barge in, but I wanted you to know what we found. Now take one of these capsules now and another when you go to bed. How good of you to be here, Will. You are surely an answer to prayer to many families. Now goodnight, and if there is anything I can do - anything at all - don't hesitate to call. All our staff thought a great deal of Mr. Sanders."

The Allens were throwing clothes in suitcases, and trying to comfort Judith. John called his closest Neuro M.D. and told him what had happened. "I have no surgery today, but could you look in on my patients? I trust your judgment. You have my cell number and I can get back from Boston fairly soon if you need me. I'll call my office nurse in the morning and have her readjust my schedule. I'll be back in two days or sooner, if needed. Thanks a million. I owe you a big one!"

They threw their bags in Jonathan's trunk, and some in Dr. Allen's. They would need to take both cars in case he had to return quickly. Judith was still crying softly as she and Jonathan drove out of the driveway with the Allen's following them. It was after 1:00 a.m., there was little traffic, so in less than two hours they were parked in the Sanders' driveway.

As the Allen's and Judith entered the living room, every emotion from the family was released. Judith held her mother and sister. The Chaplain introduced himself. More coffee was brought in, and after tearful hugs and a wastebasket full of tissues, they all sat down. Words seemed so futile. John and Laura knew their son ached for Judith. It was a time for families to hold each other close in support and caring. Words did not seem important at that moment.

Shortly, the chaplain said he would be leaving, but would come back the next morning, if they wanted him to come. Martha thanked him and held on to him. "I'll call you tomorrow if there is a need. You have been so wonderful. We can never thank you enough. We'll be in touch." Then she remembered they had all come in her car.

"How will you get back to the hospital for your car?"

"Oh, I'll take a taxi."

"Indeed you will not," said John Allen. I'll drive you to your car. So they left together.

Completely exhausted, the families dispersed and trudged upstairs, found their rooms, and after a few words, went to bed. It was 3:00 a.m.

Judith lay in her bed. Maybe her final promise to herself had been met. The chaplain was there. Maybe he would have the funeral service. Maybe - just maybe - words spoken so long ago to David would be heard again. Could God really be in all of this heartache? Was He really a God of love? Her eyes closed and she slept. Only God knew how much a part of this He really was!

When John returned, he slipped quietly to the guest room where his wife was waiting for him. After all that had happened, she clung fiercely to him as she kissed him goodnight.

CHAPTER 33

At breakfast, her eyes red and voice hoarse, Martha said, "If only I had gone and seen him before we left the hospital. If only I had been there when he died. If only I had tried to understand him better. If only . . ." Her voice could no longer utter a sound. Consolation came from each one, but her heart ached because she felt she could have done so much when she had done so little.

John Allen spoke up. "I have begun making a little list of things that should be done today. Any, or all of us, will go with you and help in any way we can."

Martha nodded and gave a gentle, weary smile, and thanked him for all he had done already and was doing now.

It suddenly occurred to her that Bill's flight had never been cancelled for the Law Convention, and none of his partners had been informed of his death. John offered to call the airline and the office to notify them of this.

David called from Chicago saying his flight would leave at 9:00 a.m., and he would be there at 12:10 on

Delta flight 609. "I'll try to meet you, but if I can't get away, one of us will be at Logan to bring you here. It will be so wonderful to have you with us. I need you so much," Brittany sighed. "We have to go to the funeral home and the cemetery, so I may not be back in time, but I'll do my best. Do your parents feel terrible that you have to leave now?"

"No, they both understand and wouldn't have it any other way. Through the years, we have had to part many times, and our love has been strong and we care for others. My mother has always felt we should do all we can for those who are hurting, or we should not be in ministry. Both my parents and my brother know I love you, and they would never stand in the way, so please don't worry about that. You have enough on your heart already, and I will soon be there with you."

By the time calls were made and various things decided, 15 gentlemen were at the door - all of them from law offices in the area, and good friends of Bill. They hugged Martha and introductions were made. Some brought flowers - others food. Many had changed their flights for the convention so they could be with this family.

John Allen called his office and there were no emergencies, so he made appointments at the Hancock Funeral Home for 1:00 p.m. and at Fenway Cemetery for 3:00 p.m.. When he told Martha, she was grateful and relieved.

Chaplain Garrett called to see if there was anything he could do. It had occurred to both Martha and

Judith that no one had been asked to preside at the funeral. So Martha said, "We don't know yet when the funeral will be, but we would like for you to give the message. Could we work out the details later?"

"I'd be honored to speak, and whenever you want to go over the details, just let me know. I want to give you my cell phone number so you can reach me any time. Now is there anything I can do for you this morning?"

"Friends are with me. We will go to the funeral home and cemetery this afternoon. May I call you tonight with the details?"

"You can call me any time. I'll be at the hospital this morning, and if you need me, call the main number and they'll page me. That's no problem. Please don't hesitate to call." His voice was extremely kind and caring.

More lawyers, and Bill's secretary arrived with more flowers. Each wanted to know the time and place of the funeral. All the lawyers wanted to be present, and since they were headed for the Convention, they wanted to be back in time. So Dr. Allen called the Funeral Home Director and asked if Saturday, August 31st at 2:00 p.m. would fit their schedule. The Director assured him that would be fine.

With the help of the family and friends, information for the obituary notice was written down. All at once, Martha realized how well-known her husband had been. At noon, the Alumni Office at Yale called with condolences and to ask for information.

Brittany realized what time it was, and with a hug for her mom, she tore out of the door to head for the airport. She knew she would be late, but David wouldn't leave until someone picked him up. As she drove to Logan, Brit remembered that when she and David were at camp, he often sang for the services. What a beautiful tenor voice! She wondered if he would sing for the funeral service.

Parking was difficult, as always, but she found a spot, locked the car, ran through the garage to the escalator, and headed for the baggage area. Standing by the door and straining to see every car was the handsome, tall man she loved. Without noticing anyone else, she ran into his arms. "Oh David, you are here and I'm secure in your arms and your love. Forgive my being late, but with a house full of people, time got away. All that matters is that you are here and I never want to let you go."

The whole family felt that David belonged, and his caring and concern were felt by all. After the introductions, it was time to leave for the funeral home. Martha wanted the Allens to be there as well. They met inside the old, gold and dark blue majestic lounge. Details took some time, but the Directors were gentlemen with obvious knowledge and experience with the trauma death brings to families.

The largest room available held 400 people, and chairs could be added. A stained glass window behind the moveable pulpit caught everyone's eyes. It pictured Jesus holding a lamb in His arms. Beneath His feet was dark green grass next to a small, deep blue river. The walls of the room were deep purple trimmed with gold. The carpet was gold with strands of blue. In its majestic serenity, it brought a calm and peace to the crushed and heartbroken family.

Martha spoke with the Director and the details were finalized. The staff, dressed in gray and black, brought refreshments to the family, and in the quietness of the place, they were strengthened.

A little after two o'clock, they left for the cemetery office. Long before that day, Bill had chosen a plot for himself and for Martha. Two large weeping willows moved gently with the breeze over the site. A tiny hill with few tombstones around it was his choice.

By 4:30, they were back home. Dr. Allen was called for an emergency, and he left immediately. But Laura stayed.

The Chaplain called again and asked Martha if he could stop by the following morning to work out the details for the service. "It will be my pleasure to come. By the way, have you given any thought to music, or can that wait until tomorrow?"

"We'll discuss the details in the morning, Chaplain Garrett. My daughter's sweetheart arrived today, and I believe he will be singing. There is an organ available, but I don't know an organist."

"My sister teaches piano and organ at Boston University and plays the organ in a church. I'm sure she will be happy to play, if you would like."

Martha marveled at how smoothly details were working out. "Oh, that would be wonderful. After we talk tomorrow, perhaps she and David can get together. You've been so kind. Tonight is sort of a come-as-you-are supper, and we'd like to have you join us, and you could meet David at the same time."

"That would be great. I'll be happy to come. Around 6 o'clock?

"Things are a bit chaotic, so I'm not sure when we'll eat, but do come at six, or when you can. I know you have much to do."

David and Jonathan shared a guest room, so they were able to get acquainted. Brit had given her room to the Allens. She and Judith were finally alone and could share their feelings, and that gave Martha some time for rest before supper. It had been a long day. Bodies were worn out. Bleeding hearts do not heal readily, and tears came easily.

Just before anyone came downstairs, the phone rang. Judith answered. It was her uncle calling from England. Her cousin had received the message in Seattle and she had contacted her dad. He would fly over on Friday and be there for the service. It had been years since he had seen his brother, but he felt he should be there.

The Funeral Director called to remind the family that they needed to bring a suit for Mr. Sanders. Martha assured them someone would be there right after breakfast the next morning. It had completely slipped her mind.

"I wonder how many other important things I've forgotten? Please, all of you, help me to remember what I may have overlooked." It was an earnest plea from a broken lady who was having trouble putting things together. She felt she was part of a jigsaw puzzle with some of the pieces missing.

"Judith, dear - please make hair appointments for all of us on Friday. Also, we need to see if we have the proper clothing, or if we need to shop. Let's look at our things in the morning." Her mind wandered from one detail to another.

Chaplain Garrett arrived on time. Having had so little all day, everyone ate the carefully laid out food, including the lemon meringue pie. David and Chaplain Garrett had a long talk and then the Chaplain left.

Bed was calling everyone, but Brit wanted some time with David. They stayed on the sofa for a while after everyone had gone to their rooms. Dr. Allen had called to say he would be back Thursday, as far as he knew, barring another emergency. Calm reigned at last, and a sense of peace encompassed the home.

CHAPTER 34

Chaplain Garrett arrived to speak with Martha and her daughters about their wishes for the funeral service.

"I've been to several funerals, but have spent only a short time in any church, so I really don't have any suggestions. But this has been your ministry, as you call it. Perhaps you can give us some ideas of what would be best." Martha looked apologetic.

"Through the years, it has been my custom to read the family's favorite passages of Scripture, or verses pre-chosen by the deceased. The music is usually requested by the family. If you have certain familiar verses you want read, that will be fine. Naturally, we will use your choice of music. David has a fine voice, and I know he will sing the hymns and songs you want. Please understand, we want these things to be your choice, not mine. If you have a special passage such as Psalm 23, or others that would be fitting, let's use them. David has sung in churches and will pick hymns that fit in with the Scripture we read. I would be so grateful if you and David planned these things together and then shared it with me. Would that be all right?"

"I've never had to do anything like this. My parents died when I was very young and I remember little of the services. Bill's brother is not a religious man, and I am sure he will be content with your choice. You, of course, know by now that we have never attended church as a family, except going to a service on Easter, or attending a Christmas presentation. I regret this, but it is the truth and I trust you'll understand." Martha's voice was full of regret and lack of assurance.

"I understand, Mrs. Sanders. Then will it be o.k. if David and I put this together - and then you can change, add to, or do anything you wish with what we decide. You haven't mentioned the length of time for the service, but I am sure it will be best not to prolong it. By the way, would any member of the family, the law firm or Bill's brother wish to say a few words? If so, that can be fit in at any time during the service."

Martha and Judith nodded in agreement, and Brittany added, "Could I request one song? When David and I were at camp, twice he sang THE LOVE OF GOD, and it was so meaningful. Would that fit into such a service?"

"That's always a favorite and would certainly be appropriate. Since part of my message will be on "love," it will fit right in."

For more than an hour, the Chaplain and David sat in the den and planned the details of the service. They had prayer before they began and Chaplain Garrett told David that Mr. Sanders had accepted the Lord just hours before he died. The hurt is deep right now for the family, but we know their loved one is safe at Home with his Savior.

They wrote out the order of service - the Scriptures, music, short message, and time for others to speak if they wished. They showed the draft to Martha, Judith and Brittany. Chaplain Garrett then took his Bible and read the verses they had chosen, and David shared the words to three hymns he felt would fit the message. After reviewing all this, the family agreed that Bill would be happy with their plans.

"How much has to be said at the gravesite?"

"Very little, and there is no need for music. We usually say a few final words. If you like, each of you may lay a rose or other flower on the coffin. It should take no more than 10 minutes. Also, I understand that some lawyers are providing a small reception for the family at one of their homes following the services."

Martha then remembered that there should be a time for visitation at the funeral home the night prior to the funeral. "Perhaps we could have visiting hours from 7:00 to 9:00 p.m. Friday night. Does that seem best?"

"Oh yes. I forgot to mention that I had given that information to the Funeral Director today. I also gave him the information for the program. Would you like the words of Psalm 23 on the opposite page?"

"That would be nice and very appropriate. Thank you so much for taking care of all this. I'm afraid I've been no help. No words will ever be able to express my deepest gratitude for all you are doing."

Chaplain Garret left and David went to the funeral home to practice the music with the Chaplain's sister. Brittany went with David. Mrs. Allen left for the Cape to get her clothes for the funeral. Jonathan said he would find what he needed in Boston so he could be with Judith. Then the two went hand in hand for a short walk in the

Common. Martha drank a cup of tea and lay quietly on the couch. Somehow she felt very good about the service and hoped Bill would have been pleased. She could still not believe that he was gone - and the house which had once been his palace, was cold and empty. She was so glad the girls had their men with them. What a comfort for them and for her. And then, in her solitude, she fell asleep.

CHAPTER 35

The family members arrived at the funeral home just after 6:00 p.m. on the 30th. Friends came and went. Bill's brother was friendly and comforting. Flowers banked the mahogany casket, and since Bill had not lost weight, nor been ill long, he looked just as all remembered him. Two hours of sympathy and encouragement flowed over to three, but the parking lot was empty by 10:00 p.m.

Back home, the conversation was warm and friendly, hiding the hurt and emptiness. Dreading the next day, yet knowing it must be faced, good nights were said, hugs shared, and the families slowly climbed the stairs. Sleep was badly needed, and by midnight, restful peace came.

Large black vehicles arrived at one o'clock the next day. When they arrived at the funeral home, Chaplain Garrett was there, greeting all with warmth and gentle understanding. David had left earlier to practice, and as they entered the room where Bill lay, soft music was coming from the organ. Just before two o'clock, the Chaplain ushered the family to the front pews. Martha sat directly in front of the casket and before the service began, she rose, stepped forward and kissed her husband for one last time. Sobs could be heard throughout the room.

As the service began, the Chaplain thanked the people for coming. "This is never an easy time, but 'God's grace is sufficient.'"

Let's bow our heads and hearts in prayer. "Our Father, You know the hearts of this dear family and their friends. We ask just now that Your comfort and grace will sustain them at this difficult time. We thank You that You have also stood by a loved One at His death, and You understand. We commit these moments to you. In Christ's name, Amen."

David then went forward and sang, "Nearer my God to Thee." His glorious voice filled the room as he focused his eyes on Martha, Judith and Brittany.

"Our Scripture is a favorite of mine. I trust it is one of yours, too. John 14:1-6. 'Do not let your heart be troubled. Believe in God, believe also in Me. In My Father's house are many abiding places. If it were not so, I would have told you. I go to prepare a place for you, and I will come again and receive you unto Myself, that where I am, there you may be also. And you know the way I am going. Thomas said to Him, Lord, we do not know where you are going. How can we know the way? Jesus said to him, "I am the Way, the Truth and the Life. No one comes to the Father but by Me.'

"I would like to share with you the conversation our dear Bill Sanders had with me the night he died. We had been together a few times and I had shared with him about my faith in Christ. He asked me to explain how I came to put my trust in Him. I told him of going to a Billy Graham Crusade meeting and hearing that we have all sinned and come short of what God wants. There is no way we can ever go to Heaven, or have our sins forgiven or see the Father unless we accept Christ's sacrifice on the cross as an atonement for our sins. When we do, we are His children, and He is our Lord and Savior. That night, Bill bowed his head, held my hands and asked Christ to cleanse him and come into his life. When he opened his eyes, the joy of the Lord was on his face, and he said it was the first time in his life he had been at peace. When I was told of his death, I knew he was more alive than ever and safe in the arms of Jesus in Heaven. For all of you who knew him and loved him so dearly, may this be your greatest comfort. And if you believe in Christ, you will see your loved one again. It is my earnest prayer that each of you will come to love Jesus."

The Chaplain sat down, and David rose. "Before I sing the final song, I would just like to say a short word. When I was in high school, I was a troubled youth, and often told my parents lies and did things that hurt them. A chum of mine took me to a Youth for Christ service, and there I heard how much God loved me - so much that He gave Jesus to die for my sins. That night, I asked Christ into my life and I found peace and joy that I had never known. The words to this song will reassure you that God really cares, even in the midst of sorrow." Without further explanation, his melodious voice rang out with THE LOVE OF GOD.

The Chaplain closed the service with prayer. The Funeral Director spoke a few words for those going to the cemetery. The room was hushed as the casket was rolled down the aisle. The family left first. Guests followed. The black limousines were waiting for the family. At the open grave, only a few words were said. Many talked with the family. Tears and gentle sobs abounded. The words spoken in the funeral home were still very fresh in their minds.

Martha spoke with the Chaplain and asked, "Do you really believe my husband did what you said?"

"Oh yes, my friend, he said all that I told you in the service, and I know he is in Heaven. Be very sure, dear, that God loves you even in the midst of your heartache and loss. He will never leave you or forsake you. He will always be there waiting for you to love Him, too." He put his arms around the grieving widow and they stood by the open grave for some time. David was holding Brittany as she cried. Judith and Jonathan stood with his parents. After some time, they all went to the home of a lawyer friend, subdued, but with words from the music and Scripture still fresh in their minds. They shared daintily fixed sandwiches, cake and coffee, after which friends left and the family went home. Few words were spoken, but many of the guests thanked the Chaplain and David for their words of comfort, spoken and sung.

Dr. Allen and his wife left for Sandwich. Bill's brother was staying in a nearby hotel and would fly out early in the morning. The Chaplain left after a short prayer of comfort - and the family was alone. It had been the most difficult day they had ever faced. But somehow there was peace. God surely had not forgotten them.

CHAPTER 36

Martha awoke early and stretched her arm across the cold pillow.   The bed was empty and the hand she usually held was no longer there.   She wanted to call Bill's name, but without looking, she knew he was gone. Twenty-two years had slipped by with its joys and sorrows, love and emptiness.   Yet the man she had married was the man she loved.   Where does one begin living without the phone calls from the office, waiting for that late dinner, re-warming the food, hearing the door open to a loving, "Hello, Martha. I'm home." Listening for the automatic closing of the garage door. The call which said he would be late and not to wait up - but she did anyway.   She remembered his first smile as he held Judith a few minutes after she was born and the dozen red roses he had sent to her hospital room. Memories, memories . . . all welled up within her and the tears came freely.   Yet life had to go on - and she had to live.

As the sun arose, Martha got up, showered and dressed.   Jonathan and Judith were already sipping coffee as she entered the kitchen. They made breakfast and David and Brittany came in from a walk in the Common.

"Mom," Brit said, "David wants to see his folks one more time before they leave for Pakistan. I know it is an awful time, but I so want to meet his mother and dad. Could I please go with him for just a day or two? It would mean so much to him and to me."

"Of course you can go. Make your flights as quickly as you can and one of us will take you to the airport. Brit jumped for joy and David ran for the phone. There was a 10:00 a.m. flight on American Airlines. They had just time to throw things in suitcases, and Judith and Jonathan got the car. With hugs and kisses, they were off.

Alone! All alone! And with both girls in love and one soon to be married, what would her life be like? Martha cleared the dishes and put them in the sink without energy or will to do anything else with them. The newspaper lay on the table where Judith had left it. She glanced at the headlines but had no idea what she read.

Just then, the phone rang. It was Brit from the airport. "Oh, Mom, we didn't mean to leave you alone. Judith and Jonathan are on their way back. I'm so sorry. But thank you again for letting me go. I promise not to be away long."

"It's all right, dear. Have a good time and don't worry about me. I'll be fine. Don't hurry home on my account. Spend time with the family and enjoy each other. You know we can only live one day at a time. I love you."

She hadn't really thought of it that way before, but we do only have today to live. Tomorrow is not promised to any of us. Maybe it's best we can't see the future. As the thought stayed in her mind, the door opened and Judith came running to her and hugged her. "Oh, Mom,

I'm so sorry we left you alone. It was thoughtless of me. Please forgive me. We just ran out without thinking. Are you sure you're all right?"

"Yes, dear, I am fine and I'm glad you were both able to see the kids on their way. David's family will be so happy to see him and to meet Brit. It will be great for all of them."

"Oh, Judith, when I was upstairs I thought of your father's clothes. What should we do with them?"

"I have no idea," Judith answered. "I'm sure there must be places where clothes are needed. Who would know?"

"Maybe Chaplain Garrett will know. He must have been through this many times before. I'll call him later and ask."

Just as she had finished her sentence, the doorbell rang and the dear Chaplain was standing there holding a large box of fresh coffee cake.

"We were just talking about you. Did your ears ring? Thank you so much for the goodies. Maybe we could have some coffee, and we'll ask you what we intended to ask you just before you came! I've been in Bill's closet and looked at all his clothes. His drawers are full, too, much of which has never been worn. He has new ties and shoes and lots of shaving stuff. Do you know what we can do with his things? I hate to have them gone, but I know it has to be done." Martha's voice weakened as she finished her last statement.

"One of the places in the city where the need is great is the Salvation Army. There are hundreds of homeless men who go to their buildings and attend their services. The Army gives them food and clothing, keeps them overnight when necessary, and helps many find work. I am sure that would mean a great deal to them. Would that be something with which you'd feel comfortable? I'd be glad to help you, and I'm sure Judith and Jonathan would join me and that would take the burden off you."

Martha smiled and sighed. It seemed such a relief and it would help so many. Bill would like that. "Oh, that relieves me, and sounds just right. You don't need to do it today, but whenever. Is it far you have to go? Should I rent a U-Haul or something to help you so you would only have to make one trip?"

"Their Headquarters are on Route 9 not far from 128. It would be easiest if we had some kind of small truck. Then we could do it all in one trip. Perhaps you would like to visit them first so you would know how dear Bill's things will be used."

"That's very kind, but I can go sometime later. I'm not really up to it now, and I know you understand."

Jonathan volunteered to get the U-Haul and take everything to them early in the coming week.

"I'll naturally want to go through his jewelry. I'd like for you, Jonathan, to have one of his watches, as well as one for David. If you want any of his ties, wallets or things like that, it would please me so much for you to take them and enjoy them. I know this would please Bill, too. Why don't we go upstairs now and see what is there. I really don't know myself, for he had so much."

"Are you sure you want to do this now, Martha?" the chaplain asked. "Maybe you would rather wait?"

"No, it's best to get it done since you and Jonathan are both here. We'll save things for David as well."

They climbed the stairs and stood amazed at the enormity of the task ahead. So much was still hanging in plastic covers. Boxes of wallets, ties, shirts, caps, hats . . . It was like walking through a Men's Department store. Martha took some special things - jewelry and other mementos. Then she left the room for the three of them to place things where it would be easiest to box up or carry out. It was nearly one o'clock before they returned to the living room.

Little was said, but all knew that a new life had begun, and the widow had already found joy in giving. It was a brave start. Martha Sanders was going to make it!

CHAPTER 37

The plane was on time leaving Boston. Every seat was filled, and it seemed that each family had at least six children all under the age of one! David knew Brittany was tired, so he was quiet. Juice and stale peanuts tasted good, but soon the lights came on to fasten their seat belts. The Captain announced it would be bumpy for a short time as they were encountering heavy weather. Brittany didn't like to fly, and soon her head was buried in David's shoulder. Her emotions were raw, as well. So he just held her quietly. The babies seemed to quiet down, but the rough weather continued.

"We'll be all right, dear, and it won't be long before we're in Chicago. It will be great to see my family."

The plane took a sharp drop. Some people screamed. Outside it was dark, and there was lightning nearby. The pilot announced, "We have requested to change course to avoid the weather, so it will soon be smooth."

Shortly after he spoke, the plane was on an even keel and the rough weather had passed. Due to the change in their route, they were late arriving, but it felt good to be taxiing down a long runway at O'Hare. It took a while for people to make their way off the plane, but David's eyes gleamed when he saw his folks leaning over the rope looking for him and Brittany.

"Oh, how wonderful to have you here. Welcome, Brittany. We're thrilled that you could come and we can finally meet."

The Wilkersons were friendly and already loving toward Brittany. Mrs. Wilkerson spoke tenderly, "We're so sorry about your father. We would have gone to you if there had been anything we could have done, but with leaving so soon, it seemed best if we just let David go. We stayed home and prayed for you and your family many times a day and each evening when we had devotions before going to bed. I'm so glad David could sing at the funeral and I know the messages meant much to you and your dear family. It must be so hard for your mother. I know you and your sister will be a great comfort her, and many friends will comfort her, too. Your father must have been a very famous lawyer, so many of his colleagues will spend time with her. We certainly always need friends, but especially at a time like this."

They quickly found their luggage, and Gene Wilkerson went to get the car. It was a small, old Pontiac, but everything fit in just fine. Soon they were on their way out of the city headed for Lombard. The church where they were members had given them a nice little home where they could stay for their time in the States. The stopped for lunch, and Brit called her mother to let her know everything was fine.

David's dad had a meeting with the Missions Committee at 3:00 p.m. It gave Brittany a little time to catch her breath, and she and Mrs. Wilkerson had a long talk.

Much was shared about Pakistan and their work there. About 4 o'clock, David's younger brother came bounding in - his baseball in one hand and mitt in the other. He hugged his brother and was introduced to Brittany.

"Not bad! Wish I had a pretty girl like that! How did you rate anyway?" Before anyone could answer and after everyone had laughed, he bounded up the stairs.

David said, "He's the happy-go-lucky one in the family, but with all his fun, he has a heart of gold. I shall miss him when he goes back home with mom and dad."

Brittany could see at once what a wonderfully close knit family this was, and she almost envied them. Maybe one day she would be part of the family. But she remembered David saying they could never be married until she loved the Lord.

Dinner was over and after the dishes were safely in the kitchen, Mr. Wilkerson took out his Bible. Everyone had one, so Brit looked on with David. He read Psalm 23 and 24. After reading, each one gave a prayer request or praise. Then they prayed around the table. Brittany felt alone and in the wrong place. Yet she knew what was said must be true. She didn't understand it, but the 23rd Psalm had been printed on the folder they had at the funeral and she had re-read it many times. It had comforted her.

"Brittany, please don't feel left out. We have learned to love you through David, and we want you to feel part of our family. We may do things differently than your family does, but that doesn't mean we don't care. We love the Lord with all our hearts and we owe Him our lives, and we want you to know Him, too. He loves you and so do we."

"I'm so happy to be here, and I do want to know more. I just feel so very ignorant, and this is all so new to me. Please forgive me if I seem to act strangely. I don't mean to. I want to believe as you do. But it may take time."

"We're praying for you and we do not want you to do anything in a hurry. It took me a long time to learn this, but I do know God is never in a hurry," said Gene. "It's been a long day for you and a long flight. Why not get a good night's rest and we'll have more time to get acquainted tomorrow."

David took Brit to her little room and kissed her goodnight. "I love you, Brit, and so does my family. Goodnight, dear."

"Good night, David. I love you, and your dear family, too."

CHAPTER 38

Gene Wilkerson was a man of perception and, having come from a family who did not know the Lord, he was very concerned for Brittany. He had no thought of pushing her in any way, but he wanted her to understand why the family did some things that might be unfamiliar to her.

"Wednesday night, the church is having a little farewell for us after Prayer Meeting, and we surely want you to be with us. Our meetings last about an hour and the fellowship time follows that. Would you like to come?" Gene asked Brittany.

"I've never been to that kind of meeting, but I do want to be with all of you, so I know I will enjoy going. I promise not to say anything that would embarrass you or your family."

"We are proud to have you with us, and we know how much you and David mean to each other, so we feel you are part of the family already."

Brittany had not been used to such loving kindness from her father, so she turned red and thanked him for his kindness.

David had to drive to Wheaton College, 30 miles west of where they were, as he was entering in the Fall as a freshman and had information to sign, books to buy, Orientation to attend as well as other matters.

"Would you like to go with me?" he asked Brittany. She quickly smiled and nodded her head. Every minute with David was special and she wanted to waste no time in being apart from the man she was learning to love more each day. She had never heard of the College, but that didn't matter. She wanted to see every area where he would be while they were apart.

Wheaton College is an on old, Christian College, surrounded by huge trees, filled with beautiful ivy-covered classroom buildings and dorms, set a little higher than the City of Wheaton itself. There had been several famous Presidents and the faculty was comprised of an abundance of scholars. Many, many majors were offered, but David was enrolled in the Theology program, since he felt God wanted him to have a good background in the Word before he followed his parent's footsteps. Having been raised in Pakistan, he loved the people and had learned the national language, Urdu, as a child. Ever since he was in school, he knew God wanted him back there. In every sense, it was home to him.

Brittany and David drove to the campus. She went with him from Registration, to the book store, to the dorm, and walked through several of the departmental buildings. Everywhere, she saw beautiful paintings and many Bible verses in bold relief on the walls. The Chapel was a special place, and when they entered it, many young men and women were kneeling at the altar. David took Brittany's hand and together they knelt. Nothing was said, by somehow Brittany felt she was standing on

Holy Ground. After everything was finished, she asked, "Isn't this a very expensive college?"

"Yes, it is. But God, in his wonderful love and provision, has given me a 4-year scholarship. I applied months ago and really never thought I would receive it, but without it I could never have come here. God answered the prayers of my family and many friends and 6 months ago, I receive a letter with the wonderful news. My parents were as thrilled as I. My dad is a graduate of Wheaton, too.'

After a late lunch, they drove home, and his dad insisted they go shopping for some of the extra things David would need for college. So the two drove off while Jessie and Brittany sat on the little porch, drinking lemonade and homemade cookies fresh from the oven. Mrs. Wilkerson wanted to know about Brittany's family, and for the rest of the afternoon, they shared with each other.

After dinner, David asked Brit if she would like to see a video of their ministry in Pakistan. What a thrill for her to see the people, the towns, the heart-breaking poverty, the little chapel where they held their meetings, and the small house that was their home. In the tiny front yard there was a small sign in Urdu, "Welcome to our Home."

When the video was finished, Brit said, almost without waiting, "Oh, I'd love to see that place and meet those people. I can't even imagine all the help they need."

The family smiled and David gave her a quick hug. "Maybe you and I will go there together. That would be some glorious answer to prayer!"

But suddenly, Brittany remembered his words spoken at camp, "I can't marry you until you believe in Christ and love Him with all your heart." The thought left an empty place in the pit of her stomach, but she said nothing.

Wednesday evening came quickly, for the day was spent in last minute packing, arrangements, checking passports and visas, airline tickets, weight of luggage and other things. After a light supper, they drove to Lombard Bible Church. It was a large, white building with a beautiful cross on the steeple. As soon as they were inside, people from everywhere greeted the family, and David introduced Brittany to as many as he could.

The service began at 7:00 p.m. and the pastor read from his Bible and spoke on the need for people to know Christ. He asked Gene to pray, and then pieces of paper were given out. Each had a name and information on it. People broke into small groups and prayed for those needs. The service was closed with several choruses. Then the Reception was in a large room next door. Tables were filled with flowers, gifts, food and a huge banner in the middle of the room which read, "WE LOVE YOU AND WILL BE PRAYING FOR YOU."

It was after 10:00 p.m. before the family had said goodbye to each one. At the door, the pastor took their hands and prayed for them - for safety, health, ministry, witness, and the difficult separation from their son. How glad everyone was that Mike was going back with them, and he would be entering the Missionary Kid's School.

Many gifts were packed in shoes, side pockets, and even inside socks. Tears of gratitude flowed as they saw the love gifts going with them. Several people had written notes with dates on them to be read later.

David and Brittany sat on the couch for a little while after the family had gone to bed. It had been a wonderful day. Surely God was in that place.

The next day, Brittany's flight was to leave for Boston at 3:00 p.m., so they drove off before noon. Gene prayed for her, and David's heart was so full, he could hardly say a word. They had a bite to eat at O'Hare Airport, and they took Brit to the checkpoint. It was a tear-filled farewell. Each hug was special and her heart longed to be a part of that family. She didn't know how to pray, but decided she would start on the plane and maybe God would hear her.

The door of the plane closed and the sign for the flight was removed as the family stared through the window at the airliner. Soon it pulled away from the gate. They waved, even though no hands could be seen.

As they turned to leave, David took his parent's hands. "Could we have one last prayer for her?"

Both Jessie and Gene prayed. David could only hold tightly to his parent's hands. And tomorrow he would be back again, saying goodbye to his precious family. It seemed like a lot for the heart to take in two days. BUT GOD! He knew their hearts and He would comfort and support them - each one.

"I will never leave you or forsake you," God had promised. David found it was easier to quote it than to live it right at that moment, but he knew it was true.

CHAPTER 39

A close friend of Martha's invited her to the mountains for a long weekend. She was sure she needed to get away from the house for a time of quiet. It gave Judith a welcome opportunity to go to the Cape to be with Jonathan and his family. She knew she would be welcome and Jonathan would be thrilled.

After her mother had left on Thursday morning, she drove to Sandwich. She was greeted with open arms and all she could say was "Bless your hearts for making me feel so welcome."

During lunch, the subject came up about Jonathan's soon departure for Yale, and also about the wedding, keeping in mind the feelings of Judith's mother.

"Would your mother feel bad if you went with us to New Haven to see Jonathan settled in college? Would she be alone, or would Brittany be with her?" asked Laura.

"Brittany will be back tomorrow as David's family leaves for Pakistan and he enters Wheaton College. I'm sure Brit will be glad to be with mom. She'll need to attend her classes at school. This is her last year of High, but other than that, she'll be home. I'm sure mother would understand my going to Yale with you folks."

That much was settled. Although there was still concern about Judith's mother, and then Judith's leaving home for good in December.

"I know your mother must feel very alone."

"But Brittany will be home all this year. She won't see David except perhaps for Christmas or a long weekend. Mom knows our wedding plans and I'm sure she wants us to go ahead. I only wish there were several close friends with whom mom could spend time," Judith said with a slight sense of remorse.

John Allen spoke up saying, "She would always be welcome here and we could have her come for weekends or special holidays. Even though her heart is raw and hurting now, time will help heal the loss. It's not really any of my affair, but were your parents very close?"

"Dad was more interested in his practice and making money than he was in spending time with his family - even mom. I'm sure he loved her in his own way, but to Brittany and me, he seemed distant. I think when they were first married, and when we were little, he was at home much more. But the more famous he became in his practice, the less any of us saw him. The shock of his death was traumatic to us all, but even though we shed tears and were deeply sorry he didn't make it, neither Brit nor I grieved as we might have. I'm not sure how mother really felt. Does that answer your question? I'm not trying to hide anything. I hope you know that."

Laura said, "We never mean to pry, but we care so much for you. We want the best for you and the whole family. Our family has been so close. But we sensed that was not the case when your father so definitely refused to accept your engagement and never seemed to even want to get to know Jonathan."

As they were talking, the phone rang. It was Brittany. "I'm leaving tomorrow for Boston and my plane arrives at Logan at 6:15 P.M. I'm on Delta flight 106. Can you meet me and take me home? I know mom is away for the weekend."

"Sure, I'll meet you. I'm in Sandwich with the Allens, but will get you, take you home, and then come back here. I'm sure Jonathan will go with me." He nodded an affirmation to her.

"Oh, Sis, I hate to have you make that long trip. I'll just catch a cab. That will be no problem at all. I'll call when I get home. Have a great time with the family. I can't wait to tell you all about David's family. They are so neat - and loving. And he's the absolute greatest!"

"Are you sure you don't mind taking a cab? We would be happy to come ."

"No, please stay there. You need time with Jonathan, just as I did with David and his family. Oh, Sis, my dream now is to marry him and serve with him in Pakistan. You can't believe all the pictures I saw and all the things they shared. They are the kind of family you dream of all your life. I shouldn't say that, for you have found that same love with Jonathan and his family. I love you and will see you soon."

"That was so kind of Brit. Now we can have more time together just to relax and enjoy," Jonathan said as he hugged Judith.

Dr. Allen had to leave for the hospital and the others went swimming. It was a great afternoon. All were together for dinner. Judith tried to call her mom but there was no answer. She hoped she was enjoying the quietness of the mountains and finding a really close bond with her friend.

Judith and Jonathan spent the evening talking about their wedding, and felt in their hearts that nothing should be changed unless Mrs. Sanders had strong objections.

From all the weary days and night, funerals and partings, they were overjoyed to have had a day with no interference and no problems. At sunset, they walked along the beach, leaving footprints in the sand. The moon glistened across Cape Cod Bay and there were no ripples on the sea, nor in their hearts.

Before leaving the beach, Judith said, "Have you thought at all about the message at the funeral - and the music? It has never left my mind or my heart. Jonathan, is it possible to look at the calm sea, enjoy the beams from the moonlight, look at the stars in the heavens, and not believe Someone created it all?"

"You're right. But how can we be sure there is a God? I've seen such tragedy with dad's patients - so much sorrow. How can a loving God let the world hurt so much?"

"I don't know any answers, but when I watched the life of the Chaplain - his love and care, his always being there when needed, his comfort to all of us, and then listening to what he said and quoted from the Bible - I can't believe the man doesn't know God in a very personal way. In my heart, I would like to have what he has. Do you think we could talk with him some day, together? After all, we have asked him to give us our wedding vows. I have to believe there is more to life than I have heard all my life from my family. I never even went to church or had a Bible. I really do want to hear more from Reverend Garrett."

Jonathan watched her face and listened intently to her words. "I guess I've been so happy with US that nothing else has mattered. But you are right. We do need to talk with him. When you go home, will you call him and see if we could see him before I go to Yale?"

"Why don't we call him tomorrow, since time is short before you leave. Maybe we can see him the first part of next week. Would that be O.K. with you?"

"Of course. That would be great. We can even talk about the wedding at the same time. Judith, you are one wonderful gal. No wonder I love you so much!"

It was late. The house had a light by the front door and one in the living room. They tiptoed in and kissed goodnight. It had been a VERY good day.

CHAPTER 40

New Hampshire is one of the most popular vacation spots in New England. It has high, winding roads and deep valleys, gorgeous lakes and quaint little villages full of gift shops and stands full of home-made goodies.

It was to Newfound Lake that Martha and her friend, Wendy Seely, went for their long weekend. It was an easy drive from Boston, with little traffic. They stopped at a tiny tea room for a sandwich and cold drink, and chatted about the countryside and the lovely weather. Boston had been warm and the cool breezes to the North were a treat.

They registered at a lovely cottage with a large picture window facing the lake and before unpacking, they watched skiers, ski-dos and even some brave enough to swim near the shore in the cold water. Making use of the coffeemaker in the room, they enjoyed a freshly brewed cup as they sat by the window to rest and relax.

"Martha, I don't know if you remember, because of the large crowd, but I attended Bill's funeral service. I know it was so hard for you. But surely you were encouraged by Rev. Garrett's message. And the young man who sang gave us a taste of Heaven. Did this help you, or did it make you feel more alone and empty?"

"It was a hard day, because Bill's death was so unexpected. I'm sure I was still in shock at the service. But the Chaplain from the hospital had been so gracious and kind to the family that it warmed my heart as he spoke. You don't know our family well, but in our hours together here, I can explain more. I was pleased with the service, but much of it is just a blur to me even now. I'm so grateful for your planning this time together with me. I've known you for a long time, but I really don't know you, and would love to share with you. I'm sure I haven't really answered your question. I'm not trying to be evasive, but when some of the fog lifts, I will share my feelings as much as I can."

"I can certainly understand how you feel. My husband of 28 years died three years ago, and for months, I was still trying to put things into perspective. He was a lawyer, too. Came home one night saying he was tired. He lay on the couch as I finished getting dinner ready. When I went into the living room to tell him he could come to the table, he didn't move. I knelt by the couch, touched his cheek and called his name. He never moved. I called 911, but when they arrived, he was already gone. We were very much in love. We had no children, but we spent much time traveling and enjoying just being together. Perhaps I thought we should come here, for it is a solace to me, too. We came here often and spent hours fishing and taking boat rides on the lake. One Christmas we came and joined a group of couples staying nearby - and sang carols from house to house and even at motels. It was one of my happiest memories. Even though Jim loved his law practice, I was first in his life - and when he was gone, it felt like half of me would never return. So I do know how you feel, and when you want to share, I'll be listening with an understanding heart."

For dinner, they went to Laconia and enjoyed some fresh fish, home-made warm bread with lots of pure butter and strawberry jam. Fresh, hot apple pie with vanilla ice-cream topped it off. Afterward, they wandered through little shops, and later watched the fading sunset from their room.

The phone rang and it was Judith wanting to know if everything was all right and if they had found a nice place to stay.

"It's beautiful here. You and Jonathan must come sometime, for both the mountains and the lakes almost take your breath away." And then she asked, "Are you having a good time - and how is everyone there?"

"We're fine, mom, and I'll be talking with you tomorrow. Enjoy every minute. And I'll be sure to give the family your love."

"Martha, how wonderful of your daughter to call," said Wendy. "She must love you dearly and care where you are and how you are. We wanted children so much, but I was unable to have any. I'm so glad for you. And I think you said the young man who sang at the service is a friend of your daughter?"

"David is a wonderful young man. He and my younger daughter, Brittany, are almost engaged. She has been with him near Chicago. His parents left today to return to their work in Pakistan. They are missionaries there. He will be going to college in Illinois, and my daughter has one more year of high school in Boston. It will be so good having her with me."

"Does coffee keep you awake?" Wendy asked.

"No, I'd love a cup. We should have stolen a few rolls or something!"

"I have some brownies with me that I baked last night. How about one or two of those?"

"Sounds perfect!"

As the moon shimmered over the lake, they drank and ate and enjoyed just being quiet. Martha knew she had found a real friend. It had been a wonderful day. Tomorrow they planned a trip around Lake Winnipesaukee. Lunch would be at Alton Bay. They could watch the sailboats and the Mail Boat. What a nice thing to look forward to. Martha's heart seemed at peace after a long time in cold storage.

The Chaplain had said that God loved people. She really felt that night that He might even love her. It was a good feeling and her nerves were less tense. As she put her head on her pillow, taut muscles began to relax, and for the first time since Bill's death, she slept soundly through the night.

CHAPTER 41

Before Brittany and David parted at the airport, David held her close and said, "I long to put a ring on your finger and say we're engaged - but I just can't do that until I'm sure you know the Lord. Oh, Brit, if you only knew how wonderful it is to belong to Him, and have His peace in your heart. I know we love each other, but I also know that the gulf between us would only widen if one belonged to Him and one did not. The Bible is very clear when it says, "Can two walk together unless they be agreed?" God never makes mistakes and He wants us to be happy - but we must be one in heart and one in Christ. I love you, Brit. I'll never stop. But He is on the throne of my heart and my life, and HE must stay there. Please, please look at your heart, read the Bible, listen to His words. He longs to come into your life and make you His very own."

On the flight back to Boston, Brittany could not forget David's words. With all her heart she wanted to marry him - but would her mother and sister understand? Would she be alienated from her family? Would it also mean her entire life would be in Pakistan, 14,000 miles away? Her emotions were in turmoil and she felt so lost and so completely confused. David's family had been wonderful to her and she loved them dearly. But how could she change to accept their beliefs and ways? And what of her friends at school? What would they think?

As her thoughts ran rampant, the plane took a sharp drop and the FASTEN YOUR SEATBELTS sign lit up. Quickly afterward, the pilot's voice came over the loud speaker. "We have hit a slight storm. Please remain in your seats until we give you clearance otherwise. Don't be concerned for this will last only a short time." His voice was reassuring. The passengers went back to reading, talking - and yet Brittany felt uneasy. Was everything all right with the plane? Was she afraid to die?

The plane climbed and then descended, rolled a bit, and soda on the little tables fell into the aisle. The clouds were thick. It became very dark outside. Brittany had chosen a window seat. She stared through the glass, hoping to see the ground or some ray of light, but the darkness persisted. They had been in the air two hours now. People stopped what they were doing. The stewardesses did not come by. Finally, the pilot came over and said, "We are going to land in Newark in just a few minutes. The weather around Boston has worsened and we have been advised to land. Please make sure your seat belts are securely fastened and your seats are in the upright position. We will be on the ground shortly. Thank you for your patience during this inconvenience."

As the plane descended sharply, the sky did not lighten. Everyone heard the lowering of the landing gear. Brit felt the flaps go down - and then all she felt was pain. All she heard were screams. All she saw was fire. And then she felt nothing at all.

When she opened her eyes, a man was standing by her. All she felt was stabbing pain and she felt she was moving. The man explained, "We are taking you to a hospital. Please don't move. Are you having pain? What can you remember?"

"My head, my head! Oh, my head. Where am I? What happened to me? Where is David? Where is my mother? Oh, my head!"

Baptist Hospital Emergency Room was full. There were people dressed in white and green uniforms. Screaming came from every direction. Phones were ringing. Doctors arrived. Stretchers bumped into one another. There was confusion everywhere.

Brittany opened her eyes and saw an unfamiliar face. She felt something pushing on her tummy. Bright lights shone in her eyes. A needle was put in her arm. A muffled voice said something that sounded like "surgery." Then there was less pain and she was rolled out of the Emergency Room.

"Can you feel this?" she heard a voice ask. "Move your leg for me. Good, now move the other one. Good. Other than your head, do you hurt anywhere?"

"My head hurts so. But I can see your face. My arms feel hot like they were burned or something. That's all I feel. Where am I? What happened to me? Please tell me. And please call my mother."

Dr. Allen was at the Cape Cod Hospital making rounds when he looked at a patient's TV. All he could see was what looked like a plane on fire and people everywhere. He started to ask the patient questions, but not wanting to upset him, he headed for the doctor's lounge. The room was full of nurses and doctors. A Delta plane which originated in Chicago, had crashed trying to make an emergency landing in Newark. The plane had burst into flames. Few details were given as newsmen were trying to get stories. Smoke filled the air and nothing was really definite as to what had happened, how many were dead, how many injured, etc.

Then in a flash of recollection, Dr. Allen remembered that Judith had said her sister was leaving Chicago for Boston that day. He couldn't remember her saying what time or what airline, but he raced to the phone and called his wife.

"Laura, please speak softly as you answer my questions. Do you know what flight Brittany was taking from Chicago and what airline? When you ask Judith, please don't say anything. Just use general conversation." He went on to say, "A Delta flight from Chicago has crashed near Newark. Many are hurt. Some may have been killed. I've only seen a little on TV. Maybe it's best not to turn on the TV right now. Call me when you can with details. My cell phone is in my hand. I'll be home as soon as I can get away. Love you."

Judith and Jonathan had been out for a walk along the shore in Sandwich and had just come in. As casually as she could, Laura greeted them and asked about their afternoon. "By the way," she asked curiously, "when does Brittany get to Boston? I've forgotten what you told me. Is it today or tomorrow?"

"Yes - remember she called last night and we agreed she would take a taxi home tonight. She's on Delta Flight 106 which was to leave O'Hare about 10. I know it will be hard for both David and Brit to be apart. They are so much in love. At least he'll be staying in the States for college so they can see each other now and then."

Laura tried not to show any emotion as she listened to Judith, but her heart sank. Maybe this was not her flight - or maybe she took another flight. She left the living room, quietly walked to the back yard, took her cell phone from her pocket and called John.

"Oh, John, she was on Delta 106 from Chicago to Boston. Was that the flight?"

"Laura, don't say anything. I'll be right home. Yes, that was the flight, but we know nothing about anyone yet."

Within 15 minutes, John arrived at home. Jonathan noticed his father was upset. Something must have gone wrong with one of his patients.

"Dad, did you have a rough time in the OR? Did you lose a patient?"

"No. Things went well with most of my patients - but there is something I need to share with you. I was in the Doctor's Lounge and saw the TV. A Delta flight has crashed trying to make an emergency landing at . . ."

Before he could finish, Judith screamed and hid her head in Jonathan's shoulder.
"Oh, good Lord! What was the flight number, do you know? Can we turn on the TV? Oh dear - Mom - what about her? Oh, it can't - it can't be true. Hasn't our family suffered enough? Whoever said at dad's funeral that God was kind? I hate Him. I HATE HIM! He doesn't care a thing about anybody."

Judith sobbed and sobbed when the TV was turned on and the flight was identified as Delta 106 from Chicago.

John put his hand on Judith's arm and said, "There are so many hospitals in that area, but I will go back to the office and find a listing of them. Then I will try to locate Brittany. I think it will be best if you wait just a little while before calling your mother." And then he quickly left, leaving a sobbing Judith in the loving arms of Jonathan.

Before they took Brittany to the OR to suture the torn flesh on her head and neck, they asked if she knew her name.

"Brittany Sanders. I live in Boston and my mother is Mrs. Martha Sanders." Finally a name and a contact. The doctor sent a volunteer to call the Sanders family in Boston. Then Judith was taken to the Operating Room. Thankfully, her skull was not fractured, according to the MRI. She did have a serious concussion and lacerations on her head and neck. No bones seemed to be broken, but both her arms had second degree burns.

"It could have been so much worse for her," said the doctor. When I see what else has been coming through the ER door, I'm glad we have one who will make it and be fine. So many have already been taken to the morgue."

Dr. Allen quickly looked through his massive book, trying to locate hospitals in the Newark area. He dialed one and the line was busy and stayed that way. He found a hospital in Jersey City, but they had no casualties. They told him many were taken to Elizabeth because that was close to the crash site. He looked for names of hospitals in Elizabeth, and found three. The first one was Elizabeth General, but the phone rang busy, busy, busy. Then he tried Baptist Hospital and it, too, rang busy. He went to the lounge and they had just posted a number across the TV screen where people could call to ask about relatives who had been on the plane. He dialed the number and a lady answered.

"Can you tell me if Brittany Sanders has been located, and if so, do you know which hospital she is in?"

The lady asked him to wait. After what seemed like an eternity, she said, "Yes, she is in Baptist Hospital in Elizabeth, but that is all I know. We do know she survived the crash."

John thanked her and hung up. Running to the car, he headed home and told the family the news. Judith, still in panic, cried, "We need to find Mom before she sees it on TV. She knew all about Brit's flight and everything. Should I fly down to Newark to be with Brit? Tell me, please, what to do? Do you think she will live? What about David? Should I call him? Please help me do the right thing," she sobbed.

Dr. Allen finally found a colleague in Boston who knew a doctor at Baptist in Elizabeth. He assured John he would call and find out what he could and get right back to him.

"It may take some time because I'm sure they are all doing everything they can. The last I heard, it was a full flight with some 298 on board."

Laura suggested, "Let's try to find your mother. We don't know where she is staying, but as soon as we find her, some of us can go up and bring her home or keep her here. The shock will be terrible."

Judith called David, but there was no answer.

Martha and Wendy were having a lovely snack in a little tea room in Alton Bay. All the world seemed lovely and peaceful. They were going on around the lake and shop at some of the gift shops later. It was a good day for both of them.

CHAPTER 42

David had just kissed his parents and brother goodbye and was standing by the window to get a last look as British Airways flight 1002 pulled out. It was scheduled to refuel in Frankfurt, Germany, and arrive the next afternoon in Rawalpindi, Pakistan. They would call him from Frankfurt and then from Pakistan. It was hard for David to see them go, but he was thrilled with their ministry and was looking forward to a good year at Wheaton College.

David headed for the parking garage, glad he had written down where he had parked, and then headed home. On approaching the driveway, he saw his pastor standing by the front door. David wondered why - but they were friends, so he must have come to cheer him up after leaving his family. But the pastor ran to David's car.

"I've tried to reach you for hours. Even last night, no one answered. You must have been out. I kept calling until late. Have you heard the news about Delta . . ." He didn't have to finish the sentence. David had not had time to watch TV or look at a newspaper, but he knew at once there must be bad news.

David's face turned white and he stammered, "What happened?" We were with friends last night until late and then left very early for the airport. What is it?"

"I'm sure you said your girl friend was flying to Boston yesterday afternoon. Was I wrong?"

"No - she was on Delta 106. I tried reaching her at her home last night without success, but thought she might be with friends. We were so busy with my folks leaving, I've seen nothing and heard nothing. What happened?" There was desperation in his question.

"The plane was trying to make an emergency landing at Newark. It crashed before it could land safely. I have a number you can call to see if Brittany has been accounted for - if she's in a hospital - or how she is. I'll stay right here with you until you find out something - anything!"

David's feet were glued to the driveway. He could not move, nor could he utter a word other than, "Please God . . ." In a few seconds, his pastor took his hand and led him to the house.

"Please call for me, would you? I can't."

Pastor Donaldson dialed the number. After the phone rang many, many times, a voice finally came over. "May I help you?"

"Do you know if Brittany Sanders has been located? And if so, could you tell me where she is?"

After an interminable wait, the lady said, "We have found your friend. She is a patient at Baptist Hospital in Elizabeth, a city near Newark. We have no details concerning her condition, but we do know she survived the crash."

With a most grateful "thank you very much", Dr. Donaldson hung up the phone. David was sitting on the edge of a chair, shaking violently, but managed to request, "Please pray, pastor."

Pastor Donaldson put his arm around David and prayed that God would care for Brittany and that she might not be seriously hurt. He prayed for the family, that God would give them strength and wisdom.

Just as he finished praying, the phone rang. David reached for the phone. It was Dr. Allen. "I've tried and tried to get you without success. Did you know that Brittany is in the hospital? Either Judith or I will fly down to be with her. We have tried to reach her mother, but she is in New Hampshire with a friend, and we don't know where. She usually has her cell phone with her, but apparently she forgot to take it, or turned it off. We are going to reach her somehow. Hopefully, she hasn't seen it all on TV. If she had, we know she would have called Judith. But tell me, what can we do for you, David?"

Gathering some inward strength, David replied, "Oh thank you so much for calling. I have just seen my folks and my brother off on a flight for their return to Pakistan. We were with friends last night and got home late. I had heard nothing. If I had the money, I would take the next flight to New Jersey to be with Brit - but I don't."

Without hesitation, Dr. Allen replied, "Whatever money you need, we will get it to your bank immediately. So go ahead and make your plans. Just give me the name of your bank and your account number and I will send $2,000 to your account by wire."

"Oh no, sir. I couldn't take your money. Somehow I'll find a way to get there."

Dr. Allen responded, "David, you are like one of the family. Please let us help you."

David, close to tears, thanked him and found the information he needed. The pastor realized by then there were about a dozen people at the door, all wanting to help David. He let them inside and they held David in their arms as he sobbed and sobbed. Each one offered to give money, lend a car - do anything to help. Pastor Donaldson called the airport and made a reservation for David on Delta Flight 201 leaving O'Hare at 6:00 p.m. He also volunteered to take David to the airport. He could pick up his ticket there.

David packed a few clothes. One of the church members took him to the bank and he was able to take out money for his ticket and some cash as well. He would thank Dr. Allen later, and pay him back when he could.

Not even 24 hours had passed since the plane crash, so there were still a lot of unknowns. About 100 had survived. The pilot and co-pilot died. The flight engineer was in critical condition.

Brittany was taken from the ER at 3:00 p.m. She had been there all night and all morning while so many were being treated, and even with extra doctors and nurses, only so much could be done. She was then put in a room with another passenger. Both were sedated, but neither was in critical condition.

David called the Allens to tell them when he was leaving and thank them again for the money. He said he would never be able to repay them fully, but they insisted they were more than glad they could help. And they did not expect reimbursement of any funds.

John's colleague in Boston finally got through to a doctor he knew in Newark. He said he would find out immediately all he could about Brittany Sanders. It was only an hour later when he called saying she was in Baptist Hospital in Elizabeth and doing well, with burns on her arms and a bad concussion and still under sedation. Everyone cried, but were greatly relieved that she was alive. Dr. Allen knew it was imperative to locate Martha and her friend.

Martha and Wendy had had a great day. They arrived back at their cottage, tired - yet rested inwardly. They watched the setting sun from the front window.

Martha couldn't find her cell phone anywhere to make a call home. She excused herself and said to Wendy, "I must call Brittany and Judith."

She dialed her home phone and received no answer. She decided her daughter had gone out with friends. Then she tried Brittany's cell phone number. Still no answer. Martha thought that a bit strange, since Brit always carried it with her, but she thought perhaps Brit had forgotten her phone. Then she became concerned knowing that Brittany would call her cell phone number later and would get no answer either. She called a neighbor to leave word of where she was and the phone number in their room.

Then she tried calling Judith. She couldn't get through to her cell phone, so she called the Allens' number. John answered.

"Hello! How are you, John. I'm so glad to talk with you. I'm sure Judith has tried to reach me, but I've misplaced my cell phone at home and never even gave an address of where we are. We are having such a wonderful time. Everything just got away from me. Please give my love to Laura. And may I speak to Judith?"

Dr. Allen said, "Just a minute. I'll find her."

He looked at Judith and asked, "Do you want to tell her, or do you want me to? I'll do whichever you think is best."

"You can do it better than I, for all I would do is cry, and that won't help," Judith said tearfully. "Assure her that Brittany is really all right."

Returning to the phone, John said in all kindness, "Martha, there is something I need to tell you. Brittany was on her flight from Chicago to Boston last evening. The plane crashed outside of Newark. But let me hasten to say, your daughter is in the hospital in Elizabeth. I understand she has burns on her arms, a concussion and some lacerations on her head and neck, but is not in critical condition."

He could hear Martha scream and then sob. Then Martha's friend took the phone.

"I'm Wendy Seely and we are staying at a cottage on Newfound Lake. Should we leave for Boston immediately - or what do you suggest would be best for us to do?"

"A doctor friend of mine has spoken with the doctor in New Jersey. Brittany is not in critical condition. Her friend, David, is flying to Newark tonight from Chicago to be with her. Would Martha like to come here to our home in Sandwich? Judith is here and that might be a comfort to both of them. If she would like to go to Newark later, or even now, we will be glad to help with all the details. Let me give you our home phone number and cell phone numbers."

After giving the information to Wendy, John requested, "May I speak to Martha again? We're so grateful you are with her and we know you won't leave her. If you want any of us to come there, we will come tonight. In any case, let me have your address and routing to your motel cottage."

Martha returned to the phone and heard John's reassuring words that Brittany was safely in a hospital and not in critical condition. "Dr. Allen, do you think I should try to get back tonight and fly out as soon as possible? What do you suggest?"

Martha had perfect confidence in John's judgment and would do whatever he felt would be best for all concerned.

"David is on his way from Chicago. Why don't you stay where you are for tonight, and if we hear anything at all, we'll call. Then tomorrow, why not have your friend bring you here so you can be with us and Judith. If anyone has to go to New Jersey, two of us can go together. How does that sound?"

"Yes, John, that makes sense - except I long to be with Brittany. But I suppose with all that is happening in the hospital, it wouldn't be much help for me to be there. Maybe tomorrow we'll know more, and Judith and I could fly down together. I don't think I could do it today anyway. The shock is taking its toll. Wendy has your numbers now and you have ours. If there is any change - any change at all - please call me. I'm so grateful for all you are doing. And now may I speak with Judith?"

"Oh, honey - how are you? We are all in a state of loss and questions. Please let me know you are all right. I'm so glad you have Jonathan and his caring family."

"Mom, I'm all right and feel as you do. I can't talk either, but we will in the morning. If you want to fly down tomorrow or the next day, we can both go. Dr. Allen has also offered to go, too. I love you, Mom." And that was all the conversation they could manage.

Wendy gave Martha some Aspirin and a cup of hot coffee. They sat quietly by the window, saying nothing. Martha was still trembling, and Wendy was right beside her, holding her close. They stayed there long after the lake was dark and the moon hidden. Finally, out of sheer exhaustion, Martha headed for bed.

"Do you want me to sit by you until you fall asleep? I'm sure Brittany will be fine, but I know your heart must be broken. If only there was something I could do."

"Oh, Wendy, you have been a strength and courage to me and I am so thankful for you. I'll sleep after a while. But if you'd like to stay here , that will be fine."

Soon the effect of shock and weariness overtook Martha and she fell into a troubled sleep. Wendy slipped quietly out of the room, took a blanket, wrapped it around herself and sat in a chair by Martha's bed and wondered why it was possible, after such a glorious day, to have this happen? They had enjoyed such quiet, peace and happiness.

CHAPTER 43

David's smile, along with his bouquet of a dozen red roses, brought sunshine into an otherwise bleak room. He walked quietly to Brittany's bed, touched her hand and kissed her forehead. Her blue eyes opened wide. "Oh, David! You're here."

She lifted her bandaged arm toward him and took his hand. She smiled for a moment, then closed her eyes, but held on to him. The nurse he had spoken to said she was doing well and was now listed as stable, and she was definitely out of danger.

"Her arms have second degree burns. Thankfully, her face wasn't burned. She has a concussion, but no fractures. I'm sure your coming will make all the difference in her time of convalescence. Does the rest of her family know where and how she is?"

David explained that Brittany's sister and mother knew and in a few minutes he would call them to let them know her condition.

"Her home is in Boston and her family is there. Do you have any idea how long they will keep Brittany in the hospital?"

There are still so many being treated or are in the OR, that as soon as she can travel safely, I'm sure she will be allowed to go home if there is a doctor there who could care for her and a hospital where she could go if needed.

"Oh, yes. Brittany's sister is staying with the family of a neurosurgeon right now and his practice is near where they live on Cape Cod. Could she be taken by car, or would she have to be transported by other means?"

"I'll have to ask the doctor. Naturally, it would be best if she flies, but I'm not sure that is wise after all she's been through. Can you stay through today? I'll find one of the doctors and he can talk with you and give you specific information."

"I can stay as long as she needs me and until she is in the doctor's care in New England. I'll leave the room just long enough to call her family so they know how she is. May I use my cell phone in the hospital, or must I go outside?"

"We don't allow them to be used in here, especially with all the electrical equipment being used, but if you take the back stairs, they will lead you outside. It's not far. Here, let me show you the way."

David thanked her and followed her to the stairs.

"Dr. Allen, this is David. I'm sorry to call you at this hour, but I'm with Brittany and she is doing very well. She has second degree burns on both arms and a concussion, but I talked with the nurse and she feels she could be released soon if she could be near a doctor and hospital, if needed. I'm waiting to talk with one of the doctors to learn when she may be released. Can you call her mother or do you want me to do it? I'd need the number where she is staying. Brittany had said in Chicago that her mother would be away for the weekend, but she didn't know where."

"David, let me share all this with Judith, and then she can talk with you before I get back on the phone."

David shared everything with Judith and when she offered to go, he said it might be difficult, for the motels were full for miles around, and transportation was still a problem. However, if she felt she should fly down, he would meet her at the airport or wherever.

After some discussion, Dr. Allen returned to the phone.

"We will call her mother and give her your phone number. Can you use your cell in the hospital?"

"No, I can't. But I'll call you the number in Brittany's room and her mother can call her there. I will stay as long as needed. Is there anything else I can do? Any way I can help?"

"We're so glad you are there and as soon as you see the doctor, please let us know. We'll call her mother, for she is terrified. She's with a friend in New Hampshire, but I'm sure they will return to Boston today. I'll keep you posted. We're just so thankful you are there and we know Brit is overjoyed to have you by her side."

The doctor came in shortly and told David that Miss Sanders could go home in two days.

"How do you think she should travel after all that's happened?"

"We'll give her pain medicine and something to make her sleep so she can fly. It would be too long for her to drive. Can you go with her? Is there a doctor she knows where she is going?"

"One of the finest neurosurgeons in New England is a good friend of the family. He practices at Cape Cod Hospital, but could also care for Brittany in a hospital in Boston, if that were necessary. I'm sure if nurses were needed, they could have them go to their home. I'll be with her until she is safely with Dr. Allen and the family."

Phone calls flew from one family to another and Dr. Allen told David to go ahead and make plane reservations, and the family would meet them in Boston. He also said that Brit's mother was on her way home and greatly relieved that David was with her daughter. Phone calls continued all day. In the evening, one of the surgeons had the bandages removed from Brittany's head and neck. The lacerations were re-bandaged. David then explained to Brittany their plans for flying her to Boston, and although afraid to fly, agreed she wanted to go home, especially since David would be with her.

On David's flight from Chicago, he had spent almost the entire time praying for Brittany and asking the Lord the best way to witness to her and her family. He read his Bible and also prayed much for his parents as they headed for Pakistan. He was sure they would understand if they tried to call him from Frankfurt and couldn't get through. They had traveled so much, they were content to leave things in God's hands, for they were His servants and trusted Him with every detail of their lives.

David found a room in a motel not far from the hospital, ate dinner and went to bed. His mind and body were weary. But his heart was at peace as he fell asleep praying for the girl he loved.

Brittany was released two days later and was given medicine for the flight. She was taken by ambulance to the plane and the stewardesses were kind and helpful. As soon as she was settled, the other passengers boarded. David gave her the medicine, and before the plane left the gate, she was asleep. In less than an hour, they landed at Logan in Boston.

Brittany was taken off by stretcher. She was still sleepy, but genuinely glad to be with her mother, sister and the Allen family. Placing her in the back seat with pillows and a blanket, they drove to Sandwich. Dr. Allen had arranged for Home Health nurses to come daily to check her and change her bandages. He tested her reflexes and found they were perfectly normal. Her only complaint was the burns on her arms. Pain medicine was given as needed. And within three days, she was able to sit on the porch. Much that had happened was, mercifully, obscured from her memory. She only remembered the plane going down - then the screams - and the pain. They later learned that there had been 80 mile an hour winds with lightning everywhere. Then the wind hit the plane with such force that it went straight down within a few miles of the runway. Many passengers were in critical or serious condition in Newark, Elizabeth, and New York. That same evening, several planes had been diverted to airports as far west as Detroit and South to Washington. They said it had been the worst storm in over 50 years.

David was thanked many times by everyone for all he did for Brittany. He told Dr. Allen again that he would repay the money which had been sent to him, but that was refused.

At dinner, David asked if he could say the blessing before the meal and thank the Lord for taking care of Brittany. All agreed enthusiastically.

"Father, we praise Thee and thank Thee for protecting our loved one and caring for her through this terrible ordeal. We know that there are no accidents with you, for you are in control of our lives and know us completely. We praise Thee for the care given by the doctors and hospital personnel, for the concern of her family and the many details worked out by Dr. Allen. Thank you, Lord. In Jesus' Name. Amen."

Nothing was said, but Martha hugged David and thanked him many times for all he had done. He was already late for Orientation at Wheaton, but he had contacted them and they expressed understanding.

The next day, as hard as it was, before saying goodbye to Brittany, he took her by the hand and led her to the living room couch. Then he knelt and prayed for her, again thanking the Lord for sparing her life.

It was Judith who drove David to Boston to catch his flight. He promised to call the minute he got off the plane.

The Wilkersons had arrived safely in Pakistan. It had been a good trip. They talked at length to David and told him that on the plane, they had had special prayer for him and for Brittany. As they discussed the time, it was exactly when Brittany was flying to Boston. God had abundantly answered.

Within a week, Brit felt almost normal. She told the family that she really believed God had answered David's prayers. She said she knew in her heart that God was real and loving and He cared for her. She didn't understand any of it, but she was alive and cared for, and she felt only God could have done that.

Martha spoke up, "I didn't understand your father's death, but when I listened to the Chaplain, I knew there was a reason. Now that you were saved and not badly injured, I am sure God was in control. I want to believe as David does."

It had been a long day and the family was quiet. Nerves were less frayed and hearts beat more normally. Bed was welcomed.

David was safely back in Lombard. His family was home in Pakistan. Brittany was getting well. The pieces that had fallen apart were coming back into place. Surely God had protected this family. They didn't know why or what to believe, but they did admit that the universe had a Creator, and surely He must care for the people He created. The Sanders were determined to search for the Truth and embrace it -- whatever it took.

CHAPTER 44

The alarm was set for 6:00 a.m., but Chaplain Garrett was wide awake an hour earlier. For some reason, his thoughts went to Martha, and he realized it had been some time since he had called her to see how the family was doing. It was still far too early to reach her, so he read his Bible and prayed, then had a bowl of cereal, some rye toast and a cup of coffee. At 8 o'clock, he phoned, and Martha answered.

"Please forgive me for calling so early, but you have been on my heart and mind ever since I woke up. How are you and the girls?"

"I'm so glad you called, Chaplain. I wanted to ask you to come for lunch or dinner so we would have time to talk. So much has happened since I spoke with you last. Could you come tonight or tomorrow for lunch?"

"It would be good if we could make it tomorrow, as I have a Staff Meeting at the hospital today, and I never know how long those will last. What time should I be there?"

"About noon would be fine, if that's all right with you. Then we could have some of the afternoon to talk."

"Fine. I'll look forward to seeing you tomorrow. Thank you for asking me." He sounded pleased with the invitation.

Martha spent the day shopping, cooking, having her hair done, and looking forward to the next day. Judith had only two more days before Jonathan would leave for Yale. Brit was already getting things for her senior year in high school. Her scars were hardly noticeable now and she seldom had headaches. After the week at the Allens and a week at home, she seldom talked about the crash. At first, she had had nightmares and cried in her sleep. Then she had trouble sleeping at all. But now she was working hard at getting ready for school. Martha often thought she had a lot on her mind, but she said very little.

The accident was reported at length in the Boston Globe, but even when the names of the crash victims were given, it was usually on a page near the end of the first section and most did not look there unless their family was involved. Martha had bought all the issues reporting the accident both in New Hampshire and in Sandwich and she was eager to read all about the circumstances and devastation. Apparently the Chaplain had not read the names of the passengers, or surely he would have said something to Martha.

When Brittany came home for dinner with some friends who would be in her class at school soon, she told her mother a group of them were going to a movie.

"I'm so happy you are back with your friends. It makes me feel good to see you so much more like yourself. But please tell me, are you really better in your heart, or is this a mask you're wearing?"

"As you know, mom, it hasn't been easy, but I have to get on with my life. Since David calls twice a day, it helps a lot. But I miss him so much! He has a week off at Thanksgiving and, even though it's a long way off, we are both looking forward to it. He's willing to fly here to be with us if that's all right with you."

"I'd be happy to have David here anytime, and I know he has little money, so why don't you surprise him by sending him an airline ticket? I'll be so happy to give you the money, and when he comes, there is so much you could do together. I don't know if Jonathan will be home then or if Judith will go to New Haven for Thanksgiving. I know she is already planning a big weekend in late September for the Yale-Princeton football game. She's already excited. I can hardly believe she'll be getting married in December, but I'm so happy for both of them. You and your sister have picked the best men, and I am so glad for each of you."

"Oh, mom, it would be great having David come for Thanksgiving. Thanks bushels for letting me send him the ticket. He has his scholarship, but not a lot more, so it will mean so much to him. How soon can I tell him?"

"Anytime you want. We can get an electronic ticket here and all he has to do is make a reservation and pick up the ticket at the airport, or you can buy one and send it in a card if you'd rather."

They had a light dinner and Brit left with her friends for the movies.

Martha heard her daughter come in - but she had always trusted her girls and was never worried about them staying out or going to places where they should not go. Neither of them ever smoked or drank. For this, Martha was exceedingly grateful.

The doorbell rang a little before noon. Martha hurried to the door and was happy to see Chaplain Garrett standing there and he seemed pleased to be there. It only took a few minutes before Martha was telling him about the plane crash and Brit being injured. But spared. He was shocked and expressed his sorrow in not knowing about this before. He told her he would have come at once had he known.

"How is dear Brittany now?   Is she all right physically and emotionally?"

"At first, she was traumatized, of course. But David -- you remember he sang at Bill's funeral - flew in to be with her in the hospital and brought her home. He had to return to Illinois for college, but the rest of us stayed with the family of Judith's fiancé in Sandwich. Brit had a bad concussion and there are still a few scars on her arms where she was burned, but she says little about it all. I don't really know how she feels inside. She's going back for her last year of high school and is doing things with her friends - but I'm not sure everything is right within her heart."

Chaplain Garrett looked at Martha and said, "You know how I feel about trusting the Lord. I only wish and pray she will find Jesus and take Him as her Savior. At times like these, the only real peace and security we can have is in accepting God's will and being grateful that He cared - and continues to care - for us. I'm sure David spent many hours praying, for he is a godly man and mature for his years. He will be a great son-in-law when they marry."

Martha smiled at the thought.

"But how can I help you?" Chaplain Garrett asked. "You've been through so much these past weeks, and I'm sure this plane crash tore your heart into pieces."

"Chaplain, ever since you spoke at Bill's funeral, I've thought about all you said in the hospital and afterward when you came here to help us. Those things have weighed heavily on my heart and mind. I believe what you said is true. And David has not only said a lot, but his life shines forth what he believes. I truly want what you both have - but I don't know where to start or what to do. Life has been spiritually on the other side of the world for me, and all this is very new. I guess we thought as a family, if we didn't murder or steal, were kind to our neighbors and gave money at Christmas for poor children - all that was enough and we would automatically go to Heaven. Until you prayed with Bill and spent time with us and him at the hospital, I never had heard about why Jesus was sent into the world, or anything like that. Oh, please forgive my ignorance, but I am being honest with you."

Chaplain Garrett smiled and said, "You never need to apologize for being honest. That is a great virtue. For many years, I didn't know the Savior, but once I turned my life over to Him, my whole being took on new meaning. I felt as though I had come through a dark tunnel into glorious light. I covet that experience for you and your family. I know David does, too. Is there some way I can help you to understand? Something from the Bible I can read to you? Something I can pray for you? I want so much to help you realize that we have all sinned. It is sin that keeps us apart from God. But in His mercy, God gave His Son, Jesus, as the perfect sacrifice to eradicate our past sins. He came to die so we could live -

abundantly. I can't make that decision for you, Martha. I can only pray and ask Him to work in your heart and bring you to Himself. I long more than anything else to have you know His love, His joy and His peace."

For several minutes, there was a comfortable silence. Then Martha suggested they eat lunch. Afterward, she asked him to pray for her and the girls. He prayed a long prayer and assured her of his continuing prayers. Then he turned to her, looked into her tear-filled eyes and said, "Would you like to ask Christ to forgive you and come into your life right now, Martha?"

"Oh, yes, I would. But I need a little more time. Maybe the next time you come."

With a note of sadness, Chaplain Garrett replied, "Martha, God only gives us today. We have no promise of tomorrow. I would never push you into a decision. But I want His best for you. I'm sure that once you accept Christ, your whole life will change and God will lead you every step of the way. Now I will leave you with that and continue to pray. Please tell Brittany and Judith that I'm praying for them, too."

Martha and the Chaplain had a delicious luncheon together, sharing some of the best and worst moments of their lives. They both enjoyed the time together.

Then this godly man stood, thanked Martha and was on his way.

As the door closed, Martha knew in her heart the Chaplain was right. She didn't understand theology. She had read very little of the Bible. But in her heart, she knew Chaplain Garrett was right, and she determined she would kneel by her bed that very night and the best she knew how, she would ask Christ into her life to be her Savior.

CHAPTER 45

For a long time, Martha thought about the conversation with Chaplain Garrett. She knew in her heart what she should do and wanted to do, but there were so many questions. What would her family think? What about her friends? What about her lifestyle? She knew she would have to go to church, and Sundays had always been a fun day or a shopping day. If she went to church, where? She would feel so ignorant and so alone. The persistent ringing of the phone interrupted her thoughts.

"Hi! I said I'd call so we could make plans for lunch. What about tomorrow? We could go somewhere on the ocean and then go shopping, or whatever you'd like to do. If you have other plans, we can make it another time."

"Oh, I'm so glad you called, Wendy. I think tomorrow would be great. Let's go to Gloucester and eat lobster - then do some window wishing. It sounds like just what the doctor ordered."

"Good. I'll pick you up about 11 o'clock and we can have the rest of the day. Lobster makes my mouth water already. I haven't had any in a long time. I'll see you tomorrow, then."

Judith called to say she and Jonathan would be leaving for New Haven the next day, and after he was settled in, and they did some apartment hunting, she would return home.

"Oh, Mom, when I get back, can we look for a wedding dress and clothes for the honeymoon and for what you and Brit will be wearing? I'm so excited, I can't think of much else. Jonathan and I are counting the days until December 22nd!"

Brittany arrived home with boxes and bags full of special things for school and showed them to her mother. She was getting excited about her final year in high school. Her color had brightened, and her mother was pleased to see her looking happy and well.

At bedtime, Martha thought of her promise, but surely one day wouldn't make any difference. She'd wait until tomorrow night. Maybe she could discuss it with Wendy.

Before she got into bed, she took the Bible the Chaplain had given her and opened it to the middle where she found the Book of Psalms. She read the 23rd, the one that was read at Bill's funeral, and she thought how beautiful it was. The Chaplain had said that Bill believed, and she pictured him now sitting beside those still waters and enjoying the green pastures. If only she could have heard it from Bill himself.

She lay awake a long time. Her heart was not at peace and she knew it. But was the only answer to be found in Christ?

CHAPTER 46

The evening before Judith and Jonathan were to leave for New Haven, they took a long walk on the beach by the Coast Guard Station in Sandwich. They talked a long time about the wedding, stopping occasionally to kiss, and wandered along with their arms around each other. Finally, Judith said, "Jonathan, my love, do you remember what the Chaplain said at Dad's funeral? And the words David sang? And all the times the Chaplain prayed for the family?"

"Of course I remember, nor have I forgotten all David did for Brit after the crash. He not only went to her, but stayed with her, and even when he was here, I saw him many times on his knees in the early morning, and I knew he was praying. He's very special. I do believe he has an answer in his life that we haven't ever talked about - and we really should. I've not gone to church and I guess you haven't either - except at Christmas or Easter. But even the other night, I was thinking that we will want children - and we'll want them to go absolutely straight. We live in a drug-infested world and it's essential that we set the right example for them."

Judith remembered how far her own father had wandered from his family and how he had hurt them all.

He had loved her mother and the girls when they were small, but what happened? Could that happen to her and Jonathan, even though they adored each other right now?

"Perhaps we should read the Bible together, and when we get to New Haven, find a church and attend every week. I'm sure the Chaplain can tell me where I can buy a Bible for each of us, and we could read the same thing each day, even though we are apart. Maybe the Chaplain could even help us by suggesting where to start reading. What would you think of that?"

"You're right, Judith, and I agree completely. But I know with studies and other activities and writing you every day and our talking by phone, time will fly. Do you think we could keep that promise if we made it to each other? You'll be busy with the family, planning for the wedding, visiting New Haven as much as possible We have to be committed and honest. How can we be sure we'll keep our promise?"

They walked a long time without words until Judith spoke. "When we marry, we'll make our vows. We'll promise to love and care for each other, whether sick or well, rich or poor, and we'll forsake all others and cleave to one another. We'll make those vows to each other with all our hearts because we're in love. But those vows will also be made before God. Should we not keep the same promise about reading the Bible, even before we're married? Or am I wrong in pretending to promise something we can't carry out?"

"You get the Bibles and talk with the Chaplain," said Jonathan after a slight hesitation. "Maybe he can suggest something that will help us. But one thing is sure. If we make promises to each other, we MUST keep them as long as we live."

They walked back to the car and drove in silence. It was late and they kissed goodnight and went to their rooms. Both of them thought about what they had discussed.

Jonathan wondered what his parents and friends would think if he suddenly became some kind of religious freak. He remembered what David had sung at the funeral. "The love of God is greater far than words or pen could ever tell." How much would he have to give up to know that love?

Judith wanted to talk with her sister about David and learn how she felt about the man she was going to marry. David had said that they could not marry until she believed as he did. How did Brit really feel and what did she believe? Sleep wouldn't come to Judith, so she got up, put on her robe and tip-toed into the living room. Behind the sofa was a bookcase. She turned on a small light and looked at the books. There were shelves of paperbacks, novels, medical books - and near the bottom, she saw a small black book. Taking it carefully from the shelf, she saw that it was a New Testament. She turned off the light and went to her room to read Psalm 23. She discovered that the Psalms were at the back of the book. She always thought she saw people open big Bibles to find them in the middle. Oh well, it didn't matter. She read the last verse over and over. "And I will dwell in the house of the Lord forever." How did you get there? She had to ask Brittany and the Chaplain as soon as possible. And with the little book in her hand, she fell asleep.

Before breakfast, she found Jonathan and said, "Guess what I found in your living room last night?"

He looked at her strangely and replied, "I can't imagine. What were you doing in the living room? I thought you had gone to the guest room."

"I couldn't sleep, so quietly came here and found a New Testament on the bookshelf. I read Psalm 23 over and over again.. Then I fell asleep.

Laura called saying breakfast was ready, so they joined his parents and a busy day began.

Everyone helped pack Jonathan's computer, small TV, boxes and bags into the car. They knew it would be hard to say goodbye, but it was harder than any of them had imagined. Tears were shed. Many hugs were given. Lots of advice was shared about driving slow, eating well, studying hard, and calling home often. After a final wave, they drove out, crossed the Bourne Bridge, up I-495 and eventually to I-95 to New Haven. They sat close to each other until they arrived at Jonathan's dorm about 1:00 p.m. The car was unpacked, and they went to a little café for a late lunch. Swallowing did not come easy, for they knew Judith would soon have to leave. Even though it was not that far to Boston, they had been together so much, and been through so much together in these past short months, it seemed like a million miles away.

Before dinnertime, Jonathan met his roommate, Fred Jenkins, from Albany, NY. He seemed like a nice fellow, friendly and happy to be at Yale.

Jonathan took Judith to a lovely spot on the water for dinner. It was late when he took her to Hampton Inn, near the college. They would meet for breakfast. Then while he was in orientation, Judith planned to look in the newspaper and perhaps visit an apartment or two which might be appropriate for them by the first of the year.

She hated the thought of saying goodbye, but would take the train to Boston in the late afternoon.

It was a hard night for both of them. She was glad Jonathan was settled in - and after all, December was not too far away. She would call the Chaplain as soon as she got home, and also spend time with her family - especially Brit. She loved Jonathan more than life itself, and wanted their marriage to be perfect. She really wondered if even God could make life better for her. It was already so perfect, did they really need HIM?

Alone in the Motel, she looked at a little folder which told about New Haven. Then she opened the night table drawer, looking for something else to read. And there it sat! A Bible with a gold cover - given by some group she had never heard of. The front page indicated it was a Gideon Bible, whatever that meant! Opening it, she found the 23rd Psalm. This time the book of Psalms was in the middle of the book, not at the end. Maybe in one Bible it came at one place and in another it came somewhere else. But that didn't matter.

She not only read Psalm 23, but kept reading. The more she read, the more meaning it seemed to have. If only she could take the Bible home - but that would be stealing. So she put it back where she found it, turned off the light and fell asleep. Her last thoughts were of dread for tomorrow. But it had to be faced with courage, strength and love, and she was certain both Jonathan and she could do that.

CHAPTER 47

As promised, Wendy picked up Martha just before 11 o'clock. It was a lovely day with a twinge of fall in the air and the blue sky and white clouds made New England the most beautiful spot on earth. Other areas are nice, but this was home, and it was best!

Hot, creamy New England clam chowder followed by broiled, stuffed lobster, made the perfect lunch. They sat by a large window on the waterfront and watched the fishing boats enter and leave the wide harbor. The women chatted about their family and friends. After lunch, they browsed through some shops, looking at jewelry, fancy purses, miniature sail boats and carved ships' wheels.

For a long time, they sat on a wooden bench overlooking the water, each lost in thought about many things.

After a short time, Wendy asked, "Martha, I meant to ask you this while we were on vacation. Where do you go to church?"

Martha turned, looking a bit astonished, and answered, "I regret to say that our family does not go to church. I have thought many times since Bill's death that I should start going, but I've put if off. I have no excuses. Why do you ask?"

"I attend services every Sunday at St. William's Catholic Church and wondered if you would like to go with me. I could pick you up, and after the service, we could have dinner. Would you like to go with me to see if you like it?"

"Well," Martha started. "It would be nice to go with you. The Chaplain from Mass General had Bill's funeral service. It was so encouraging. And the fellow Brittany has fallen in love with, David, sang at the service and his message still stirs my heart. But so much has happened recently that I just haven't attended any church. It's hard to go alone."

"Great. I'll pick you up about 10:30 Sunday morning. I'm sure you will enjoy the priest. He has a wonderful sense of humor and really cares about his parishioners. He has traveled everywhere and loves to share some of his experiences with us each week. I'm glad he's so human and never pushes us to make decisions or change our ways. That kind of religion turns me off. I've been a Catholic all my life, and our priest suits me just fine. Many of my friends attend the same church, so we have a lot in common. I'm so glad you'll go with me."

The ride from Gloucester back to Boson was lovely. After Wendy left, Judith called from New Haven and talked a long time about their trip there, and about the Yale campus, and all they had done that day. She told her mother she should be home the next day late in the afternoon. She would take a taxi from the train station.

Brittany walked in, wearing a high school shirt and red cap, showing off her school colors and telling her mother about her first day back in classes. The rest of the day was taken up with normal household duties. David called after dinner and talked to him for more than an hour.

"Oh, Mom, I miss him so much. I want to forget about school and marry him and just be his wife. I don't care about an education or anything else, but I know he won't propose until I believe as he does. I'm going to call Chaplain Garrett and ask to see him. I have to stop wondering and wandering and find out what I must do to know the Lord. I'm sure David is right and his belief in Christ is real. It just has to be real for me, too. You said you wanted to talk more with the Chaplain, and I know you spent time with him a couple of days ago. What did he say, and does any of it mean anything to you? Mom, are we right in never even going to church? We keep hearing the same thing from two people we admire and respect, but we listen and that is the end. There has to be more to life than what we've had. Even daddy made us unhappy, and the Chaplain said Dad believed before he died. I don't know about you, but I MUST find out how to know Christ. David has told me over and over again, but somehow, I just put it all off. I can't do that any longer."

"Dear, I'm going with Mrs. Seely to her church this Sunday and I'm sure she would be happy if you came along. Would you like that? It's a Catholic church, but I imagine all churches are pretty much the same and must preach the same. How about it?"

"I'd like that, Mom. I want to hear more of what we've already heard. David will be so happy if he knows I'm going to church. I'll really look forward to Sunday."

Wendy picked Martha and Brit up as she had said, and they drove to a large stone church with a huge cross on the top. When they went inside, Wendy bowed her head and made the sign of the cross. They watched everyone do the same. In front of every pew there was a little wooden bench. Maybe that was to kneel on, Martha thought.

As the service began, young men with candles walked down the aisle to the front of the church. The hush was so great, Brittany was afraid to whisper anything to her mother. The priest wore a black robe. A huge silver cross hung from his neck. Everyone knelt on the little slab of wood and prayed something together, but neither Martha nor Brit could make out the words. The music was very solemn. Then the priest spent a half hour telling about his latest visit to the Holy See, and the special time he had there.

At the close of the service, the priest greeted the parishioners at the door. It all seemed very strange to the Sanders, but little was said at dinner. Wendy took them home, stayed a short while, and left.

Brittany then spoke to her mother. "Mom, David told me all about his worship services, and when I was with him in Lombard at their Wednesday evening service, it was a happy, uplifting time of singing songs about the Lord. Different people prayed and you could understand every word. The pastor welcomed everyone, and when he spoke, it was just a short message about God's care and protection. Then he had a special prayer to ask God to take care of David's family as they were to leave for Pakistan. He also prayed for David and for me, and when the reception was in progress, he came over and talked to me very kindly and warmly. It was so different from today. Frankly, Mom, I didn't like the service today. I think they worship Mary. David said Mary was the mother of Jesus, but she worshipped her Son and loved

Him. I think Mrs. Seely is nice - but I'm not sure I could believe or worship as she does."

Martha answered, "Yes, it was very different from anything Chaplain Garrett has told us. I'll be honest with Wendy and tell her how I feel. There must be a big difference between churches and what they believe. Today made me feel unloved and so alone. It felt like we were all required to conform to what everyone else did. When you talk with David, ask him how he feels about worshipping in a Catholic church, and if it's anything like his church. I think he must believe differently from those we were with today. But do ask him. He'll be happy to explain it to you, I'm sure."

Brittany went shopping later that afternoon and her mother took a nap. The morning had made her weary and also very confused. Obviously, religion is not easily understood.

Before going to bed, Martha and Brit ate some cheese and crackers and drank a cold drink. In many ways, they were glad the day was over.

Before Martha climbed into bed, she thought about her promise to herself, that she would kneel and ask Christ to come into her heart. She knelt and was very quiet. Tears rolled down her cheeks. But no words would come. TOMORROW she would ask Him - first thing in the morning.

CHAPTER 48

By mid-September, several new developments had occurred. Some were expected. Others not at all.

The Chaplain had become a frequent visitor to Martha's home. At first it was his desire to make sure she really understood the Gospel. He was faithful in explaining it to her in many different ways. After that, he found that his reason for seeing her and taking her to dinner was more than just for the sake of witnessing. He had been alone for so long - and he felt so completely at ease with Martha - that he felt terribly lonely when he was not with her.

At first, Martha was sure the only reason Will came was to give her more reasons for accepting Christ as her Savior. But as she got to know him better, and found being with him a joy, she had to admit to herself that she liked his company, and whenever he called, she was delighted to hear his voice, and she wanted to see him. After the past years of loneliness, even though she was married to Bill, Will's warmth and caring spoke words and actions her heart needed and longed for.

David found life at Wheaton exciting and challenging. Courses in Theology and Introduction to the Old Testament thrilled his heart. One of his classmates

was Ashley Brown. They sat together for both classes and walked together from one building to the next. After their classes, a group would rush to the dining room and the same group often ate together. It didn't take long for each to share a little of his or her past and plans for the future. Ashley's parents were missionaries in Niger, West Africa. She had been born and raised there. MK's had a lot in common. Two fellows were also Missionary Kids -
one from Bolivia and one from Germany. There were prayer groups each Friday night and the Asian and African Prayer Bands met together. It soon became obvious to David that, even though he loved Brittany, Ashley was already walking the same path as he was - with the same vision and calling to the mission field after graduation.

When David called Brittany day after day and begged her to accept Christ, he began to grow weary of pleading, and doubts about her being converted occupied much of his mind and heart. He knew she was pulled aside by her family. She had no Christian friends, so it presented her with a difficult path. Ashley was not only one with David in purpose and belief. She was warm and outgoing and he couldn't help being attracted by her broad smile, and her large, blue eyes that sparkled when they were together. David's heart became confused and guilt sometimes overcame him. So many times he had told Brit they could never marry until she believed and now he began to wonder if she would ever come to Christ. It seemed like a true battle between God and Satan, and he knew Who would win. His fervent prayer was that God's will be done in all of their lives.

The first football game of the season was Yale vs. Princeton. Judith drove to New Haven for a long weekend. What a time they had! Friday night there was a bonfire. Saturday morning was the annual parade featuring the Yale band and cheerleaders. And never had Judith heard such yelling and screaming at the afternoon game. And Yale won by three points! Then there was the prom in the evening with everyone dressed to the hilt. It was a chilly night, but she and Jonathan stood outside the ballroom, stealing kisses and talking.

Jonathan held her close and asked, "Dear, do you think we have to put off our wedding until December? I need you with me. I love you so much and I miss you every minute. A weekend now and then is fine, but it's not enough. Do you think our parents would object if we moved it up to the long Thanksgiving week? We couldn't have a long honeymoon then, but - what do you think? Maybe they would let me take a few days away from classes, and we could still take a cruise. Please tell me what's in your heart."

"Oh, Jonathan, I've dreamed and dreamed that we might be together sooner, but I didn't know how you felt. I'd never push you, but it would be wonderful. In October we could find an apartment, and the timing of our honeymoon wouldn't matter. What means the most is that we would be together as husband and wife. Every day I don't think I can live another day without you. I don't know what our folks would think about that."

"Tomorrow before you go home, we'll call Mom and Dad and ask them. And when you get home, you can ask your mother. Then we'll know how they really feel. I know they will be honest with both of us."

It was settled, and when they went back to the ballroom and began to dance again, the world took on a new and exciting meaning for both of them. The party began to break up just after midnight and the lovers walked slowly to the Hampton Inn. They stood on the steps a long time, then finally kissed goodnight. They would meet at 8:00 a.m. for breakfast, and then call the Allens. Judith's train would leave at 1:00 p.m., so they would have a little time before she had to leave.

On the same Saturday night, David had asked Ashley to go to a Youth for Christ meeting with him and have dinner before the service. It was a short train ride to Chicago, and the speaker was a well-known missionary from Ecuador. Ashley was pleased, and readily accepted David's invitation. It was the first night he had not called Brit since he had started college. In some ways, he felt like a traitor. Yet, his heart was light and, as he returned to his dorm, he was humming a familiar song, "The love of God is greater far than tongue nor pen could ever tell." He had not sung it or even hummed it since he had sung it at Mr. Sander's funeral.

About 8:00 p.m., Brittany tried calling David, but there was no answer. She decided he was studying in the library, and no cell phones were allowed there. She missed his call, but knew he would phone the next day, as he always did. At bedtime, she picked up her Bible and thought about going to church. But some of her buddies were going to the Cape for the day and she had promised to go with them. That sounded like much more fun than church. She felt a prick in her heart, remembering David's words. But maybe - one day - he would let down on those words, and they could be married anyway. She was so glad her mother seemed happier than she had seen her in months, and wondered if it had anything to do with her spending more time with Chaplain Garrett.

Dr. Allen came home from the hospital that Saturday night, and without saying a word, he took Laura in his arms and told her how much he loved her.

"Tomorrow, I'm taking the day off, and we're going to Provincetown together and just enjoy each other. I miss our times alone, and we are going to have more time for each other. I got to thinking as I was making my rounds today, it must be terribly hard for both Jonathan and Judith to be apart when they love each other so much. Do you suppose they have ever thought of moving up their wedding date?"

"So many times, I have been so glad you and I have such a deep love and can be together, and I want the kids to be happy," Laura said. "As you said, it must be hard for them to be so close and yet so far apart. Maybe they have thought about it and have been afraid to say anything to us for fear we would object. I would be happy if they decided on another date - maybe even the week of Thanksgiving. What do you think? Should we say anything, or should we wait for it to come from them?"

"I think we should wait at least a week or two. Maybe by then they will have thought about it. If not, maybe we could ask them if they would feel better about having the ceremony sooner. I'm sure Martha wouldn't mind. They would still not be that far away."

When the lights went out in Wheaton, New Haven and Boston, several hearts beat with more joy than any of them had ever known.

CHAPTER 49

David's feet felt like lead as he started for the dining room. His heart was weary with heaviness - more than it had ever been before. He had given Brittany all he knew to give of the Gospel, but every time, her decision was to put it off until tomorrow. When he flew to her after the plane crash, he thought the entire experience would make her realize that the Lord had protected her and sustained her life when she could have easily been one of those who lost their life. There was so much about Brit to love, and he felt totally frustrated. He questioned his witness. He asked himself over and over again where and how he had failed. He realized she came from a family that never went to church, never read the Bible, and didn't know anything about God. But after Mr. Sanders's funeral, he felt sure Brit's heart was touched. His emotions had been on a roller coaster, and now that he had met Ashley, so much had changed so quickly.

For breakfast, all he could manage was a banana and a cup of yogurt. As he left the dining room, he heard a friendly, "Hi!"

"Ashley! You have certainly come at just the right time. I needed a smile and a friendly face."

"What happened? Is your family all right? Everything o.k. in Pakistan? Did you get a bad grade on that stupid History test?"

"No. I'm just having a battle in my life, and with all my heart, I want the Lord to win. But Satan is pulling so hard. I think tonight after dinner, I'll go down to Lombard and talk with my pastor. He doesn't know me well, but he's a mature man of God, and I need some wise counsel."

"Is there any way I can help," Ashley inquired. "Or am I wrong in thinking I'm part of the problem?"

"Oh, Ashley - you're not part of the problem. I am. My heart is torn. I want to be loyal and truthful before God and to others. You and I have so much in common that it gives overflowing joy to my heart. But, as you know, I've spent much time with Brittany, and I don't want to hurt her. To be honest, I'm lonely and can share so much with you. We have the same goals and plans and every time I'm with you, it means more to me. Yet, I don't want to make Brittany feel that I have forsaken her just because she refuses to accept our Lord. Please pray for me. I only want His will - above all else."

David and Ashley walked to class together in silence, but afterward, they went their separate ways.

David called his pastor and was relieved to find him in and willing to see him that afternoon. So after his last class, he drove his rickety car to Lombard and spent nearly two hours there. The last 15 minutes was spent on their knees, and when David turned his car toward Wheaton, his heart was light and his whole being was at peace.

When he returned to campus, David called Ashley and asked if they could go for a walk. She enthusiastically agreed to do so. David shared with her that his pastor had understood, and really believed that God would undertake for Brittany as well as for him. The last thing he told David was this: "ALL things work together for GOOD to those who love the Lord - to those who are called according to HIS purpose." David told Ashley he couldn't tell Brittany all of that, but he would write her a long letter and pray that she wouldn't be too hurt.

When Brittany came home from school on Friday, she was too excited to talk. The star football player had asked her for a date. He was the envy of every girl, and she couldn't talk fast enough to tell her mother everything. Never once did she mention David, and although her mother was surprised, she did not interrupt her daughter.

Brittany and Phil Briggs were going to a movie. After only a bite of dinner, Brit tore upstairs and found her prettiest dress, matching shoes and a small purse. When the doorbell rang, Martha greeted a tall, handsome man with a broad smile and deep voice. He introduced himself and shook Martha's hand just as Brit bounded down the stairs. He put out his hand and took hers, and after she had kissed her mother and said goodnight, they were out the door. It happened so fast, it almost took Martha's breath away. She was, however, impressed by the young man with good manners and a warmth that she could feel filling the room.

Phil Briggs was the big man on the football team and he was so good looking. He had, however, come through the school of hard knocks. His father had abandoned the family, and three boys were more than his mother could handle. Since Phil was the oldest, he was sent to work early and came home late - delivering newspapers in the morning and cleaning out super markets in the afternoons. His two younger brothers finally went to live with an aunt, and his mother found a good job as a secretary. All this enabled Phil to finish school, and even though a bit older than his peers, he found his niche in sports. He had no goals beyond high school, so grades were not that important, except to keep him on the team. He had been deprived of real love, and it was easy for him to start looking for someone who would care about him. He had met Brittany in Math class and also in English class. They sat together and often ate lunch before he had to go off to practice. Three weeks is not a long time, but her friendliness and his caring attitude, along with his good looks, worked their way into Brit's heart.

"I guess as much as I care about David, I'll never fit into his world. I don't want to give up beautiful clothes, fancy cars, movies and sports to live in some far off place where there would never be any fun and all would be religion and more religion," she told herself. "I guess it would only be fair to write David and tell him that. I truly appreciate all he has done for me, and all he gave of himself when I was in the hospital. But I really want life to be fun - filled with going and doing. Christianity sounds like too much of the same thing day after day - and what fun could we possibly have in some little village in Pakistan among people you can't even talk to?"

Brit knew in her heart that David was right about getting things straight with God, but that could wait a few years until she had had some fun and done lots of things with fellows in Boston. Maybe she could even travel to Paris, London, or the Riviera.

She was so filled with her own thoughts and plans that she forgot that David hadn't called her as he usually did - nor did she try to call him.

The next day Brittany would see Phil play in his football game, and then they were going out to dinner together. After a good day with Phil, Brit came home swinging her back pack and whistling.

Martha was waiting to find out about Brit's day and about the fellow she had been with. She also wanted to know about David.

"Surely you don't want to hurt David after all he's done for you, and the ways he has shown his love and devotion."

Oh, Mom, it's not that. But I've been thinking so much these days about David, and even though he is wonderful, I can't see myself as the wife of a missionary stuck off in some land where I have no family and where there is nothing to do but preach all day, or clean dirty kids, or try to avoid awful diseases. I'm not sure my love for him is strong enough for all that. I want so much to have fun and enjoy life and have all the good things we have here. I'd never have any of that in Pakistan, or India, or wherever. I don't have David's commitment or his "call" or anything. I'm just not prepared to give up everything to be a missionary."

Brit went on to tell what a great day she had had with Phil, and how much she liked him. She was the envy of the entire school, and she liked that a lot, too!

CHAPTER 50

Sunday dawned crisp and clear in Sandwich and John and Laura drove to Dunkin' Donuts for French crullers, orange juice and coffee, before heading for the tip of Cape Cod.

Martha had promised Will Garrett she would go to church with him, after which they would have dinner. She was up as the sun arose, trying to decide what to wear, and making sure her new Bible was next to her little purse.

Brittany threw on some jeans, a shirt and sneakers, met her friends for breakfast, and was off for the day. When she hugged her mother goodbye she said, "Mom, you have a sparkle in your eyes and you are getting all dressed up, even to special makeup. Where are you going, and why are you so happy?"

"Well, dear, I have promised to go to church with Will Garrett, and then we'll have dinner together. He has begun to mean a great deal to me, and I hope you are glad. His obvious warmth and special attention have touched my heart. It has been so lonely for so long, and I think we are beginning to care for each other."

Brit hugged her mother and held her hand. "Oh, Mom, that is the best news you could have ever given me.

Both Judith and I have been so concerned about you and longed for you to be happy. The Chaplain is a wonderful man, and I think you would make the greatest couple! Oh, Mom - that's fantastic! Have a wonderful day and enjoy every minute. Please tell me all about it tonight. Judith gets in this afternoon. Everyone will have special news. I need to run along, but I need to call David first. I love you, Mom, and I'm happy for you."

Brittany tried to call David - then realized Sundays at Wheaton would be filled with church and church activities. She would call him tonight, or maybe he would call her on her cell. So she grabbed a jacket and ran out the door.

Jonathan and Judith had breakfast together. Then he took his cell and called his folks. There was no answer at home, which was unusual. So he tried the cell phone number. His dad answered.

"Hi, Dad. Where are you so early this lovely morning?"

"Hi, Son. Your mother and I are taking the day off and going to Provincetown. We wanted a day just for us. And how are you and Judith doing? Did you have a good weekend? I heard our Yale beat Princeton. Great! What does Judith think of Yale, and did she have a good time?" Then he quickly added, "I guess that's a foolish question!"

"We had a great weekend, and we have something to bounce off you and mom. Judith and I spent a long time between dances discussing our marriage. We want so much to be together and wondered how you and mom would feel if we moved the date up to Thanksgiving, and then took our cruise over Christmas for a real honeymoon?"

"That's absolutely amazing you should ask, son. Last night, your mother and I said almost the very same thing, knowing how much you love each other and want to be together. I'm sure the few changes we would have to make in the chapel date, invitations, etc., wouldn't make any difference, and we would be so happy for you. Both you and Judith will need a weekend here to finalize everything and she will have to talk it over with her mother, but I don't think that will be a problem, either. We can spend time making lists, final plans, working on announcements, invitations, being sure the Chapel is free, etc. Do you still want Chaplain Garrett to have the ceremony? Would you want it on the Saturday of Thanksgiving weekend, or on Friday afternoon or evening? These are things you'll have to decide with Judith. We can do the leg work for you. I'm sure Brittany will be thrilled, too. When do you think you can get away for a long weekend? It will soon be October, so we can't put it off too long."

Laura listened as her husband spoke on the phone. Her heart beat a little faster. Her mouth fell open. It seemed that they had all been thinking the same thing!

"Oh, Dad, I'm so glad you and mom feel as we do. I can get away in two weeks. I'll drive up Thursday night and maybe Brit and her mother can drive down with Judith so we can make all our final plans together." He continued, "Yes, we want Chaplain Garrett to perform the ceremony and we want to marry in Roger Williams Chapel. Judith will talk with her mother when she gets home this afternoon. We are too excited to think, but I promise to study hard and do my best. So far, I have an A in every subject except History. That's a B."

After a few more pleasantries, Jonathan closed his cell phone. He and Judith were elated with what had been accomplished. They knew Judith's mother would agree with this new schedule. And it would only be a couple of months before they could be together forever!

Martha and Will went on to church, and at once, Martha felt a warmth and peace that she had not experienced in a long, long time. Somehow in that quiet place - the sun streaming through the beautiful stained glass windows, the friendly people, the singing of hymns, reading the Scripture and listening to the preaching of the Word - made her realize how very much she had missed out on in her life. She was truly sorry when the last hymn was sung, and the service was dismissed. But, of course, she was looking forward to having dinner with Will.

Will had made reservations for the two of them at the Copley Plaza Hotel dining room. It was a quiet place - typically New England. In all her years in Boston, Martha had never been there before.

After they were seated in the far corner of the room, Will spoke.

"Martha, we have come to know each other through sorrow and joy. For many days, I have prayed that we could have this time together, and I'd like to ask you two questions."

"Of course, Will. You know you can ask me anything."

"Well, the first is - and this is VERY important - have you accepted Jesus as your Lord and Savior so He can live His life through you?"

There was a short pause, a bowed head - then a soft smile. Martha replied, "Somehow I knew you would ask me that. I have given so much thought to all you have said - ever since Bill's funeral. I've tried to read my Bible, but I fear it has been with far too little understanding. But in my heart I knew that all you have shared with me is the truth, and your godly life has been such a blessing to me in so many ways. Yes, Will, I want to know Christ as you do and have His peace and joy in my heart as you do. To answer your question - yes, I do accept Christ as my Savior. I think I even did it a few nights ago, but this makes it more final and real. I can never thank you enough for leading me to the foot of His cross."

Will leaned across the table, and taking her hand in his, bowed his head and tearfully thanked the Lord for making Martha His child and for giving her a whole new and abundant life in Christ.

Coffee and hot rolls had arrived and the waiter asked them twice if they were ready to order. He was told they would look at the menu and tell him in just a minute or two. When he came back, they ordered broiled, stuffed shrimp, salad, baked potato and buttered asparagus. The waiter left sighing - glad they had finally made up their minds. He wondered what took some people so long to decide on something as easy as ordering a meal!

After eating their salad, hot coffee was poured, and Martha said, "You said you had two things you wanted to ask me. What is the second?"

"Can you wait for that until we've finished our dinner and are in the car? It would be quieter there - and no one would interrupt to ask if we wanted more of anything.

"Of course I can wait, Will. That sounds like a good idea. When I get older and wiser, I'm going to open a special dinner spot, away from everything, where each patron can tell the waiter or waitress, 'I'll call you when I want you.'"

They both laughed and decided that would be a great idea.

Dinner was especially delicious. It was topped off with strawberry shortcake and another cup of coffee. There was no hurry, and they both enjoyed being together and talking about mundane things as well as deciding on solutions for the present world situation!

When they went out to the car, Will didn't turn the key. He simply leaned toward Martha and took her hands in both of his.

"You've probably already guessed my second question. Martha, I want to marry you. I love you and want you to be my wife."

Martha's face grew crimson, and then turned very pale. It had never occurred to her that Will loved her. They enjoyed being together - yes. But in love? She looked longingly into his beautiful hazel eyes and squeezed both his large hands. Then she leaned over to him and kissed him with the kind of kiss she had never experienced before.

"Oh, Will - if salvation is the greatest thing in life, then certainly you are the next greatest! The girls will be so thrilled and I can hardly wait to tell them. Yes, Will. Yes, yes, yes. I would love to be your wife. And I shouldn't even say this, but how soon may I become Mrs. Will Garrett?"

Will held her in his arms for a long time, and then said, "Since Judith and Jonathan are going to marry in

December, how about Thanksgiving? Too soon? Or would you like more time - like Valentine's Day?"

"I don't want to wait any longer than we have to. Right now, I think eloping would be so much fun! Wouldn't that amaze everyone?!"

When they finally arrived back on Beacon Hill, it was late afternoon. They had discussed many things and had made all kinds of possible plans. They were in love. No one could have doubted that!

CHAPTER 51

Judith boarded the train with a heart far lighter than it had been previously. Now she could actually count the days and they could get their wedding clothes and make real plans. It all seemed so right and good. They had been through a lot since early summer. But all of a sudden, the clouds had rolled away and the sun shone brightly over Eastern New England. A tiny bit of color could be seen in the maples and birches. The drier air was crisp, clear and welcome.

It was hard to say goodbye to Jonathan, but their excitement overshadowed everything and they hugged and held on tightly. It made it all easier to know they would soon be together and not have to part.

"I love you, I love you, I love you," whispered Jonathan as he kissed Judith one more time as she boarded the train. What a glorious weekend it had been!

It was after five when Judith opened the front door of her home in Boston. All was quiet and she wondered where her mother could be. She was quite sure Brit was off with her friends, for she often did that on Sundays. But her mother was almost always home. She called out, but silence echoed in reply. Then she saw a note on the coffee table. "I've gone to church with Will Garrett and then we're having dinner. Should be home by five at the latest. Love you, Mom."

She was surprised that her mother called the Chaplain, Will, and also that she had gone to church with him, but she was glad. Her mother deserved happiness and she hoped all the best for her. Life had not been an easy road for her in recent years.

Judith took her bag to her room and flopped down on the bed. Her mind had raced all the way to Boston. Soon she would grab paper and pen and begin making lists. How exciting! She couldn't wait for her mom to get home.

No sooner had that thought crossed her mind when she heard the front door open. She ran downstairs and hugged her mother - then realized the Chaplain was standing there as well. She greeted the Chaplain warmly and asked him to come in. He said he would only stay a few minutes.

All three began talking at once. Finally Martha said, "Oh, dear Judith, I have wonderful news for you. I have just promised Will I will marry him!"

Judith grabbed her mother and hugged her hard and long. Then she ran to the Chaplain and told him how thrilled she was for both of them. When is the wedding? You have to tell me everything!"

"We haven't discussed the date yet. We thought maybe around Christmas, but I wondered how you would feel about that since you're planning a Christmas wedding."

"Oh, Mom. We've changed our plans. We've decided to have our wedding the Saturday after

Thanksgiving. We really didn't see any reason to wait. We talked it over with Jonathan's parents and they are in full agreement. I hope it's all right with you."

"Oh, that's wonderful. You love each other so much. There's no reason to wait. That would mean Will and I could still plan a small ceremony around the Christmas holidays. Would that be all right with you and Jonathan?"

"That would be just great! What a way to celebrate Christmas. I'm so happy for you both - and Brittany will burst her britches when she hears. She'll be happy for Jonathan and me, too. Will David be coming here for Christmas - or hasn't she said?"

Just then, Brittany bounded through the door, excited to see her mother and Judith - and Chaplain Garrett.

Before even a proper greeting, Judith burst out - "Mom and the Chaplain are going to be married! Isn't that the best news we've ever heard?"

They talked and talked and finally everyone went into the kitchen to get supper. Judith felt like she would have a real dad, and her heart was thrilled. She finally went to Chaplain Will and asked, "May I be your daughter? Would you let me walk down the aisle on your arm? Oh, dear, I just remembered - you're going to perform the ceremony. That wouldn't work, would it?"

"Of course it will work. I don't have to say anything until you are at the front of the Chapel, so both will be perfect, and I am honored to have you as my daughter."

Judith squealed with delight. She couldn't believe all that was happening.

"Tell me all I must have missed today," Brit stated excitedly. "Mom, you look absolutely radiant! Come to think of it, so do you, Sis. And I must admit, you do, too, Chaplain." Brit was thrilled with the prospect of having a close, loving family.

It was dark by the time they finished eating. Will Garrett hugged the girls and kissed his bride-to-be goodnight. Then he took all their hands, bowed his head and thanked the Lord for all HE had done. He walked with Martha to the door. He would see her the next day, for they had to find a good jeweler! He kissed her again.

As soon as Will left, Martha called Laura and John to share the news. They were almost as excited as she was! They suggested that perhaps there could be a double wedding.

Martha shared this with the girls when she hung up.

"Oh, Mom, a double wedding would be terrific. It would be icing on the cake! We could have our reception together - but no way will we let you go on OUR honeymoon!"

What an exciting day it had been! When they had gone upstairs, Brit shared with Judith all about Phil Briggs - and her reason for not feeling it was right for her to marry David. Judith understood and said she was sure that though David's heart might be broken, he would understand and accept her decision.

Brittany determined to write a letter to David the next day rather than trying to explain it all by phone. She really didn't want to hurt him because she was very fond of him and admired his commitment to His Lord. They just weren't on the same wave length and marrying under those circumstances could never work out.

It was after midnight before all the lights went out in this happy home.

In Wheaton, David was writing a long letter and he was still typing as the sun came up the next morning. Soon he would have to be in class. But before he would mail the letter, he would read it over and over, and pray that he was doing the right thing and that Brit would understand.

In the middle of the night, Brittany woke up screaming with pain in her tummy. Nothing seemed to help, even though she vomited. At 3:00 a.m., they headed for the ER at Mass General. The M.D. on duty knew after testing that it was her appendix, and by 6:00 a.m., she was on the Operating Room table.

Judith called Jonathan as well as the Allen family. Dr. and Mrs. Allen left Sandwich at 7:00 a.m. for Boston. By 8 o'clock, Brit was in the Recovery Room - groggy, half-awake. Will immediately arrived at the hospital and had prayer with the family. They all went to the Coffee Shop for a muffin and coffee. When they went upstairs, Brit was still in the Recovery Room because of a developing fever.

By noon, they moved Brit to a private room and the doctor told them she was doing much better, even though she still had a low grade fever.

Dr. Allen returned to Sandwich. Laura stayed with Martha. Judith called Jonathan and told him not to drive up, since there was nothing he could do. Martha called the school to tell them why Brittany would not be in class.

By late afternoon, Martha, Judith and Laura went to the Sanders' home for a short rest and something to eat. Then Martha called Brit's room. She said she felt a little better, but was sore and scared. Martha promised she and Laura would be there soon.

Before they left the hospital, they talked with the doctor, and he assured them all was routine and Brit would be up the next day and walk a little. Will arrived again to have prayer with them. They all went home for the night. It had been a long day.

Martha tried to sleep, but her heart and mind were with her daughter. About 3:00 a.m., she got a glass of milk and some cookies. Finally, she dozed off and slept until the sun was shining brightly in her window.

Before Martha dressed, she called Brit's room and there was no answer. Finally, a nurse answered and said they had taken Brit to X-ray, as she still complained of severe pain in her lower abdomen.

Martha dressed hurriedly and she and Laura drove to the hospital where they found the doctor in Brit's room. He said he thought she had an infected ovary and they were giving her antibiotics. They had given her pain medication, and she was now asleep. Laura called her husband and Judith let Jonathan know. By noon, the fever was gone and the pain had lessened considerably.

Will, Judith, Laura and Martha went out to get some fresh air and a bite to eat. And after lunch, Laura and Judith went home while Martha and Will went to a jewelry store to pick out her diamond engagement ring.

CHAPTER 52

Brittany appeared to be gaining strength, and after three days, was up and eating a little, but from a really small surgery with no complications, she was not gaining as expected. The surgeon ordered a sonogram, and it revealed a large cyst on her left ovary.

After consulting with Martha and Dr. Allen, it seemed wise to remove the ovary. The emotional impact upon Brit upset her and the fear of never having children gripped her heart with dread. Even though the doctor assured her that she could become pregnant with just one ovary, yet tears came as her mother held her. The nurse came with a doctor-ordered tranquilizer to calm her quivering and fear.

Phil Briggs came to visit every day and brought flowers and sent cards. Martha was pleased for Brit's sake, and she liked the young man. He appeared to be the perfect gentleman, and he certainly cared for Brittany.

After the surgery, healing occurred quickly. Brit was on her feet and able to go home. It felt good to be out of the hospital and to eat her mother's good cooking. After a week she was able to attend school half days.

Judith spent as much time with her sister as possible, encouraging her and delighting in the fact that Phil cared for her. Even at school, he carried her books and made sure she was all right through the day.

Brittany recalled that before her trip to the hospital, she had promised herself she would write David. Two nights after being home, she sat at her computer and wrote a long letter. It was a kind letter - in no way hurtful. She explained her feelings about saying "yes" to finding Christ just to please him, her not wanting the life of a missionary, and her longing to be near her family. She thanked him for all he had done and all he had meant to her - especially after the plane crash and his flying to be with her. She would never forget all his kindnesses. And yet with all that, she did not feel it was enough to try to live as he wanted and to change in a way that was against all she felt and believed. She went on,

"David, as much as I appreciate your care and concern for me and all your kindnesses in so many ways, that is not reason enough for me to marry you. I could never be the Christian you would want, and I cannot lie, thereby being dishonest to you as well as to the Lord you love.

I have earnestly tried to read my Bible. I've tried to pray. I've spent much time wondering how to ask Christ into my life - but nothing is real, and I just cannot live a lie. I want to be honest in my life and not pretend. And I know you feel that way, too. Please forgive me if I have hurt and disappointed you - but I must live as I see best.

One day I even spoke to Chaplain Garrett, and though he was sad about my decision, he agreed that Christianity cannot be forced. It must come from the heart and with a deep conviction that one needs a Savior. I don't fully understand all that right now.

If I knew how to pray, I would certainly ask God to give you a mate with your same beliefs, vision and love. I want God's best for you and hope one day you will be back in your beloved Pakistan with a wife who loves you and feels, as you say, called to be a missionary. Again I ask your forgiveness, and hope you will understand.

Thank you , David, from a grateful heart, and may God bless you.

Fondly,

Brittany

After the letter was written, she read it through many times, then placed it in an envelope, sealed it, and with tears in her eyes, affixed a stamp to the right upper corner. With a great deal of difficulty, she addressed it. She knew in her heart she had done the right thing. From both parents she had learned integrity, if nothing else.

After she crawled into bed and the light was out, she tried to pray for David, but the words just would not come. Finally she managed to say, "God, I don't know how to pray but please help David to understand."

Sleep came slowly, but her heart was at peace and her body was pain free and relaxed.

The next morning she placed her letter to David in the mailbox for the postman to pick up at the front door. When she returned to the box a few hours later, she found in the day's mail a letter from David to her. She did not know at that time how long he had labored over writing it, and how many days he had kept it on his desk before finally putting it in the mail. It was thick, and she was afraid to open it. She supposed he was proposing to her again, or telling her he was coming for Thanksgiving. Or perhaps it was an explanation of why he had stopped calling and writing to her.

Alone in her bedroom, Brittany opened the envelope and held the folded sheets of paper in her trembling hands. Then she opened the pages. His letter seemed to her to be an answer to prayer, though she didn't really believe in that. But David's words were so gentle and kind that her heart bounded within her as she read each word. He had always understood her feelings, and even more wonderful, he had met a Christian girl who was called to the mission field and together they were happy and excited. Immediately Brit knew he would understand her letter, and in a mysterious and wonderful way, it had all been worked out for the best. The thought occurred to her that maybe God does, after all, hear and answer prayers.

At lunch, Martha and Judith read David's letter. To Martha, God had, indeed, answered prayer. To Judith, things just worked out for the best, and she hugged her sister, knowing that none of this had been easy on her. But relief was obvious.

Now that everything had been settled for Brittany and David, the three of them sat at the table with a calendar in front of them. Dates were being marked.

Lists were being made. All were eagerly looking forward to Thanksgiving and Christmas. The question came up again about a double wedding, but both Martha and Judith felt it best for each to have her own special date and ceremony.

While they were engrossed in all this planning, Will Garrett arrived. Brittany quickly shared with him about her letter to David, and let him read David's letter to her. Will's only words were "It's best all around, Brittany. But my prayer for you is that you will come to know the Savior."

The afternoon was spent at the kitchen table. In the late afternoon, Jonathan called to see when the two families could get together and decide on many things. A Saturday meeting would be best for his dad, and the Chaplain was more free that day than on others. So it was agreed that they would meet at the Allens' home early on Saturday, and spend the day making plans and firming up things. Jonathan would arrive from Yale late Friday night and spend the weekend in Sandwich.

Early Saturday morning, Martha, Will, Brit and Judith piled into Martha's Cadillac and headed for Sandwich. Joy was spilling over and the trip was glorious and quick.

A hearty breakfast awaited them at the Allens. Judith was thrilled to be with Jonathan, and she realized more than ever how much she truly loved him and had missed him during these past days.

They sat at the living room table with lots of paper, pens, pencils, and calendars. It was one o'clock when Laura fixed a luscious salad followed by home-made apple pie and coffee. No one was offended when Will asked the blessing. They ate in the midst of merriment and joy. It was less than two months before Jonathan and Judith would marry, and just a short month after that, Martha and Will would say their vows. Will attended Calvary Chapel in Boston, so their wedding would be there. It was where Martha had attended that beautiful church with Will, and had rejoiced in the pastor's message. He would marry them. There would be many who would attend because the Chaplain was so well-known at the Hospital. They decided on a small reception in the Education Building of the church.

The Allens plans were pretty well worked out. They would have their reception at the Sandwich Country Club Inn.

Judith decided to go to New Haven the next weekend so they could look for an apartment, her first search having turned up nothing. Neither Martha nor Will had decided where they would live, but it seemed best for Will to leave his small apartment and they would live in Martha's Beacon Hill home.

At the close of the day, they listened to the bells ringing from the Roger Williams Chapel. Hugs all around and joyous faces made the day one never to be forgotten. Judith begged to stay until the next evening to be with Jonathan. Naturally, it was fine with both families, so just three drove back to Boston. It was late when they reached home.

Brittany left Will and her mom in the living room while she went to her room to study - and to call Phil Briggs. Maybe - just maybe - one day she would wear his ring!

CHAPTER 53

October arrived quickly, and hearts not only beat faster, but with so much to be done before the Saturday after Thanksgiving, days were often lengthened. Nights went by, but not fast enough.

Jonathan and Judith found a small apartment near the college. It was in an old, brown, wooden building. One bedroom had a double bed and two upright dressers. The bathroom was so tiny, if you put two porcupines in it, their quills would stick together for life! The kitchen had a good electric stove, a new fridge, metal sink, dishwasher, and a place big enough for a microwave, can opener and coffee pot. Underneath the counter there was plenty of space for everything vital to a kitchen. The stairs to their new home were short. On the first floor, there was a new washer and dryer for use by all the tenants. Judith picked out new drapes, yellow decorations for the bathroom and curtains to brighten the kitchen. Dr. Allen and his wife drove a van to New Haven with a new leather couch with two matching chairs, a glass-topped coffee table and linens for the bed. Laura chose bright blue for the bedspread and curtains for the bedroom. Soon the little apartment began to look like a real home. The bride and groom-to-be were thrilled and excited. The manager of the 6-apartment building was pleased to have such good tenants, and especially grateful when Dr. Allen paid him three months' advance rent.

Martha and Judith shopped diligently for their wedding dresses and special evening clothes for the dinner before each wedding. Martha chose a floor length dress of bright red velvet with a sweetheart neckline and an Italian lace veil for her wedding attire. Her shoes would be dyed to match the dress, and she would carry a Bible with one single rose across the cover.

When she put the dress on, the saleslady called others in the Bridal Shop to see. Oohs and aahs came from everyone. Martha had always been a beautiful lady - but this wedding gown brought out even more of that beauty. She was absolutely radiant.

Along with the wedding dress, since she and Will were going to Miami,Key West and the Florida Keys for their honeymoon, she purchased two brightly-colored dresses and three pant suits in case they went sailing or did some other casual things. Three other dresses were purchased - one light green trimmed in pale yellow, a baby blue satin, and a black chiffon with white scarf and tiny streamers of white down each side of the skirt. These she could wear when they went out for dinner in the evening. She couldn't even remember what she had purchased for her wedding to Bill, but this would be far more exciting, and no matter what she bought, she wanted it to please Will. They had decided that since the ceremony was to be on December 22nd, the chapel decorations would be red, white and green.

Jonathan's favorite color was blue, so Judith decided the bridesmaids should wear blue. All the dresses were satin with lace down to the finger tips. They would have small, blue, flowered oblong hair pieces with satin ribbon touching the back of their dresses. Bouquets would be yellow, rose and green with centers of roses matching the girls' dress who stood next to her. Brittany would be her Maid of Honor carrying yellow and Phyllis, Jonathan's best man's fiancée, would carry green flowers with roses in the center. Judith wanted Jonathan to tell her what he would like her to carry. He decided on three orchids with long satin ribbons falling gently from each.

It took many days in several bridal shops for Judith to decide on her dress. Finally, she found exactly what she wanted. White satin, tightly fitted to her waist, a slim skirt with a three foot train, lace gloves trimmed with satin borders, and a thin lace veil covering her face and falling just below the rounded neckline of her dress. She would wear white satin shoes, a pearl necklace and small pearl earrings. As Judith looked at herself in the full length mirror, her mother could only wipe her eyes, and without hesitation, kiss her precious daughter.

Brittany was very quiet, and in awe of her sister. "When it's my turn, will you go with me and make me look as lovely as my sister?" she asked her mother.

Martha hugged her daughter and after Judith had taken off all her finery, she kissed her sister, assuring her they would make her the prettiest of the three!

The lady at the Department Store brought out dozens of clothes for a cruise and Judith bought something special for each day - including a stunning black bathing suit trimmed in light blue. Evening clothes for the rehearsal dinner were found and Judith chose a velvet blue suit to wear after the reception. Her mother gave her a long white ermine jacket to wear, since it would be cold, and that would make her look even more beautiful.

After nearly a week filled with shopping, two invitations arrived. Wendy was giving Martha a shower and so was Laura. The next day, Judith found two invitations by her night table. Her sister was giving her a shower and another by her mother-in-love.

Having promised Jonathan and Judith that they would supply the flowers for the ceremony and see that they were arranged properly, Laura and John went to the Roger Williams Chapel, looking carefully at every part. The Chapel had stained glass windows about 10 feet apart. This gave the church its own beauty and it seemed a shame to add much else. Yet they wanted the flowers just right, and Jonathan and Judith wanted a wooden altar on the platform to be covered with fall flowers. The carpet was mauve and the pews were dark brown. Small bouquets on the end of each pew would be fitting and would match the altar flowers. After seeing the chapel, they drove to Hyannis. There was a florist there who had been a friend for years, and they told her what they wanted.

"I'll certainly go to the Chapel myself and make everything as you wish. It should be a magnificent wedding." It was now seven weeks before the big day.

The following weekend, Martha and Will were arriving to hear about the flowers and decorations to see if Martha would like anything different. The families were now such good friends, they pretty much thought alike, but the Allens wanted to make sure Martha was in full agreement. Besides, it would give Will and Martha an opportunity to get out of the City for a brief time to enjoy a day by themselves.

It was becoming harder and harder for Jonathan to put his mind on his studies. Every page shone with Judith's face. His dad reminded him that he must work really hard if he wanted to be a doctor. He found the best way to deal with his stress was to call Judith each night and talk for half an hour or so, and then buckle down until the wee hours of the morning. His room-mate helped him as much as he could by a gentle slap on the shoulder, and a "Get with it, friend. Your new wife won't want a drop-out for a hubby!"

By the middle of October, almost all the details were in place. The bridal suite at the Marriott in Boston had been reserved. The flight to Miami had been confirmed and tickets were in hand. The balcony suite on the ship was confirmed, paid for and shore excursions determined and pre-paid. The Allens were giving their son and new daughter the trip as their wedding gift.

Jonathan's number one question for his parents was, "What do I give Judith for a wedding present?"

Many suggestions were made, but nothing seemed just right.

"It has to be forever. It has to be something she will cherish. Maybe a bracelet with hearts for charms - each engraved with a different word of love."

Ah yes, he had found the answer to his question.

Will pondered the same question and finally decided on cultured pearls and earrings to match. He had never seen Martha wear them, so maybe that would be something special. Will found just the right ones at Bailey, Banks and Biddle in Boston.

Martha and Judith talked for hours about what to give their grooms. No decision was made, and they decided to let it go for a while to concentrate on other things.

It had never even occurred to either of them that it could snow on their wedding days. What a horrible thought. But this was New England, and winter is winter!

CHAPTER 54

The light fall breeze was kicking up little white caps in Boston Harbor. The green leaves of summer were now turning to gold, deep brown, yellow and brilliant red. The cars were bumper to bumper on every highway in the Green Mountains of Vermont and White Mountains of New Hampshire. It was the weekend of October 12th - the time of year that ALL of God's majesty and glory could be seen in His creation. Thousands drove from everywhere to see the spectacular mountains, shimmering blue lakes, the gift shops overflowing with hand-made ships in bottles, taffy, paintings of schooners under full sail and real maple syrup. People took boat rides around Lake Winnipesaukee. Myriads of powder puff clouds roamed about in the crystal blue sky. Autos of every kind gently, slowly and carefully climbed Mt. Washington. The narrow road with barely a foot between the car and eternity was well-kept but in many places, cars could not pass. The mile high mountain often had snow squalls at this season of the year. All along the highways, one could see bumper stickers proudly declaring, "I climbed Mt. Washington!"

As crowded as the roads are, every New Englander waits for this time of year. And so it was that the Allens took Martha and Will in their car, while Jonathan and Judith took Brittany and Phil Briggs in theirs. They left Boston before 6:00 a.m. The air was filled with freshness. Natural beauty surrounded them. After many short stops, the two cars met at the foot of Mt. Washington, then following each other, climbed to the very top and stood in awe at the glorious handiwork of a Painter whose name is God.

It was almost 8:00 p.m. when they arrived back in Martha's driveway. After a quick snack, Jonathan and Judith joined the Allens and headed for Sandwich. Phil went home, as did Will. Martha and Brittany fell happily into bed. It had been a never to be forgotten day. Brittany had taken over 100 pictures on her digital camera which all would enjoy at a later time.

Before Martha was asleep, Will called and asked, "Could we meet for lunch tomorrow. I not only want to see you, but I have a question or two that need your answers."

"Of course we can meet, but you may have forgotten, tomorrow is Sunday. Would lunch after church be all right? I plan to meet you at the church before 11!"

"Oh, Martha - my mind was still on the gorgeous scenery we've witnessed today. Of course - we'll meet at church and then go out afterward. What about Brittany? Would she want to come with you, or does she have other plans?"

"Brittany is going to spend the day with Phil. I think they are going back to see more of the color. She said she would be leaving early and they both wanted to take the boat ride on Lake Winnipesaukee. I've tried many times to have her go to church with us, but she always has other plans, and I don't want to push her. I'm praying much for both my daughters. I know neither knows the Lord and it breaks my heart. I'm sure you're aware of that, as well. But I'll see you at church. I love you."

Before 6 o'clock the next morning, Martha heard Brit go quietly down the stairs She always took her shoes off until she got to the door. She never wanted to wake her mother. But her mother was usually awake anyway!

The church service was excellent. The pastor spoke on the theme of suffering. He seemed to know there were many hurting people among his parishioners. Martha was sorry that the service wasn't longer. She loved to hear the Word of God preached in such an absorbing and personal way.

After the service was dismissed, Martha and Will had dinner at a quiet restaurant overlooking Boston Harbor.

Just before the dessert arrived, Will turned to Martha and with a furrow on his brow he stated, "Martha dear - something is bothering me and I need your help and wisdom. Since I'm marrying Jonathan and Judith, I'm concerned that neither one knows our Lord. I have always counseled couples before the ceremony and talked to them about marriage and commitment and that this is a covenant which ought never to be broken. I know they love each other and I admire both of them - and I love your daughter as though she were my own. But I feel I must talk with them before the wedding. Please tell me what you think, or if I'm wrong in what I think is right.

Many times I have learned that my thoughts are not God's thoughts, and my ideas were purely human, and I have been wrong. So I need your thoughts and feelings concerning this whole matter."

"Will, you are completely right, and I believe you should talk with them. I have spent many hours with Judith talking about relationships, love, faithfulness - and have even mentioned that I long for her to know the Lord as her Savior. She has listened and I have no doubt she and Jonathan are in love and I have no fear that this marriage will not last. Laura and I have discussed their marriage, but I have never talked with her about the Lord. I feel ashamed that I haven't, but I'm such a new believer myself, I didn't feel it was right to say very much, for I know so little. But I'm 100% behind your desire to talk with Judith and the whole Allen family, if you feel led to do so."

After dinner, they sat in the car and read Scripture for a period of time and then spent several minutes in prayer. When they were back at Martha's home, Will called Jonathan and asked if he could meet him and Judith later that day, or the next weekend.

"Judith is going to New Haven with me this afternoon, as we are still doing things in the apartment. She'll be back on Tuesday, but I have class and will still have to study next weekend. If it's important, could you come down on Saturday and we could talk? I know it's a long trip for you, but you wouldn't have called if it hadn't been important. Could you give me an idea of what this is about?" Jonathan sounded confused and non-committal.

"Jonathan, ever since I was called into the ministry, I have believed in counseling couples before they wed. I would like to have that privilege with you and Judith, and I certainly don't mind driving to New Haven on Saturday if that is all right with you and Judith."

They all agreed to meet the following Saturday, so Will would pick Judith up early and they would be at Yale for lunch and have several hours together.

After Jonathan hung up, he explained to Judith the importance of the meeting, but she was afraid Will could force them into his beliefs.

"I don't think so," replied Jonathan. "He has never come across as that kind of man and I have never heard him do or say anything to make anyone uncomfortable. It sounds like a good idea, just to hear this thoughts, even though both you and I have spent many hours with the family discussing these things. After all, he does have the ceremony, and I believe we should hear what he has to say and maybe he'll give us some very good advice. He's been doing this for years, and he's a very wise, astute man."

"You're probably right, Jonathan. And since I have promised that you would always be the head of our house, I want this to be a wonderful experience - not one of which we are afraid. Thanks for setting me straight. I've done things on my own for a long time, and I'm glad I have you to keep me in check. I love you for it."

The following Saturday, Will and Judith had a great time as they drove to New Haven, and she really came to appreciate him in an entirely new way. She loved him and often called him "Dad," so there was no fear in her heart.

At lunch, the three talked of many things and then they went to a quiet corner of the College Library and Will began, "Since I have the ceremony for your wedding, I want to share some thoughts with you. You have decided to take Communion before your final vows, and I would like to ask why you want to do this?"

Jonathan replied, "We've been to many weddings and have seen others do it, and we thought it would be fitting for us - sort of a promise to each other and, I suppose, to God - a token that we love each other and it will be forever."

"Have you ever stopped to think what Communion is all about, such as who takes it and who does not?"

"Well, no," said Judith. "I guess not. Yet it seems the right thing to do in church. But I don't really know what it means. Would you tell us about it?"

Will saw open hearts before him. They seemed ready to listen. And he was certainly pleased to be able to speak to them openly about this.

"In the Bible," he began, "We are told that the night before Jesus died on the cross for our redemption, He took bread and wine and told his disciples that they were to do this is remembrance of HIM. He would die the very next day as a sin-offering - an offering which God had required from the beginning of time. It had always before been the blood of a sheep or goat sacrifice which God had required. And those who wanted their sins forgiven performed this sacrifice to atone for their sins. But this had to be done every year, and God determined that He would send Jesus to die as a sacrifice for our sins. It would be death just once - and for everyone, everywhere. The only requirement would be that sinners would accept this atonement for their sin. If they did not, there was no other way.   So Jesus, on that last evening together with his followers, shared this with them. And He asked them to continue the service of Communion so they would never forget that He came to die for their sin problem. By believing, they could be saved from sin and its penalty - eternal death - and be redeemed to eternal life. Communion is not something anyone should take unless he has a personal relationship with God through Jesus Christ. I'm aware that you do not believe as I do, and I respect that. But I cannot perform the ceremony if you take Communion without placing your faith in the One Who gave His life to bring you to God. Otherwise, if you don't take Communion, I can marry you and I have no problem with that. I hope you understand what I'm saying, and don't take offense at it."

Jonathan replied, "We really never knew what Communion is all about, so we would be just as happy if we left that part of the service out and said our vows and promise to love and cherish one another as long as we live.   Would   that   offend   you?"

"No, that would be fine. But I did not think it fair to you to do something or say something unless you truly understood what it meant. Marriage is so sacred and so totally giving of oneself, it is best to promise only what you actually mean. You will find that even all those promises are not easy to keep when you become husband and wife."

The afternoon was quickly gone and after a few goodbye kisses and friendly words, Judith and Will drove back to Boston. Judith spoke very little on the way. She asked no questions. And Will didn't expound any further on what they had talked about with Jonathan. When they arrived home and Judith had gone to her room, he shared with Martha a little of what had been said. He said he felt relieved, even though he felt bad that Jonathan and Judith did not know the Lord. But Communion had been taken out of their ceremony and they seemed to understand why that was a priority to Will. Then he kissed Martha goodnight and told her he would call her the next day.

CHAPTER 55

As time flew by, family and friends brought life and excitement to the apartment in New Haven by their gifts - a shower curtain with a seascape and mat and towels to match. Martha found an antique rocking chair with a tiny footstool. Brittany wandered through Filenes and found a lace runner for the dining room table plus a bouquet of artificial silk flowers. The little place was beginning to look like the haven it was intended to be.

Martha and Will would live in the mansion on Beacon Hill. Each day he brought books, pictures, his computer. There was plenty of space. One guest room was turned into his office. The Allens gave him a large oak desk and a special stand for his computer, a bright lamp and a comfortable leather chair. Not being used to all this, he was completely overwhelmed and deeply grateful. Martha replaced her out-of-date pictures with his special paintings. The office looked masculine, spacious and filled with love.

The second week of November, cars flew back and forth, every detail was checked, wedding clothes and honeymoon outfits were set aside. Final details were confirmed with the florist. Reservations at motels for friends, and special separate rooms at the Hyannis Marriott for Will, Martha and Brittany were reconfirmed.

Cold weather arrived early in New England, and even though the bride and groom had been planning a cruise, they were buying woolen sweaters, heavy gloves and socks, and Jonathan gave Judith a full-length mink coat!

"Oh, Jonathan, you should never have done that. You have been too wonderful. You spoil me far too much."

"That's because I love you so much. I want to give you more and I will when I finally have that M.D. after my name!"

Three days before the wedding, Brittany and Judith were carrying a large box of books down the stairs at their home in Boston. Judith slipped on a step and fell, hitting her back on the stairs and her head on the banister. She got up immediately and assured Brittany she was fine.

Martha heard the crash and ran quickly to find her daughter beginning to get up.

"Oh, Judith, are you hurt," she asked anxiously. "Did you hit your head very hard? Should I take you to the Emergency Room for x-rays, or maybe call our doctor to come?"

"No, mother, I'm only bruised. Just let me sit for a few minutes. Perhaps you could get me a cup of hot cider."

Judith walked slowly to the couch and moaned as she sat down. Brittany put the books back in the box leaving it on the stair where it had fallen.

After Judith drank the cider, she rested her head on the back of the couch. Martha gave her two aspirin, and in a short time she fell asleep.

While Judith was sleeping, Martha went upstairs and called her doctor. He suggested she take Judith to the Emergency Room for x-rays to make sure nothing was broken.

Martha woke Judith and brought some warm clothes for her to put on. Snow was gently falling as they pulled out on the street, and the wind was whipping through the trees on the common.

The x-rays proved to be negative. The doctor checked her pupils, reflexes, made her close her eyes and touch her nose with her right index finger. The only sign of any damage was a small lump on the back of her head. The doctor told her to take two Aspirin every four hours. If her headache persisted, he would see her in the morning.

As they drove home, Judith made her mother and Brittany promise not to say a single word to Jonathan or the Allens. Without much conviction, they each agreed.

Almost all her packing was done. Her wedding gown hung in the closet. There were only a few things left to do. They next day they were all going to Sandwich and Jonathan would be arriving from Yale after his last mid-term exam.

At dinner, Judith looked pale, but when her mother questioned her, she said she was fine - just very, very tired. Will came for dinner and would stay in the guest room overnight since he would be driving his car to Sandwich the next day so they could all ride together.

In the middle of the meal, Judith excused herself and went upstairs. Martha quickly followed her.

"Judith, you must tell me the truth. What is the matter. You have to be honest with me."

"Oh, Mom, my head hurts so. Maybe if I just take my medicine and go to bed, I'll be fine tomorrow."

Martha stayed in the room while her daughter undressed. Then she gave her the Aspirin that was ordered, and opened the bed.

"Are you sure you wouldn't like some tea and crackers, or some soup?"

Judith thought for a moment and then said, "Oh yes, Mom. I'd like some chicken noodle soup and a few Saltines."

Martha and Brittany took the tray upstairs, but Judith was asleep. She did not feel feverish, but looked very pale. They didn't wake her.

Returning to Will, Martha pleaded, "Will, please let's have prayer." Judith isn't at all well."

Will prayed deeply and sincerely for Judith, the trip the next day, the wedding - and when he was finished, Martha's hankie was wet with tears.

Martha checked on Judith again, and she was still sleeping. Going quietly down stairs, she asked Will to pray again.

Brittany and her mother were finishing their packing when the phone rang. It was Jonathan. Not wanting to break her promise, Martha said, "Your bride-to-be is soundly asleep. Excitement has worn her out. May she call you first thing in the morning?"

"Of course she can," said Jonathan. I'm as excited as she is. We'll see you tomorrow. The weatherman tells us it will be sunny and in the high 40's. Goodnight. I love you."

When Judith woke up, her headache was gone. She was excited, called Jonathan and finished packing. By 10 o'clock, they were on their way. The beautiful leaves had blown off the trees, it was cold, but the sun shone brightly. It was to be a perfectly wonderful day.

CHAPTER 56

By 10 o'clock on Thanksgiving day, all could smell the turkey roasting. The aroma of mince and pumpkin pies wafted through the living room. There was a gentle crackling noise coming from the large stone fireplace. There was a horn of plenty in the center of the coffee table surrounded by several kinds of nuts and candies.

Laura had heated spiced apple cider and made corn fritters covered with confectioner's sugar. Judith and Jonathan drank a cup of cider, grabbed a hot fritter, and headed out into the cloudy, cold, foggy Cape Cod air for a walk on the beach. Martha, Brittany and Laura stuffed dates and celery with cream cheese and peanut butter. John Allen and Will drove to the Chapel to make sure everything was in order. The Chaplain left his attire hanging in the church office so all would be ready for Saturday's long-awaited ceremony. The window sills had been decorated with gold and green velvet ribbons. On the piano was a large bouquet of fall flowers, and satin bows adorned the end of each pew. All was in readiness until the last minute details were to be finished the next morning.

John was joyful, and his enthusiasm filled the Chapel. Will, who was not known as a musician, walked quietly to the piano, lifted the cover, touched the ivory keys of the Steinway, and softly played the hymn, "In the Garden." The music - so tenderly and lovingly played - filled the little chapel with reverence, and even John could not speak. Will closed the piano, and he and John stepped into the damp air - refreshed and excited.
Jonathan and Judith were walking toward the Chapel as Will and John were leaving.

John said, "You mustn't go inside. The beauty has to wait until your wedding day."

Then all four jumped into John's car and were soon in the Allen's living room.

At 2:30, they were all ushered into the dining room. The centerpiece was a miniature wooden model of the Administration Building at Yale. A gold colored tablecloth was almost totally covered with dishes full of mashed potatoes, winter squash, dressing, gravy, cranberry sauce, celery, olives, pickles and hot buttered rolls. Then came the immense turkey. The only sounds to be heard were "oohs and aahs and yummy!"

After Will asked the blessing, John carved the turkey. For a full hour they feasted, shared thoughts, told jokes and enjoyed each other's company.

At 3:30, Brittany screamed out with delight - "Look, look! Snowflakes are falling." Before the dishes could be removed, all ran outside to catch a snowflake. The sky was very gray, and the temperature hovered right around freezing. The snow began to stick to the lawn and the trees. It was early for a real storm to come, and the ground was not yet frozen, so no one felt there would be more than a few flurries - just to make their day perfect!

Now they returned to eat their dessert. All were stuffed and happy. The dishes were rinsed and placed in the dishwasher. The table was cleared. The living room chairs were full of contented people. Jonathan turned on the TV to watch football. Others dozed on and off. What a glorious day it had been for them all!

By 8:00 p.m., they all donned warm coats, gloves and woolen scarves and threw snowballs. The ground was completely white and every tree held a few flakes of snow on each branch.

Back in the warmth of their home, Jonathan could contain his anticipated excitement just so long.

"One more day! Just one more day!"

He kicked off his shoes and placed his feet on Judith's lap. "You'll have to rub my feet every night," he said, grinning.

Judith quickly tickled his toes and threw his feet to the floor.

"You're awful! Terrible! But I'll get even!" Jonathan assured her.

Will took Martha and Brittany to their motel. The roads were still clear, even with the snow. Will held Martha a long time. They only had a month to wait and even though they were extremely excited for Judith and Jonathan, their anticipation of their own wedding was very obvious. As soon as the newlyweds were on their way, then their own preparations could begin in earnest.

They did feel for Brittany, however, because although she was happy for her sister and her mother, she seemed so very much alone. Martha and Will spent many hours on their knees pleading for the salvation of the girls and the Allen family.

"God answers prayer," Will said, "but not always in the way we ask or in the time we think is right. So we must wait patiently" - and in that, they rested.

Friday dawned bright and sunny. Anticipation filled the brisk air. The Allen family had been invited to the motel for breakfast. Already the snow had disappeared except in shady areas and in the crevices of a few tree trunks.

The whole day seemed to drag by. The clock stopped and even the sun seemed to stand still. But at last, it was time for the rehearsal dinner and then off to the Chapel. The small wedding party had a lovely roast lamb dinner at the Daniel Webster Inn. Jonathan's best man gave a witty monologue. Jokes were plentiful. Martha and Will did a short skit revolving around being wed for 50 years! Laughter rang out. Dr. Allen toasted the couple with champagne. Brittany read a brief article on being an "unclaimed blessing/old maid." It was a festive, fun-filled, full of joy evening.

The rehearsal itself was short and simple. The Chaplain's friend practiced his songs. Brittany walked down the aisle and stood with Jonathan while Judith sat with her mother. The gold bands for the double-ring ceremony were placed in Will's jacket pocket in the church office. Lists of things to remember were constantly checked. The florist arrived about 8:30 p.m. to make sure the chapel would be open very early the next day. Jonathan and Judith strolled back to the Allens home, wishing it were 2:00 p.m. on Saturday!

Although it was not late, bedtime seemed to be calling. The quicker they slept, the sooner it would be the wedding day!

A sliver of moon peeked through the overcast night sky. In the distance, a church bell tolled 10:00 p.m. Good night hugs and kisses were exchanged, words of eager anticipation were spoken and finally it was time to get some rest. The day had been a good day, but long - far too long!

CHAPTER 57

Judith sat up in bed. The clock showed 4:00 a.m. She got up, washed her face, checked her nails, creamed her neck and arms. It was only 4:10! Back in bed, she listened to her sister's heavy breathing. After more than what had to have been an hour, she looked at the clock again. It was 4:20! If she had been at home, she would have made coffee, but all the in-room coffee had been consumed the night before.

At 5:00 a.m., she woke Brittany, crawled in beside her and started talking. This woke up their mother, so they all dressed and ate their continental breakfast in the lobby at 6:00 a.m. Their hair appointments were not for three hours. The photographer would arrive at the small all-purpose room of the Chapel at 12:30. She longed to see Jonathan, but they had promised each other they wouldn't talk to or see each other until the wedding.

Jonathan grabbed his bathrobe and slippers, ran down stairs and made coffee. A stale doughnut was on the kitchen table. He ate it anyway. He looked at his watch. It was five o'clock. Outside there was nothing but pitch blackness, so he didn't know what the weather was like, though he opened the door a crack and there was no rain or snow.

The Allens barely touched their breakfast. Dr. Allen made a quick trip to Cape Cod Hospital to see his patients. When he returned, he and Jonathan went to the barbershop for haircuts, special shaves, and to have their shoes shined professionally.

The hairdressers were on time for Martha and Judith. Then Laura and Brittany were taken care of. By 11:30, the four headed for the Chapel, picking up a frappe on the way. The florist was finishing placing yellow, green and bronze colored flowers on the altar and the piano. A white satin carpet was lying to one side near the chapel door.

As they dressed, each one checked the other and everyone made sure the bride looked perfect. When she stood facing the small mirror, she could hardly believe that SHE was the bride adorned in white satin.

The photographer arrived just after noon and took picture after picture of the ladies together, each one separately - and a dozen poses of the bride. It was 1:30 before he finished and headed into the Chapel for pictures of the guests and the magnificent setting for the ceremony.

Jonathan, with his dad and best man, dressed at the Allen home. Dr. Allen was absolutely handsome in his tux. He drove to the Country Club on the way to the Chapel. Every table was decorated and the head table was exquisitely done. The 3-tiered wedding cake was in place on a round table covered with a white satin cloth. The room was more beautiful than he imagined it could be, set with elegant crystal and china. All of a sudden, it reminded him of 22 years before, when Laura - radiant, glowing and gorgeous, walked down the aisle to take his hand. She had had his heart long before that!

Guests began arriving at the Chapel by one o'clock. Lawyers and their wives arrived from Boston, doctors and their families from many areas of the Cape, a few of Jonathan's buddies drove up from Yale, school chums of the bride, Laura's sister and her husband and several close friends of the Chaplain were all there. The Chapel overflowed with happy noise and beauty. The pianist was the wife of one of John's colleagues.

Jonathan, his dad and Will arrived at one o'clock and, no matter how hard Dr. Allen tried, he couldn't stop his son from twisting his fingers and tapping his feet.

The Chapel filled up quickly. The Chaplain, Dr. Allen, Jonathan and Albert Frost (the soloist) waited impatiently in a side room of the Chapel. The clock finally showed it was 1:58. The time had arrived. The pianist was quietly playing background music when Albert walked into the Chapel and stood in front of the piano. He was tall and handsome, had black wavy hair and huge brown eyes. The Chapel fell silent. All eyes watched and every head leaned forward as the strong, yet tender, voice pealed forth, "How Great Thou Art." It would have been impossible not to have had hearts touched with the grandeur of the words and music.

Laura Allen sat silently at the front of the church. Martha was just across the aisle from her. Two of Jonathan's friends rolled the satin carpet from the altar to the back of the Chapel. Then Dr. Allen, his son and the best man entered through the front side door and walked toward the altar. The maid of honor and bridesmaids moved slowly down the aisle. Then the pianist struck the first chord of Lohengren's Wedding March.

As Judith looked straight ahead, all could see this charming, winsome lady look lovingly toward the man she loved. With beauty, love and grace, the bride, leaning gently on the Chaplain's arm, stepped slowly toward Jonathan. It seemed to many that the sun shone more brightly through the stained glass windows as she arrived at the altar and looked longingly at her husband-to-be. Will gave Judith's hand to Jonathan. Then he ascended the three steps to the altar.

Before any words were spoken, Albert Frost tenderly sang one verse of "Take My Life and Let it Be Consecrated to Thee."   The ceremony itself was one which had been used for many years. Then just before the Chaplain introduced them as Mr. and Mrs. Jonathan Allen, Albert's voice filled the Chapel with "The Love of God."   And oh, what joy fulfilled it was when Will announced, "I now pronounce you man and wife." Then turning to Jonathan he said, "You may kiss your bride."

Jonathan tore back Judith's veil and his longing arms embraced her slim body. Their kiss was one for all eternity. Then turning, they fairly flew down the aisle with a joy that almost superseded the radiance of the sun.

The Country Club Banquet Hall was simply decorated. There were a few toasts, remarks by Dr. Allen and by two of Jonathan's friends. Pictures were taken from every angle - even to all the white frosting on Jonathan's face. Brittany and Albert ate together. Before they left, he took her phone number and asked if he could call. Her eyes beamed with pleasure as she nodded a reassuring yes.

There was no bouquet to throw, but Judith took the orchid from her white Bible and threw that. It landed on Brittany's head!

Quickly the couple changed, and as they ran out the door to their waiting Mercedes, confetti flew. As they drove away, tin cans rattled from the back bumper and signs covered the back and side windows, stating boldly, "JUST MARRIED!" Even with cars following, tooting their horns, somehow they managed to escape through back lanes. At last they were alone together. Mr. and Mrs. Jonathan Allen. John and Laura took the many wedding gifts home with them. Will drove Martha and Brittany back to Beacon Hill. The ceremony had been spectacular in its simplicity. Both families were overjoyed with the entire service.

When the bride and groom arrived at the Marriott in Boston, the sun was dipping behind a bank of gloriously colored clouds. November 22nd would certainly be a day to remember forever!

CHAPTER 58

After the bride and groom were safely aboard their cruise ship in Miami on Monday, Martha and Will could finally make definite plans for their wedding. Things had been on hold for weeks, but December 22nd was fast approaching, and they were more than anxious to do all the necessary preparations for that which had been their dream for these past months. And thus, the next morning Will arrived on Beacon Hill to settle many of the last minute details.

Martha had spent many hours before that time wondering what colors would be best to use for the wedding. Since it was so close to Christmas, nothing could be more beautiful than holiday colors. She wanted a wedding that was beautiful, elegant - yet simple. Since this was her second marriage, she had chosen to wear the red velvet gown she had purchased. The ladies could wear green and red and gold. The Chapel could also be made festive in green, red and gold. This would fulfill her own dreams of a special wedding, and she hoped Will would feel likewise.

Her first wedding had been small because Bill had wanted nothing but a quiet, noontime wedding with only a couple to stand up with them. He was a student, finishing his law degree. Bill refused anything more special - even though his family was very disappointed with his choice. They had had a short ceremony, coffee and cake, and went immediately to the Green Mountains of Vermont for the weekend. As Martha looked back on that time, she realized how little she had known about Bill because their engagement had been so short with almost no time for them to be together. But now both she and Will loved the Lord and each other. This was so much more exciting and wonderful.

Brittany arrived home from school, interrupting her thoughts. "I know you and dear Chaplain Garrett love the Lord and each other and I'm happy for you both. But you haven't pushed me or shoved the Bible down my throat, and I'm grateful. I don't believe yet - but perhaps someday I will. I'm dating several senior fellows. We have fun enjoying sports, dancing, movies, and all that. Now that I'm part of the class, and do so many things with my classmates, I'm happy. For a while, I envied Judith. But after all the time we had together before her wedding, I was extremely happy for her. Someday, when I'm older, I'm sure the right man will come into my life and it will feel right. I'm content to wait. I love you, Mom. And I love my new stepfather, and I know we will all be happy living here. I'm looking forward to having a dad I can love and respect and not be afraid of. I'm thrilled for you. Your being alone worried both Judith and me. She's as happy for you as I am."

For quite a while, Brittany sat close to her mother, sharing the love between them and caring deeply for each other's happiness. Finally Martha said, "Dear, I want you to help me as much as possible with all the plans for my wedding. I'll share what I have thought about colors - and the dresses for you, Judith, Laura and Wendy - and see if you think it sounds right. Will is coming over tomorrow and we will spend most of the day making final plans. Invitations must be sent by the end of the week, and we haven't even made the list of guests yet. Please give me a list of the friends you want to invite. I have a partial list from Judith, and I'll have names from the Allens in a day or two. Jonathan may have some classmates who would like to attend. And, of course, there will be many of Will's friends, and that makes it wonderful. I guess you've guessed by now that you have a very excited mother!"

Brit and her mother had a quiet dinner, and then Brit had to leave to practice for a play in which she had a major part. She had been gone only a few minutes when the doorbell rang. Martha was pleased - but not really surprised - to find herself in the arms of her sweetheart. "I couldn't wait until breakfast to tell you how much I love you. May I come in?" Will asked boyishly. Arm in arm they walked to the couch and talked until Brittany returned.

"Love birds together. Cool! I'll make us a drink and we can share goodies with it." Brittany didn't seem surprised to find Will there.

It was after 11 o'clock when Martha and Brittany ascended the winding staircase. It had been a good day for both of them. And a warmth of love seemed to fill the home which for so long had been cold and empty.

CHAPTER 59

The aroma of waffles and sausage filled the home as Will walked in. After a morning hug and warm kiss, Martha and Will enjoyed sharing breakfast and chatting about events going on in the world.

The phone rang, and the excited voice of a jubilant Judith literally sprang forth. "Hi, Mom. We're in Nassau and having a glorious time. The sun is bright and we're going surfing and water skiing. Wow! This is some honeymoon."

Before Martha could say much of anything, Judith went on, "Have to rush. The tour bus is leaving. Thanks again for a great wedding. Jonathan and I love you. Talk with you soon." And that was it. Martha was so pleased they had called. She wanted the very best for her daughter and new son.

With the dishes in the sink and the table cleared, Will and Martha took a Bible, paper, pens, coffee - and set to work. Will had a friend who was a printer, so they worked on the invitations first. Martha called Laura to see how many friends they wanted to invite. Wendy said

20 of her friends would love to be there. Calvary Chapel held a few more than 250 people, and as they counted those who should be invited, they decided 250 invitations would need to be printed.

After reading I Corinthians 13 and having prayer, they began to work on the details of the ceremony itself. John Allen was to be the best man. Jonathan and Will's close friend - Bob Jenkins - would be in the wedding party. Bob had been a Chaplain in the Navy, but was now a pastor in Lexington. Another friend of Will's - Paul Rivers - would also be in the party. They had gone to Seminary together and Will had been his best man while they were still in school. They had been close friends ever since. Of course, Judith, Brittany, Laura and Wendy would be standing up with Martha.

Those details didn't take much time. So now they started with the music. Since Will had been going to Calvary, he had learned to appreciate the ministry of a disabled young man, Timothy Woods. He had been severely burned in an auto accident. His face was severely scarred and he limped noticeably. Will said his voice was soft and gentle - and love shone from his eyes. When he sang, the whole church became hushed with awe and worship. The Chapel's organist had been there for many years and Will was sure she would be happy to play for the wedding.

They had decided some time before that they would have Communion just before they were pronounced man and wife. The Pastor of the Chapel had said that would be no problem.

While Martha was fixing a mid-morning snack, Will called Bob Jenkins and Paul Rivers. They were both in their church offices, and were pleased to be asked to be part of the wedding party. They would discuss details later. Tim was a voice teacher in a Christian school, and would have to be called in the evening.

Martha's favorite hymn was "Amazing Grace." Will shared his thoughts on the hymns he would like. He felt "There's a Sweet, Sweet Spirit in This Place" would be very appropriate before they took Communion. They both agreed on "How Can I Help But Love Him." Three hymns would be enough. Each gave a beautiful message, and they certainly wanted the ceremony to bear a testimony to the Lord they loved.

Martha shared her thoughts concerning the colors for the ladies to wear and the Christmas décor for the Chapel. Neither one knew a florist, but some time before, Wendy had said her sister had been a florist, so Martha would ask her. Otherwise, maybe someone at the Chapel would know of someone.

It was already lunchtime, and although it had been a blessed morning, it had been tiring, so they decided to leave the rest for another day. The most important thing had been covered. The invitation had been written out, and Will would take it to the printer on his way home. At one o'clock they went out for lunch and a brisk walk in Boston Common. After going to the printer, Will would need to stop by the hospital to see several patients. Martha went home and rested!

Martha decided to use the same Bridal Salon that Judith had used. She would discuss the wedding attire with Wendy. Then she and Brittany would go together to look at gowns. She and Will had decided to honeymoon in Miami Beach, so she would need some outfits for that and clothes for travel as well. She and Brit would go to Filenes and other stores to shop. She thought perhaps

Laura would like to drive up for a day and they could go to the Mall together. Laura had beautiful taste in clothes and she loved to shop.

She made the call to Sandwich. "Laura, would you like to come up one day next week and shop with me?" Martha asked. "I need your wisdom and great ideas for what I'll need for my honeymoon."

"Oh, I'd love to come. Maybe Tuesday would be good. John has an all-day seminar at Mass General. You and I could shop and then all have dinner together when John is finished. That would work out great!"

So the date was made. Martha's little calendar was fast filling up. She lay back on the couch and looked across the room through the large picture window. It had begun to snow and flakes were gathering on the pane. She called Will and asked him to be careful driving home. He promised her he would.

When Brit came home from school, they had a cup of hot chocolate with a fresh baked pumpkin muffin. Since they both loved snow, they donned their coats and walked though the Common until their heads were white and the street lights were struggling to shine through. They headed home and spent the evening going over Brit's script for the play she was in. The ground was white when they said goodnight.

Martha called Will to make sure he had arrived home safely. He did not answer on his home phone, so she called him at the hospital. "I'm sorry, dear. I've been praying for and staying with a family who needed encouragement. I'm about ready to leave now. I'll call you the minute I get home."

Martha read a while and waited for the phone to ring. She dozed off. The sound of the phone woke her.

It was after 1:00 a.m. and Will was finally safely home. She thanked the Lord for His protection, and then fell asleep.

Tomorrow, Will would be at the hospital all day, so she might just go shopping alone and see what she could find. God had been so good to her. She praised Him for His faithfulness. She was 48 going on 16 - and it was a wonderful feeling!

CHAPTER 60

Wendy called the next day just after breakfast to say that she would be in Boston, and she wondered if Martha would like to have lunch and then shop for an hour or so. Martha was happy about this. They met downtown and after enjoying hot tea and a salad, they went to Filene's. The store was crowded. Christmas decorations adorned every aisle. A long line of children were waiting to have their pictures taken with Santa. Christmas music was playing in the background.

Martha found two suits - one green gabardine trimmed with yellow and the other navy trimmed with white, perfect for traveling South. They passed the shoe department, and sitting right on top of a large display case were blue and white spectator pumps and a pair of white beach shoes.

Wendy enjoyed Martha's excitement, and before they left the store, they found three pairs of slacks with matching knit tops. Bundled into Wendy's car, they laughed and talked of wedding bells and sandy beaches. Then Wendy became silent.

"Did I say something wrong?" asked Martha apologetically.

"Oh, no - of course not. It just brought back memories of my wedding to Tom. My mother went shopping with me. We were very poor, and although Tom came from a wealthy family, I had to be careful to find the right things and also remember that each purchase should please him and make him proud of me. I didn't know his family very well and was so afraid I was not all that they had hoped for in a daughter-in-law. The wedding was in a little town in Vermont - and we went to Niagara Falls for our honeymoon. On the way, we stopped in Buffalo and Tom insisted that we go shopping. It seemed as if he bought me everything in the store! At first, I was completely embarrassed - but then I realized it was only because he loved me and wanted to give me things I had never had. His parents were warm and wonderful to me. I felt totally at home as soon as I met them.

When Tom went fishing with his best friend the following summer, something happened. We never knew what - but Tom's lungs were full of water even though he was a good swimmer. In the hospital in Burlington, he collapsed. His strong body seemed to waste away almost overnight, and in three days he was gone." Wendy wiped the tears from her face as she continued, "The doctor said it was pneumonia, but no one really believed it. No autopsy was performed, so we never knew the actual cause of death. The shock of it all caused me to go into labor, and since I was only five months pregnant, I lost our little boy.

Tom's parents did everything for me, as did my parents. After a few months, I began to feel more like myself, but the biggest part of me was gone. I never dated again and left men out of my life completely. It was a difficult time. I took special courses and became a Legal Secretary. I worked in the same firm for 25 years, and then retired. I did some volunteer work in a local hospital, and was athletic director for several years at a nearby camp for girls. I was so glad to meet you during that last year at work, and finally found a friend I could trust. You have been so good for me and I am grateful. Being with you today has put a spark in my heart, and I've enjoyed every minute. I do hope we can do it again, soon."

Martha put her arm around her friend, and on the way home they stopped for a sundae and hot chocolate. It was the first of many times they spent together before and after the wedding. Wendy's heart was soft at this point, and Martha took the opportunity to relate her Christian testimony to her. Wendy listened, but said nothing. Then she stated, "I wish I could believe, but I always felt God took my husband and my son. I wanted no part of religion. I guess I need to stop and realize that God was not the one I should fear or hate. There had to be a reason for what happened. Thank you so much for sharing with me."

Will called after Martha arrived home and asked her if she'd like to go out for dinner.

"Oh, Will, I'd love to meet you. Or do you want to pick me up?"

"I'll pick you up at six and we'll have the whole evening to enjoy."

They ate in a little restaurant near the hospital. The couple who owned it were Christians. Soft, beautiful music was playing. Candles lit the tables. There was a manger scene in the middle of the main dining room, which made it very special. They enjoyed a delicious meal, and lingered for a long time over mince pie and coffee. It was late when Martha kissed Will goodnight. "Call me when you get home. I have to know you're safe."

It was only a few minutes before the phone rang. Will was home. Knowing he was fine made so much difference.

Brittany had already gone to bed. After reading her Bible, Martha fell asleep. What a great day she had had. She loved the clothes Wendy had helped her pick out. It was now only three and a half weeks until the 22nd. Time flew in some ways, yet in other ways, the clock stopped.

The invitations were mailed exactly three weeks to the day before the wedding except for those which were to go to Judith and Jonathan's friends from New Haven. The honeymooners were now home after their week's cruise. They would need to get those addresses to Martha soon.

Laura called Martha and asked if she could drive to Sandwich the following Saturday to spend the day. Martha had no idea a surprise personal shower had been planned. Judith would drive up from New Haven. Brittany would drive her mother to the Cape. And what a happy occasion that turned out to be. Martha couldn't believe all the beautiful satin negligees, slips, summer knit tops and slacks, scarves, stockings and slippers she received. The bows from all the gifts were placed in a box top to make a beautiful remembrance and a life-long keepsake. The finger foods and winter drinks were special, as well as the eggnog. The entire afternoon was perfect. Judith was so happy for her mother, and guests made Martha feel radiant and special. How good the Lord was to give her such wonderful friends.

Best wishes and hugs were the order of the day. And after many words of gratitude, Brit and her mother drove back to Boston with a car brimming over with gifts. The following Monday, Wendy gave a surprise luncheon for Martha and more gifts were added for her enjoyment.

Now time was really passing rapidly. Martha and Brittany shopped for two evenings, and Wendy joined them at the Bridal Salon. Brittany found a forest green velvet dress she liked. And they had one in her size and one in Judith's size. The shop owner found red velvet dresses for Wendy and Laura and said she would hold them until they could come in to be fitted.

Tuxedos were easily obtained for the men. They would wear red ties and cummerbunds. Will shopped for clothes for Florida and found a number of things he liked. Because he was so handsome, everything looked nice on him, but blue was his favorite color, so his wardrobe consisted mostly of sea and sky shades!

They planned for the Reception to be held at the Marriott Hotel near the Chapel. It would be very simple - with only a decorated wedding cake, coffee and tea, along with some nuts, candy and wedding cookies. Laura asked if she and John could have the joy of providing the wedding cake. Little by little, things were coming together. Will made reservations in Miami Beach in a Hotel overlooking the Atlantic. The first night, they would, of course, stay in Boston.

For weeks, Martha had continued to ponder what to give Will for a wedding gift. One day a few weeks before, he had mentioned in casual conversation that he had always wanted a gold watch. That was the answer! Martha found the perfect one for him at Bailey, Banks and Biddle.

Martha wouldn't know until her wedding day, that Will bought her a real pearl necklace with matching earrings as his gift to her - something she had wanted all her life.

CHAPTER 61

Laura had suggested that Will and Martha use the florist who had done such a lovely job for Judith and Jonathan's wedding. But she was so far away. However, she had a friend in Boston who owned a floral shop, The Forget-Me-Not, and this florist was happy to care for the flowers. Neither Will nor Martha wanted any elaborate arrangements, so they requested a Christmas bouquet for the organ and red and green bows at the end of each pew. The girls who wore green would carry red carnations, and the ones wearing red would have green-dyed carnations. Martha chose to carry a small bouquet of red roses. The men would all wear red carnations in their buttonholes. It would be festive and elegant in its simplicity.

There had been much discussion about the rehearsal dinner, but it was finally decided that it would be catered at Martha's home, and from there they would all go to the chapel for the rehearsal. Since it was such a closely knit group, it seemed good for them just to be together and enjoy one another rather than going out to somewhere more formal but less warm and cozy.

December 20th found the entire bridal party in Boston. It was a cold, wintry day. The Allens would stay at Martha's. Will's two friends were to stay with him, so there was no problem with transportation or hotels. Since Timothy lived in Boston, he could go to his own home. The night they all arrived, they ate at Pier 4 on the Harbor. Never was roast beef more delicious! It was a happy and festive occasion. They were in a private dining area and although it wasn't planned or expected, there was a small piano in the corner of the room. So Timothy sang for the group and won the hearts of everyone with his warm smile and mellow music. Brittany sat next to him at the table and they shared a little about their families. Come to find out, Timothy had graduated from the same High School where Brit would be finishing in the Spring.

The 21st dawned crisp and clear. Christmas carols were being sung everywhere. The group staying with Martha donned warm coats, hats and gloves, and took a walk through the Common. Lamp posts were decorated. Twinkling lights adorned many of the fir trees. Strangers shouted "Merry Christmas" as they walked by.

When they returned, Brittany and Judith fixed simple chicken and ham sandwiches, made hot coffee, and cut up fruit for dessert. Clothes were being laid out, suitcases filled, dresses fluffed, suits touched up with an iron. The men watched basketball while the women fussed over perfume and lipstick.

Everyone looked well-groomed for dinner, but no one was over-dressed. The caterers did a great job. Everything went off like clock work, and by seven, they were on their way to the Chapel. Practicing for most of them was not a new thing, and except for a few suggestions and additions, everything was finished by nine o'clock. Will took his bride aside and they shared their hearts and excitement. The next time they would see one another would be on their long-awaited wedding day.

Much of the Chapel was already decorated. Timothy thrilled them all by singing "Blessed be the Tie That Binds Our Hearts in Christian Love," just as they were ready to say goodnight. Many memories filled the hearts of Judith and Jonathan. Could it be that they had only been man and wife for a month? Four weeks of wedded bliss, marred by only one short argument brought about when Judith became upset that her groom was so late getting home from the library, and dinner was cold. They were both having to learn there would be many, many times in life when plans were changed and routines upset. This was all part of life.

Goodnight hugs and kisses were abundant as Will and Martha said goodnight. It had been such a perfect evening. Before they left the Chapel, they all held hands and Will prayed for each one, and for the wedding. It was a beautiful prayer, and even Laura and John were touched by the love that filled the little church. Martha remarked as they were leaving, "Surely we have been standing on holy ground!"

Back home, Martha suggested she would love a cup of coffee and all agreed that sounded good. After a time of sharing, the frosty windows beckoned them, and they watched little snow flakes gently touch the ground. Judith said, "I know it's late, but could we just walk outside for a little while, look at the lights, and listen to the groups gathering in the Common to sing Christmas carols?"

So for almost an hour, they sang with a group here and there, watched lamp lights turn from red to green. It was like a fairyland. Everyone was jubilant as they arrived back home.

They would have to rise early in the morning. Hair appointments had been made for all the ladies. Will would be using his car for their honeymoon, so John took Martha's two suitcases to give to Will, but before they had been closed, young hearts had found jumping beans, leaping baby frogs and plenty of rice to hide among Martha's clothes. Bob Jenkins took charge of Will's car and after it was nicely deposited for the night, cans, bells, plastic bottles and tin cans were tied to the rear bumper. Will would not see his vehicle until after the wedding. Bob made sure of that!

Wendy bunked with Brittany. The Allens were in the small guest room. Jonathan and Judith were in the larger guest room. It was Martha's last night to be alone and sleep escaped her. Was it possible that the Lord loved her so much that He had made all this possible? She praised Him over and over again as she lay filled with wonder and excitement. It was long after midnight when she finally dozed off.

CHAPTER 62

December 22nd dawned after a very short night. Brittany and Laura fixed breakfast which, ordinarily, would have been delicious. But today, it was just something to eat and finish.

The clock struck eight and then it stopped! Hair appointments started at 9:30 and finished at 11:30. The photographer was to arrive at 12:30.

Will took all the men out for breakfast. They enjoyed the time together - except that the groom-to-be only played with his pancakes, but drank three cups of coffee. John teased him and said he remembered the morning of his own wedding. "I didn't fall asleep until after 4:00 a.m., and when I woke up, it was after 10. My hair needed cutting, my bags were not packed, and when I showered, I accidentally put the wet washcloth in the suitcase right next to a new green tie. When I opened the case that night, I had a multi-colored tie and a green washcloth! I never had breakfast, but my best man called and when I told him I was hungry, he brought sweet rolls, doughnuts, and plenty of hot coffee. It was a hot June day, but my hands were like icicles. I could hardly hear the minister, my heart was beating so hard. When I saw

Laura start down the aisle, I took three steps forward and my best man yanked me back. After those who had been chasing us left and we were headed for Niagara Falls, I stopped the car and said to Laura, "Are you sure you love me enough to have married me?" She must have thought I was crazy - and I was! Crazy in love!"

After breakfast, they checked at Calvary Chapel. Christmas flowers were everywhere, as well as red, green and gold velvet bows which adorned the end of each pew. The altar was covered with red and white carnations and even from inside, you could hear Christmas carols playing outside.

Back at Martha's home, it was finally time to dress. They grabbed a sandwich for lunch. Laura was already dressed. Brittany and Judith were in robes. Wendy was looking everywhere for a shoe. Surely she had not packed just one shoe! She ate her sandwich in bare feet, after which they all went on a shoe hunt. It reminded them of hunting for Easter eggs! Finally, Brit found the shoe, far under Wendy's bed.

At 12:30, the photographer arrived and took dozens of pictures before he went on to the church.

The men arrived at the Chapel before 1:30 and the women shortly thereafter. Martha peeked into the church. It was more than she could have dreamed. The organ played softly while people found their places in the pews. The place was full! All the flowers for the ladies were safely laid in a little side room, just big enough for the four of them to gather. Having taken their flowers, they quietly stepped into the foyer to await the signal for their appearance in the Chapel.

Timothy was singing "Amazing Grace" to a hushed audience. His infectious smile and gentle voice thrilled the bridal party and the men stood quietly in awe, as he sang.

The white satin carpet was rolled down the aisle. The Wedding March finally began, and Wendy, in her green velvet dress, carrying red carnations, brought every possible sound from the guests. Brittany followed in red carrying green flowers. Many whispered that they had never seen such a beautiful combination. Judith followed in her green velvet dress - and her face was almost as radiant as it had been just a month before. Her eyes were glued on Jonathan. Then Laura, the Matron of Honor, marched down the aisle. Martha entered slowly, stopping to take it all in. Her eyes were only for Will, and yet she took time to smile across the many aisles as she walked toward the altar where Will's hand was waiting for her. To him, it seemed like an eternity before she finally made it to the front of the Chapel and reached out to him.

The ceremony was brief but beautiful. After rings were exchanged, Timothy sang, "How Can I Help But Love Him?" Then the couple knelt as Timothy sang softly as a gentle breeze, the lovely voice almost in a whisper, "There's a Sweet, Sweet Spirit in This Place." Martha and Will took communion - then stood as the Pastor pronounced them man and wife. With every bit of love and admiration, Will kissed his bride and held her in his arms. The Pastor then announced, "May I present to you Mr. and Mrs. Will Garrett."

The reception at the Marriott was simple and small, but meaningful to all. Many good wishes, music, laughter, and jokes about brides and grooms were given in love. By six o'clock, all the guests had left. The wedding party spent time together, just enjoying being a family - for indeed they loved one another as a family should.

After thanking everyone, the bride and groom went to their honeymoon suite on the top floor of the hotel. All that happened there belonged only to them. Their first love gift was the exchanging of wedding gifts to each other. Then they went to their knees to thank God for making them one - one in Christ and one in each other. Their marriage had certainly been made in Heaven - they were sure of that. The next day they would leave for Miami, slowly - making every moment count. All had been perfect thus far, and they were both amazed and aware of God's gracious love for them.

CHAPTER 63

The honeymoon was more than they could have imagined - sailing on Biscayne Bay, fishing off the Keys, swimming in the blue waters of the Atlantic, wandering through little shops, and spending hours just enjoying being together. Daily, they talked with Judith and Brittany, and all was going well at home. They missed a heavy snowstorm, and it was fun sending postcards of people lying on the beach, all tanned and hot, while New England was bitter cold with snow and ice covering the trees and fields.

Brittany was enjoying school, and the newlywed Allens were spending every minute together when Jonathan was not at college. The couple who lived next door had introduced themselves and the wives shopped together while their hubbies were studying and pounding their computers to get their assignments done.

Jonathan and Judith spent a white Christmas with the Allen family, and Brittany went down to Sandwich for four days. There were gifts galore - including many from Will and Martha which they had left before the wedding. Martha and Will gave Brittany her first fur coat, and she wore it inside the heated house as well as in the snow!

Jonathan and Judith had saved enough money to give his folks a cruise during the winter. The Allens, in return, gave clothes to Jonathan and Judith, as well as a check for $1000 toward expenses during the winter months.

Laura prepared a sumptuous Christmas dinner. They had invited two doctors and their wives to join the family. Late in the afternoon, they all donned heavy winter outfits and went caroling with several others from Sandwich. It was an annual activity and when they came home, cold and happy, they delighted over hot chocolate and mince pie.

They all talked with Martha and Will, who were having a great day. The Garretts had gone to a Candlelight Service on Christmas eve, and then spent Christmas together alone. They opened gifts their family had given them - then went sailing on the Bay. Most of the large homes were decorated magnificently with Christmas scenes and thousands of colored lights. Then they drove around to see the many Christmas displays. Some homes even had ice across the lawn with little couples dancing, snow falling and carols filling the air. It was a memorable evening for them both.

By the 10th of January, the Garretts were homebound. They stopped in Charleston, SC, to view the large Christmas light display, then spent two days in Washington and one in Philadelphia before going on to Boston, spending time with Judith and Jonathan in New Haven and a weekend with the Allens in Sandwich on the way.

Brittany was jubilant to have them home. She had not enjoyed being alone in the big house, even though she had been busy during the holidays. School had now begun and she was playing flute in the orchestra and was on the basketball team. Many days she would not get home until late, but she was happy and had found many friends. She and Tommy had written several times since the wedding, and he had made a date to take her to the Boston Pops late in January.

It was a day in March, when Judith made breakfast as usual - but after Jonathan left for class, she tore to the bathroom and lost it all. It happened that way for three days, so without confiding this to her husband, she made an appointment with the University doctor.   Her excitement knew no bounds when he told her they were going to be parents!

She felt fine when she left his office, and couldn't wait to shop just a little. Maybe a blanket - perhaps some booties - and, of course, a teddy bear.

Time dragged by until she heard the front door open and her beloved came home. She ran into his arms and excitedly told him the wonderful news.   He immediately called his family and she called hers. The Allens and Garrets were overjoyed. Grandparents!

"Are you going to find out later whether the baby will be a boy or a girl?" Laura asked.

"We haven't even thought that far ahead. We're just too excited to think of anything right now!"

"Be sure you find an excellent obstetrician, Judith," Dr. Allen insisted.

As the days went by, new things came by mail. Soon the little extra room was painted yellow with a border of sailboats, fish and whales. Jonathan was sure it wouldn't matter whether the baby was a boy or a girl - as long as he/she was healthy.

At five months, Judith had a sonogram. They found out the baby was a boy. Jonathan nearly jumped through the ceiling! Dr. Allen sent a cute card with a $100 bill in it - to pay for the baby's first day in Med School!

The Allens drove down with a crib, rocking chair and some baby clothes. Martha and Will took a car seat, basinet and little blue sheets and pillowcases.

Friends from college came and went and always bought some little thing for the baby. It was obvious that Judith needed maternity clothes - so she, her mother and Brit went shopping one Saturday in Boston and found some lovely things.

Every month, Judith went to her doctor. She was in perfect health as was the baby. Occasionally she had a headache, but her blood pressure was fine and the doctor told her everything was perfect.

On a weekend visit to Sandwich, Judith told Dr. Allen about her head and the terrible pains she was experiencing from time to time. He suggested she see a Neurologist as soon as possible. Fortunately, she was able to get an appointment in New Haven that very week. She had a CT scan, and everything appeared to be normal, though she continued to have severe headaches off and on. Other than that, life was wonderful. Jonathan returned to College in the fall and was initiated into one of the most elite fraternities on campus, and was to become its President. By October, Judith really slowed down and the doctor warned her not to put on more weight.

Meanwhile, life for Martha and Will was filled with happy days. He continued as Chaplain at the hospital, and that took up many of his hours. But they also traveled to New Hampshire and Vermont for long weekends - spending days driving through the mountains or taking little boat trips around some of the beautiful lakes. They even dared to drive up Mt. Washington. At times, Martha closed her eyes and begged her husband not to get any closer to the edge, but carefully and slowly, they made it to the top. It was a crystal, clear day - and they felt like they could see forever. They bought souvenirs at the gift shop, along with a few postcards. Then they drove back down. It didn't seem quite so scary going down, but Martha was tremendously relieved when they passed through the gate at the foot of the mountain.

Dr. Allen was always busy with his practice. Laura had many friends, so life for them was very normal. They were, of course, happy about the baby and were pleased that Jonathan was doing so well with his studies. His dad was so proud of him, and always encouraged him along the way. Jonathan loved college and his biggest joy was coming home at night to his wife and soon-to-be-born son. December was not that far off, and the baby would be born at the Yale University Medical Center in New Haven. Now all they had to do was wait - and wait they did - very impatiently.

CHAPTER 64

Jonathan had laid his head on his wife's tummy many times and listened with jubilant wonder at the little thumping of the baby's heart. They had talked of the joy of having a son. The nursery was now fully decorated. The whole apartment seemed to make its own music, and many times, although the room was small, the soon-to-be parents danced from basinet to crib, elated over what was taking place in their lives.

A few days before Jonathan's party, when he would take office as President of his fraternity, Judith had made a quick trip to Boston to be with her mother and Will. They were so happy, and their home was a haven of joy.

The evening Judith arrived, Will took his dear daughter by the hand and led her to the living room sofa. "Judith, you know how much we love you and how much we long for you to know the joy we have. We have prayed so much that you and Jonathan would come to love the Savior. Just think how wonderful it would be to raise your son with God's guidance and wisdom. It's not easy these days to let children face the world without the

Savior. You have heard the truth, and you have seen how God has changed lives and given people an inward peace and joy that the world could never give. We know you have all you need materially, but spiritually, you are a pauper. I can't accept the Lord as your Savior for you - but you can ask Him into your heart, and when Jonathan sees Christ in you, I'm sure he will come to want the Lord, too. Are you sure you want to keep on living without knowing the wonder of having your sins forgiven?"

Judith sat for only a few moments before saying, "Oh, dear father, I do want to believe and I know now that I'm ready to do it. It has taken me so long - even though I have heard your messages and watched your life - as well as seeing the change in mom's life. Please lead me in prayer, and I'll pray after you."

Will bowed his head and took her hand, and with tears on both their cheeks, he prayed. After he had said "Amen," Judith prayed, "Dear Lord, I know I have sinned and I know You can do for me what I can never do for myself. I ask you to forgive my sins, come into my life and save me. I believe You died for me to save me and give me an abundant life, and You rose from the grave to give me eternal life with you in heaven. And right now I want to ask you to be my Savior and Lord."

They lifted their tear-stained faces as Martha entered the room. Judith ran to her mother and told her that Christ was now her Savior. What an occasion for thanksgiving and joy! What a miracle they had seen that day. In only moments, Martha gave her daughter a Bible she had purchased for her many months before, believing that one day she would give it to her redeemed daughter.

When Judith returned to New Haven, she took the train due to the weather. When Jonathan met her, she blurted out the wonderful news that she had asked Christ into her life. Jonathan seemed to accept this, but was not particularly overjoyed. He really didn't understand. After all, they had lived a good life. They didn't smoke, drink, do drugs, or get involved in any filth. They didn't run around with a bad bunch, and their college friends were lovely people. Why did anyone really have to have a Savior. Yes - those who committed murder, stole, came home drunk, beat their wives - of course, they needed to be cleaned up - but why would he or Judith need this. Nevertheless, Judith was jubilant over the decision she had made, and he didn't want to spoil her joy.

The night of the fraternity party, Judith looked more beautiful than ever in her blue velvet dress with its long jacket. Many of Jonathan's friends asked him where he had found such a gorgeous wife!

After dinner had been served, Judith whispered to her husband that her head ached really bad, and she felt she should go back home. He didn't want her to leave alone, and said he would take her and come right back, but she insisted she would be fine and would call him as soon as she got to the apartment. The roads were clear, and it was only a ten minute drive. So Jonathan got her fur coat, took her to the car, made sure the motor was running and the heat turned on, kissed her warmly and begged her to call as soon as she arrived home. She promised she would.

There was only one hill on the way to the apartment. As Judith started down it, her eyes blurred and headlights blinded her. She yanked the wheel away from the lights and started to turn back on the road. But her head pounded terribly, and she felt she must stop immediately. She hit what she thought was the brake, but unfortunately, it was the accelerator. The car went out of control. It tore through the trees and sand, crashed against a huge boulder, swerved, and turned over. It had all happened in less that five minutes from the time she had left Jonathan.

Two toasts were made to Jonathan as the new Fraternity prexy. He gave a short thank you response. There was clapping and pats on the back. But he quickly left the platform and ran to a pay phone. He was so frightened, he never even remembered the cell phone that was in his pocket. At any rate, there was no answer at home. He tried Judith's cell phone number, but could not get through on that. He called their neighbor, but there was no answer.

As he hung up, he heard sirens in the distance. Jonathan ran inside and asked a fraternity brother to take him home at once. Already the road was blocked with traffic. Sirens from police cars, fire trucks and ambulances could be heard. Now traffic was completely stopped. Without hesitation, Jonathan jumped from the car and ran toward the blue and red flashing lights just over the hill. As he continued, he could see his car, upside down. The police tried to hold him back, but he pulled away and ran until he reached the car. Several men were trying to tug at the doors to get one open. He saw a head against the steering wheel. Jonathan froze. He didn't want to look, but had to. Just then, many hands had been able to right the car. An officer opened the front door. The EVAC men pushed everyone aside, grabbed their equipment, threw blankets toward the car - but after only seconds, silence left the crowd shaken and still. As they pulled the lifeless body from the crumpled car, Jonathan could not believe it was Judith. He sobbed and shook until a doctor finally took him away. They were placing Judith into the ambulance. At that moment, Jonathan fell to the ground, unconscious.

Upon coming to, Jonathan cried out over and over, "My God - it was all my fault. I let her go alone. Oh God, what have I done? Forgive me. Forgive me!"

The police were able to get the phone number for the Allens. They were called with the terrible news. In their own grief, they called Will on his cell phone, knowing that the shock would be almost too much for Martha. Will was absolutely speechless. Then he said, "Oh John, only God can give grace and peace for this. When I get home, I'll call you and you can give me the details so I have it all for Martha. Meanwhile, I can only trust that God will bring good out of all this." He had just left the hospital.

The Allens were already on their way to New Haven.

CHAPTER 65

After Will spent a few minutes in prayer and started the car, he thought it might be wise to go back to the hospital to find a doctor who would give a tranquilizer prescription for Martha and Brittany. One of the doctors knew Will well and was shocked to hear the story, and gladly gave him a bottle of medicine to calm those who would be so critically wounded in mind, heart and spirit.

Will arrived home before Martha. He made coffee and fixed glasses of cold water. Then he reached for his well-worn Bible and read. Through his tears, he went from John 14 to Psalm 23, and then to the story of the resurrection.

After a short time, he heard the key turn in the front door. His hands froze and he shook inside. He never remembered shaking like that before. He quickly rushed to the door and held his wife in his arms as he greeted her. This was not uncommon, so Martha thought nothing of it - until she looked at his ashen face and felt his hands.

"Will, what's happened? Tell me quickly, please. Were you in an accident? Did something happen to Brittany?"

Will helped her take off her coat, pulled her down beside him on the couch and began to relate what had happened. He just couldn't get his words to say that Judith had been killed. Over and over he kept saying there had been an accident.

Finally, Martha looked at him, both frightened and hurt. "Will, you're repeating yourself. Please tell me who was in the accident. Where did it happen. Who was hurt?"

He looked her in the eyes and with tears streaming down his face, he said, "Judith."

Martha screamed out, "Judith? What? Tell me! It can't be true."

Judith didn't feel well and left Jonathan's fraternity party early to drive back home. She must have lost consciousness, drove off the road, hit sand while going very fast, and the car turned over several times. Martha, your precious girl is with the Lord!"

Martha stared in unbelief, and then screamed out again, "No, NO, NO! It can't be. You have to be mistaken. Jonathan would never let her drive alone at night after a party. I have to talk to him and find out what hospital she's in. We need to go there right now. Right NOW, Will."

She tried to pull away from Will, but he held her as tightly as he could. She was shaking and he knew the shock was already taking its toll. He grabbed the pills from his pocket, took a glass of cold water from the coffee table and told her to take one. She hit the glass, and the water soaked their knees.

"Don't toy with me, Will. I know she'll be all right. We just have to go. I must call Jonathan or his father!"

Will held her more strongly than ever and made her take two of the little white pills. She sobbed in his arms, then reached for the phone. But Will took it from her.

"Sweetheart, you must believe me. I'm telling you the truth. Judith was killed in an accident and it was no one's fault."

All of a sudden, Martha burst out with, "What about the baby?"

"They're both with the Savior and without pain or sorrow in His presence. We have to rest in that." And he held her warmly as she sobbed uncontrollably and tried to free herself from his grip, but he held on tightly. Just as she was starting to calm down a bit, Brittany walked in the front door.

Martha screamed, "Your sister has been killed in an auto accident, and the baby is dead, too."

Brittany keeled over and landed on the carpet. Will tore to her and picked her up in his strong arms and took her to the couch. He put a cold cloth on her head as they all sat in total silence.

In a short time, Brit opened her eyes asking where she was. Nestled in her mother's loving arms, Martha told her the story again. The room reeled and the ceiling was upside down, but Brittany tried to get up. "I'm going to call her myself. You're both wrong. She's fine. I talked with her while she was at the fraternity party, and she and Jonathan were having a wonderful time. Besides, he would never let her drive alone at night. Why would he? Why did she leave the party alone? None of it makes sense. I have to call Jonathan."

Just then, the phone rang. It was John Allen. Will answered and tried to tell him that he had told both Martha and Brittany, but they wouldn't believe it. "Would it help if I talked to them now and told them all I know?" asked John. I wish I could come up, but we're on our way to New Haven right now to make arrangements with Jonathan and the undertaker for Judith's body to be transferred, and to bring Jonathan home. We're all in shock, as I know you folks must. And you've had to bear the burden of having to tell both Martha and Brittany."

"Oh, John, please - please drive slowly and carefully. You MUST arrive safely - for you, for Laura and for us. Please, I beg of you, be careful."

Then John asked to speak to Martha. He told her everything he knew about the accident - from the time Judith had told Jonathan she had a headache and was going home, to the police finding her car, the way it had turned over, the attempts of the Medics and others to help, and the ambulance taking Judith away from the scene. John told all this as calmly as he could, but near the end, he broke down and sobbed. "My God, how could a loving God let such a thing happen? How could we not only lose a daughter, but a grandchild as well? What kind of God do you have, Will? You say He loves us, and yet He allows this?" His voice was full of anguish., Yet Will knew John well enough to know that his anger was not at Will - and probably not at God. But he had to strike out somewhere!

Will gave Martha and Brittany Phenobarbital to help them sleep, and he finally took one himself. Martha said kindly, "Dear, I want to sleep in our bed tonight with you, but I feel I must be with Brittany. Will you understand?" It was the first night since their wedding they had not gone to sleep in each others arms.

"Of course I understand, my love. If you need me or want me during the night, or if you can't sleep, please come and get me. I doubt I will sleep much, either."

Brittany was almost asleep when she and her mother climbed the stairs. When they passed Judith's old room, they clung to each other, shaken and weary, crushed and bewildered. Martha kissed Will at the top of the stairs, and he held her close to his heart. The clock in the living room struck three. With clothes still on, Martha and Brittany fell into bed, pulled the covers over themselves, and a short while later, Will heard heavy breathing, indicating they were asleep.

Then he went into the bedroom and knelt beside his bed. Before he arose, the sheet was wet with his tears, but the Lord had calmed his heart.

God gives us one day and one day only were the words he heard in his heart.

"Please, dear Lord, make this a day when we can find our peace in You. And even when we don't understand, help us never to doubt. You never make mistakes, so I ask that our hearts will try to understand - and may the Allen family find rest in body, if not in soul. Grant them Your quiet and give them sleep. Even now, comfort them for the long hours and days ahead, and may they find you as their Lord and Savior, and give them the comfort they need so desperately right now."

Will's body ached and he fell across the bed, murmuring Psalm 23. Finally, rest came to his weary body. How much more would he need to learn to be able to fully believe Philippians 3:10 - "That I may know

HIM, and the power of HIS resurrection, and the fellowship of HIS sufferings, being made conformable to HIS death." How much??

After making sure that the undertaker had made the necessary arrangements for the transfer of Judith's body, the Allens, with Jonathan, drove back to Sandwich to make final arrangements for the burial. Amidst their tears, Laura and John told him again and again how much they loved him. But even this fact could not console Jonathan at this tragic hour. Dr. Allen gave his son some medication, and Jonathan fell asleep for a short time.

CHAPTER 66

When Jonathan awoke, he stared at the ceiling, stretched his arm over to reach his wife - but there was nothing there. He wasn't sure where he was. He only knew something was terribly wrong. Then it hit him. The accident! Judith was gone. Their son was gone. There was nothing left in the world for him. Medicine didn't matter. College was forgotten. He felt a hand on his forehead, and realized his mother was beside him. Words didn't come. Nothing felt real - yet everything was all too real. His world had crashed and all he loved most dearly lay in a pile of sand inside an overturned car. Worst of all, he had let Judith drive off in the dark alone. He had not gone with her. A stupid, dumb, awful Fraternity party had kept him with some fellows he hardly knew, to receive applause at becoming president. It had meant more to him than taking his wife home. His pregnant wife! The mother of his unborn son. She had told him she had a headache, but would be fine. So he let her go. It was all his fault. He had murdered his wife and their baby. Now he only wanted to die, too. How could he ever face himself or anyone else after killing the one he loved more than life itself?

His father took him in his arms and gave him a cup of coffee and a white pill. Two of his friends from Yale were standing by the couch. His mother was rubbing his head as her tears fell gently on his forehead.

Jonathan arose and walked to the bathroom. When he came out, he headed upstairs, followed by his dad. He said he was going to take a shower, but his father stayed close by. There were no words spoken. Quietly he dressed without noticing nothing matched. Nothing was even right for winter weather. He put on one shoe and carried the other and slowly walked down the stairs. Laura had fixed oatmeal with cream and brown sugar. It was one of his favorites, but he walked by the table and opened the front door. A wintry blast hit him. Snowflakes were in the air. All of a sudden he remembered. It was November 22nd - their first wedding anniversary. He slammed the door shut, grabbed a pillow and held it to his face and sobbed as only a strong man can sob.

"Son, Martha is on the phone. Can you talk with her?" his father asked.

Jonathan took the receiver and held it close to his mouth. Words would not come.

"Jonathan, this is Martha and I'm asking if I may come down today with Will and Brittany. We want to be with you and we feel the families should be together. If you can't say anything, just let one of your parents know, and one of them can speak to me."

Jonathan nodded toward his dad, and John said, "I'm not sure what you asked, Martha, but we want you here. We are a family, and you need us and we need you.

We have things that must be discussed, and you belong with us. Our hearts not only hurt for …" John could not go on, but Martha understood, and assured him they would be there soon.

Martha, Brittany and Will got in the car. The snow was light and the roads were clear. Will drove slowly and very carefully. Route 3 was almost empty going toward the Cape, so it was an easy drive. The only words spoken on the trip were from Martha. "Will, I'm so cold. Could we stop for something warm to drink?"

Will pulled off on a side road leading to a small restaurant. They drank some hot chocolate and nibbled at some bacon and toast. But words would not come.

Thirty minutes later, they pulled into the Allen's driveway. Laura and John ran out and hugged them and took them inside. When Martha saw Jonathan, there was nothing left but tears and trembling. She held him in her arms.

"Oh, mom, I killed her. I let her drive home alone and I'm to blame. I murdered our son - your grandson - and it's all my fault. Oh God, what can I do and how can I live with myself? Do you hate me?"

His sobbing made both Martha and Brittany hold him and try to quiet him and assure him that they loved him. Accidents happen. We don't know why. But certainly it was not Jonathan's fault. Finally, John gave his son an injection which calmed him down somewhat.

Laura and John could only share their hearts with Martha. It seemed for them all that there were no more tears. Martha and Will knew their daughter was in Heaven, but even though the Lord comforted them with that thought, their hearts bled and they were raw inside.

Icicles hung from the roof over the front porch and in the hearts of both families.

There was a funeral to discuss, and as difficult as it was, somehow it had to be done. Nothing would change the heartbreak; nothing would ease the pain - yet in spite of all that, the funeral had to be planned - and Jonathan was not yet able to handle this.

John and Laura, along with Martha, went into the den while Brittany stayed in the living room with Jonathan. He could not be left alone.

The Allens and Martha felt the funeral would have to be in a larger place than either Roger Williams Chapel or Calvary Chapel. Both those places held wonderful memories that should never be tarnished. Will had been in the dining room alone, praying. He felt dead inside and knew he had to be with Martha, so he joined her in the den with the Allens.

"Maybe a Funeral Home would be the best place for the service, and have visiting hours the night before. Or would you rather have it in a church?" Will asked.

"I think that's a good idea. And would you want it in Boston at the Funeral Home where you had the service for Bill?" John asked.

Martha had forgotten all that for the time being - but then said, "That would be good - but hard for all of you from this area. For the moment, Sandwich and Boston seem so far from each other."

"No, I think that's best and it would be no trouble to have it there. Many will be coming from New Haven, the Cape, the Boston area, Brittany's school - and it seems right. Would you want Judith to be buried near her father?" Laura asked.

After discussing all this, they knew they must ask Jonathan his desires. But he was now asleep. So they would have a bite of lunch and ask him later. Martha wondered if her dear husband would have the service. Would he be able to hold up?

By mid-afternoon, Jonathan was awake, finally ate some lunch and stopped weeping. He was still in shock, but he also knew that there were things that had to be discussed. They shared with him what they had talked about earlier and he said, "Anything is o.k. with me. I only want it to be soon and short. I can't stand waiting for the finality." And though the service would be in Boston, Jonathan wanted Judith to be buried in Sandwich.

By late afternoon, the decisions were made and Will made all the necessary calls. The date was set for November 25th, the day before Thanksgiving.

That night, when all seemed quiet, Martha was alone with Will. "Dearest, could you take the service - or would that be more than you could do?"

Will waited thoughtfully for several minutes - then took his wife's hand and held it tightly. "I'm sure with your prayers and the prayers of others, I will be able to do it. Do you think Jonathan will want music? If so, do we want Timothy to sing, or would that bring back too many memories?"

"If Timmy could get through it, his music would warm hearts. I think that would be good. Let's ask the Allens, and then, if it's agreeable, could you ask Timothy?"

The gentlemen at the Hancock Funeral Home were gentle and kind. When they asked who would have the service, Will told them he would be conducting it and

Timothy Woods would be singing. The details were not essential more than that. One thing remained to be done - picking out the casket. When the funeral director mentioned this, silence fell like a bomb shell over the room - it was explosive, but still.

Finally, Laura suggested that it might be easier if she and John took care of that . . But before she finished the sentence, Jonathan blurted out, "She was MY wife and I want to choose her final resting place."

John took his son's hand and said, "Perhaps the Garretts and your mom and I could choose together."

"No," replied Jonathan determinedly. I want to go alone and choose for my wife and son."

For the moment, no one argued. All was quiet. Then Martha asked, "Jonathan, do you want to choose her clothes as well?" That was something he hadn't thought about, and in his sorrow and confused state of mind he said, "No, you can do that. Be sure it's blue. It was her favorite color and my son would have worn blue, too."

Then Jonathan picked out a mahogany casket. He came out pale and drawn, but said nothing. Martha, Will and Brittany drove home and chose a beautiful blue dress and took it and a string of pearls to the funeral home.

The Boston Globe carried a long obituary which was beautifully and carefully written. Flowers arrived at both homes. The phone rang constantly. Messages were left. People came by to visit. And several Yale fellows visited Jonathan.

The Garretts asked Timothy to sing "Face to Face" and, for the close of the service, "God be with you 'til we meet again." It seemed that two numbers were all anyone would be able to handle.

Wendy stood with Martha by the hour - fixed meals, saw people who came in, cared for all the food brought to the home, helped Martha decide what she and Brittany would wear. She was a bulwark of strength and her loving care for the family would never be forgotten.

Visiting hours were from 7:00 to 9:00 p.m. It was a bitterly cold night with the temperature hovering around 10 degrees, but nevertheless, the funeral home was crowded.

Jonathan tried to be warm and friendly, but he simply shook and sobbed every time anyone spoke to him. His dad and mother stayed by him the entire time, trying to shield some from talking too much. After an hour, Will took Martha out to a small room where there was coffee and some small sandwiches. She sat for a few minutes before returning. There were boxes of tissues everywhere, and they were soon emptied. Each visitor remarked about how beautiful Judith looked - and indeed, she was the picture of loveliness. Many times, Jonathan went to the casket and kissed his wife, only to be taken afterward to another room by his mother or dad.

By nine o'clock, strength was gone, and even though a few friends were still there, the family said goodnight and left. Everyone went back to Martha and Will's, where they donned comfortable clothes and had something to eat. Wendy and Timothy stayed in a nearby hotel. The Allens stayed with Will and Martha.

Strength was gone and weary hearts and bodies found their way to bed early. This evening had been hard on all of them, but tomorrow would be the most difficult.

Will found his wife doing dishes. He took her to the den where they knelt in prayer. Then he held her to his heart, knowing she was strong in the Lord - yet she was torn to little pieces. Only God knew and understood all they were going through.

Martha, through her tears, said, "Will, dear. I'm sorry for breaking down so much. I do know that God's grace is sufficient, but I'm finding it hard to live what I know in my head to be true."

"My beloved, He has made you stronger than I could ever imagine. And your life shows forth His love and grace. Believe me, my heart is as one with yours. But our greatest prayer needs to be for Jonathan. He has no Savior to trust and no God upon whom to lean."

No one slept that well. There were so many questioning hearts, so much inward turmoil. So much agony of a loss too great to explain. It was a blessed relief to have morning arrive. But it was bitterly cold. Snow clouds were heavy and lowering. Snow was forecast for this November 25th.

CHAPTER 67

November 25th dawned cold, but clear. Wendy and Timothy joined the families for breakfast, and they all tried to talk of anything except what would be facing them in a few short hours. After they ate, Will went to their bedroom closed the door and prayed. He loved Judith as if she were his own daughter, and he knew only the Lord could get him through his difficult task that afternoon.

The funeral cars arrived at 1:00 p.m. The families were dressed in black. They wore heavy coats and sat quietly as the cars drove to the funeral home.

All went forward to take one last look at Judith - some taking longer than others - mingling with friends, neighbors, college chums, doctors, lawyers, schoolmates. After a short time, the families went to a waiting room until time for the service to begin.

Everyone stood as the families walked to the front and were seated.

Will thanked the people for coming and for their love shown in so many ways. The sound of crying almost

made him sit down to compose himself. After a silent prayer, he took his Bible and read John 14:1-6, and then prayed. Timothy sang "Face to face," and even the strong men who hardly knew the family had a difficult time controlling their emotions. John held his son and Martha had her arm around Brittany. Will read First
Thessalonians 4 and then spoke of the beauty of Heaven, the blessings God had given to Judith in her short life, her faith in Christ, her love for her family, and her very special love for her husband, as well as the joy of looking forward to the arrival of their first-born son. Then very gently and quietly, Will walked in front of the family and spoke words of encouragement and comfort. The remarks were heard throughout the room, but they were intended especially for the families. He gave a short message on the joy of believing in Christ and the strength and the peace that only the Lord can give at a time like this. In a very few words, he explained that trusting in the Savior meant everything in death - even more so in life. All listened intently as Will Garrett spoke briefly on the words from John 11, "I am the resurrection and the life." He spoke of heaven and the joy of being where there is no more pain or sorrow, but Jonathan knew in his own heart that he was not part of what was being said. Chaplain Garrett's final words were a simple invitation for people to accept the Lord as their Savior.

When Will sat down, Timothy rose and said how the Lord had given him new life through Christ. And then he sang, "God be with you 'til we meet again."

The funeral directors explained that the burial would be in Sandwich the next day and any who wished, could join with them in that final journey.   Then the family left first, followed by more than 500 friends who had gathered for the service.

It was a very long journey to Sandwich the next day. When they arrived at the cemetery, Jonathan, his parents, and the Garretts went to the open grave. The winter blast froze their faces and their tears, but they stayed long enough to each lay a rose on the casket, and then they quietly returned to the waiting cars.

Once back at the Allen home, all strength and hiding of emotions were gone. It was now barely light outside, but Jonathan, dressed in an old pair of jeans, a sweat shirt, old sneakers and a light gray jacket, refusing to let anyone go with him, left the house. It was now sleeting and snowing. Arriving at the cemetery, he knelt beside the open grave and the casket which had not yet been placed in the ground. He placed his head against the hard mahogany box that held the two most dear to him, and wept. His hands were numb, his feet were like ice - yet he stayed there. He was angry, hurt, questioning, in despair. There seemed to be no answers. An officer happened by, went to him and insisted on taking him home, but Jonathan adamantly refused.

After darkness came, he stood. There were two roads before him and he knew one had to be chosen. He realized he could never go back. He loved his parents, but they had no answers. College was meaningless without Judith. Sandwich had been his home, but would never be that to him again. He had really only one choice - he had to run away! It was late, he was totally frozen, but he still knew he had to run away. His heart was made up. It was at that moment, in an outburst of desperate prayer, that he . . .

RAN AWAY...

TO GOD